Sam. KS + SM. Mr. and Mrs.
Sam MacInnes. Kelsey MacInnes.

Sam turned the diary toward Kelsey. "What's all this about?"

Heat moved up Kelsey's neck. "It's just something teenaged girls do. It doesn't mean a thing," she insisted, reaching for the diary again.

He immediately lifted it away as he flipped ahead a few pages. "'I dreamed about Sam again,'" he began aloud, only to pause, glance up, then start reading more slowly. "'I'd give anything if he'd kiss me. Really kiss me…'"

Kelsey heard him cut himself off as he read the rest. A moment later he looked at her with a grin that would have stopped her heart had she not been so busy being horrified.

"You thought I had a great butt?"

Her cheeks had turned a telling shade of pink. But this would be nothing compared to what color they would turn after his perusal of a few more pages would reveal him to be the subject of a few more rather specific fantasies.

Very specific, actually.

Dear Reader,

Well, as promised, the dog days of summer have set in, which means one last chance at the beach reading that's an integral part of this season (even if you do most of it on the subway, like I do!). We begin with *The Beauty Queen's Makeover* by Teresa Southwick, next up in our MOST LIKELY TO… miniseries. She was the girl "most likely to" way back when, and he was the awkward geek. Now they've all but switched places, and the fireworks are about to begin.…

In *From Here to Texas*, Stella Bagwell's next MEN OF THE WEST book, a Navajo man and the girl who walked out on him years ago have to decide if they believe in second chances. And speaking of second chances (or first ones, anyway), picture this: a teenaged girl obsessed with a gorgeous college boy writes down some of her impure thoughts in her diary, and buries said diary in the walls of an old house in town. Flash forward ten-ish years, and the boy, now a man, is back in town—and about to dismantle the old house, brick by brick. Can she find her diary before he does? Find out in Christine Flynn's finale to her GOING HOME miniseries, *Confessions of a Small-Town Girl*. In *Everything She's Ever Wanted* by Mary J. Forbes, a traumatized woman is finally convinced to come out of hiding, thanks to the one man she can trust. In Nicole Foster's *Sawyer's Special Delivery*, a man who's played knight-in-shining armor gets to do it again—to a woman (cum newborn baby) desperate for his help, even if she hates to admit it. And in *The Last Time I Saw Venice* by Vivienne Wallington, a couple traumatized by the loss of their child hopes that the beautiful city that brought them together can work its magic—one more time.

So have your fun. And next month it's time to get serious—about reading, that is.…

Enjoy!

Gail Chasan
Senior Editor

Please address questions and book requests to:
Silhouette Reader Service
U.S.: 3010 Walden Ave., P.O. Box 1325, Buffalo, NY 14269
Canadian: P.O. Box 609, Fort Erie, Ont. L2A 5X3

Confessions of a Small-Town Girl

Christine Flynn

SPECIAL EDITION®

Published by Silhouette Books

America's Publisher of Contemporary Romance

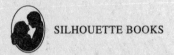

SILHOUETTE BOOKS

ISBN 0-373-24701-X

CONFESSIONS OF A SMALL-TOWN GIRL

Copyright © 2005 by Christine Flynn

This edition published by arrangement with Harlequin Books S.A.

® and TM are trademarks of Harlequin Books S.A., used under license.
Trademarks indicated with ® are registered in the United States Patent
and Trademark Office, the Canadian Trade Marks Office and in other
countries.

Visit Silhouette Books at www.eHarlequin.com

Printed in U.S.A.

Books by Christine Flynn

Silhouette Special Edition

CHRISTINE FLYNN

admits to being interested in just about everything, which is why she considers herself fortunate to have turned her interest in writing into a career. She feels that a writer gets to explore it all and, to her, exploring relationships—especially the intense, bittersweet or even lighthearted relationships between men and women—is fascinating.

This book is dedicated to every
woman who kept a diary in high school…
with the hope that she knows where it is.

Chapter One

Having fantasies about a man wasn't necessarily a bad thing. Fantasies were normal. Fantasies were healthy. Writing them down wasn't terribly bright, Kelsey Schaeffer conceded to herself, trying not to panic at what she was overhearing. Especially in detail. But she'd never dreamed that the subject of those wild imaginings would ever be anywhere near where she'd hidden her old diary. She'd had no idea that Sam MacInnes had even returned to Maple Mountain. She'd barely been back twelve hours herself.

"You going to flip those cakes, honey?"

Kelsey's mother bustled into the kitchen of her busy little diner, one eye on the spatula Kelsey held, the other on her order pad. With her silvering-blond hair in its usual braided bun, her pretty features softening with age and a white bib apron tied around her ample waist, Dora Schaeffer looked much as she always had to Kelsey. Friendly. Efficient. Enduring. Like a rock that could weather any storm or challenge and remain unchanged. The only difference about her since Kelsey's visit home last year was the white cast that ran from elbow to palm on her left arm. She had fallen from a ladder while adjusting the bunting she'd hung out front for the Fourth of July parade next Sunday.

The red, white and blue bunting now lay bundled on the storage room floor. Dauntless and headstrong to her core, her mom had pulled down the sections she'd hung rather than have them hang crooked before she'd walked down the street to the doctor's office to get her arm set. There were no half-measures with Dora Schaeffer. Something was either done perfectly, or it wasn't done at all.

Jerked from her alarm by her mom's reminder, Kelsey hurriedly flipped the two orders of buttermilk pancakes turning golden on the griddle. With most of her attention on the conversation taking place on the other side of the service window, she stacked a third order onto a plate, added a side of sausage and eggs and slid the plate onto the window's long ledge.

Amos Calder and Charlie Moorehouse, two of the community's inherently stubborn senior citizens, sat with their elbows on the lacquered pine counter, coffee mugs in hand, waiting for their breakfast. According to what she'd just overheard of their laconic conversation, Sam's sister had bought the old Baker place and Sam was refurbishing it for her and her boys. What had her mentally hyperventilating was Amos's comment about Sam tearing out the upstairs bedroom walls.

Her old diary was up there. The one she'd kept in high school. It was behind a wall in the back bedroom. Her name was in glitter on the cover. Sam's name was all over the inside.

Until a minute ago, she had nearly forgotten the thing even existed. Now, her only thought was that she would die if Sam found it.

She couldn't remember exactly what she'd written. At that moment, all she recalled was that he had been a college senior the summer she'd turned sixteen and that he'd worked on his uncle's farm. Big, buff, and totally out of her league, he had awakened her heart, her dreams and inspired a host of wild fantasies, the bulk of which she'd duly recorded, then ultimately hidden in the wall of the very house he was now tearing apart because her mom would have killed her had she found something so explicit in her bedroom.

Her then-best friend, Michelle Baker, in whose room she had hurriedly hidden her rather risqué writings after she'd discovered that her original hiding place in the old grist mill wasn't safe, hadn't had a clue what was in that diary. Since she kept a diary herself, Michelle had understood, however, how important it was for a girl to protect her private thoughts and assured her that no one would ever know the little book was there. As it was, Kelsey had never intended to leave it there permanently. But when she'd put it behind the loose wall panel Michelle had pulled out partway, it hadn't caught on the little ledge that held her friend's own treasures. It had slid all the way to the floor and they hadn't been able to get it back out.

"Kelsey?" Carrying a freshly poured glass of milk, her mom backed out the swinging kitchen door. "The cakes?"

Multitasking normally came as easily as a smile to Kelsey. At the moment, however, she could barely focus on anything other than what she was overhearing. Rattled, hating it, she grabbed a white ceramic plate from the stack near the griddle and slid the pancakes on it. The meal joined the others on the service ledge as her mom placed the milk in front of the UPS man sitting at the end of the counter.

"Wonder what's keepin' him," she heard Amos mutter.

"Keepin' who?" her mom asked. Turning around, Dora absently smiled through the window at Kelsey's suddenly frozen features, then reached one at a time for the older men's breakfasts.

"Sam." Scratching his balding head, Amos added a few more furrows to his weathered brow. "He's usually here by now."

Barely breathing, Kelsey watched the silver-haired Charlie eye his plate as her mom set it in front of him. Fork in hand, he poked at an egg yolk to make sure it was done to his liking. "Might be he drove to St. Johnsbury. Told us yesterday he'd have to make another trip into the lumberyard," he reminded the man on the stool next to him. "I keep tellin' him things aren't as handy here as he's used to in the city. Got to make lists. Pick up everything in one trip."

Amos pressed his white stubble-covered chin toward the collar of the T-shirt shirt tucked into his coveralls. As he did, he eyed his similarly attired friend through the top of his black-rimmed trifocals.

"Doing the work he does, you think he don't know about makin' lists?"

Charlie, his own glasses rimmed in silver, eyed him right back. "What's being a policeman got to do with anything?"

"He's not a policeman. He's a detective. You can tell by those shows on the TV that there's a difference," he explained, sounding as if the man being discussed hadn't pointed out the distinctions himself. "I'd think that a man who goes around lookin' for clues and such about crimes would be prone to keepin' lists of what he knows and what he don't."

Kelsey's mom gave the elderly men a patient smile. "I doubt he's gone anywhere just yet," she assured them both.

"You know he wouldn't make that long drive before fillin' himself up. He hasn't missed breakfast here in the two weeks since he arrived."

"That's 'cause he loves your cookin', Dora," came a gravelly voice from a table behind the men. "By the way, Kelsey, you're doing good this mornin', too." A white ceramic mug was raised in her direction. "Good to see you home."

Exposed by the window her mom had made wide so she wouldn't miss anything while working in her kitchen, Kelsey smiled into the half-filled room. Smiley Jefferson had been the postal carrier for as long as she could remember. His front tooth had been missing for about that long, too.

"It's good to be home, Smiley." It had been until a few minutes ago, anyway. "I hear Drew and Kathy had another baby. Congratulations."

"He finally got himself a grandson." The owner of the only gas station in town grinned as he looked up from his breakfast. "Just don't ask him to show you pictures. You get him started and the mail will never get delivered."

There was no such thing as a private conversation at Dora's Diner. Not when nearly everyone there knew everyone else. The quaint little establishment with its maple tables and chairs and bulletin board papered with handwritten notes of locals seeking to barter everything from farm equipment and labor to hay and eggs was as much the center of the community as the community center down the street. It was also the root of the town grapevine.

Much of what Kelsey had always loved about remote and rural Maple Mountain, Vermont, was the sense of acceptance and community she'd always felt there. Many of the locals were set in their ways and independent to a fault, but they protected their own. Neighbors helped neighbors. If someone hadn't been heard from in a while, someone else checked on them to make sure they weren't just busy or being reclusive. They were like extended family to her. And, like family, she loved them in spite of their quirks as much as she did because of them.

The acceptance was reciprocal. No matter how long she remained away, for a year, sometimes two, she was always welcomed back.

Her attention wasn't on that comfortable familiarity, however. All she felt as the front door opened and heads lifted to see who was joining them was a distinct sinking sensation in the pit of her stomach.

Sam MacInnes hadn't been anything more to her than a passing memory in the dozen years since she'd last seen him. Since she'd gone off the deep end for him as she had, she'd obviously thought him rather incredible back then. But she'd been a teenager at the time. Having been raised in conservative and totally unsophisticated Maple Mountain, she'd been a fairly sheltered one at that.

Years of living in cities had left her far more worldly and infinitely less impressionable than she'd once been. Still, she wasn't quite prepared for the six feet of solid muscle and testosterone in a faded NYPD T-shirt and worn jeans that walked into the room.

He totally dominated the space.

He made no effort to draw attention to himself. If anything, it seemed to her that his manner as he returned the greetings of others with an easy, appealing familiarity seemed decidedly low-key. He was simply the sort of man other men sensed as a prime example of their own, and either envied or emulated. Women simply stopped to stare and reminded themselves to breathe.

She didn't remember his hair being so dark. Its shade of sable looked so deep it nearly seemed black in the overhead lights. And his silver-gray eyes spoke more of a quiet, watchful intensity than whatever romantic notion she'd had about them all those summers ago. Yet what struck her most as he moved closer was the rugged maturity that carved lines of character in a face that had once merely been handsome—and gave him an aura of power and utter control that seemed downright dangerous.

He'd barely met her eyes when she jerked her glance away and slipped behind the wall to the grill.

The thought that he might have already found the diary sent her heart to her toes.

With her pulse pounding frantically in her ears, she heard coffee being poured into a mug and her mom's cheerful, "'Mornin', Sam. Good thing you showed up. These two were gettin' worried about you." The mug slid across shiny pine. "I just told 'em not a minute ago that you wouldn't leave without havin' breakfast first."

The chuckle she heard sounded as deep and rich as the brew her mother had just poured. "I didn't realize I was getting that predictable. But you're right." His tone grew grateful. "Thanks, Dora," he said, apparently referring to the caffeine she'd just slid toward him.

With the clink of metal against glass, her mom slipped the carafe back onto the big double coffeemaker. "What are you pickin' up from the lumberyard this time?"

"More two-by-fours. But I'm not going into St. Johnsbury until I get all the walls upstairs torn out and see what else I'll need. I've run into more wood rot up there than I did downstairs."

"That's because the roof was so bad." Amos punctuated his conclusion by stabbing a bite of pancake. "The Bakers replaced it so they could sell the place. That thing sagged like an ol' mare. Leaked in buckets, I'd imagine."

"They told Megan about the water damage," Sam replied, speaking of his sister. "She didn't care. She and the boys fell in love with the place."

"I can see why they'd do that." Silverware rattled as her mom put together a setting. "It's a pretty piece of property, with that creek and all. Kelsey used to like going out there herself when the elder Mrs. Baker was still alive. She was friends with her granddaughter.

"Speaking of which…Kelsey, I mean," she continued, her tone utterly conversational, "she got here last night. Her plane was late arrivin' in Montpelier, so we've hardly had a chance to visit. Have we, Kelsey?

"Kelsey?" Puzzlement entered Dora's voice as she turned to where her daughter had stood only moments ago. "Where did you go? I want someone to meet you."

Kelsey didn't respond. Protected by six feet of wall, she was too busy closing her eyes, shaking her head and wishing her mom wasn't so impossibly social. Dora Schaeffer had never met a stranger. Any tourist who came in more than once was remembered, along with where they were from and where they were going. She also knew every resident for a radius of fifty miles. If she didn't know them personally, she knew of them, about them and who they were related to— along with most of their business. People tended to confide in her and what they didn't confide, she overheard or pried out on her own. It was widely rumored that between her, Agnes Waters at the general store and Claire McGraw, the mayor's wife, there was hardly a secret in town.

The only person her mom didn't know as well as she thought she did was her own daughter.

There were advantages to that small failing. In a matter of seconds, it became apparent that she'd never had a clue about her daughter's wild crush on the man watching her reluctantly step back into view. Her mom didn't even seem to think she knew who Sam was.

"Kelsey, this is Tom and Janelle Collier's nephew, Sam. He's taking time off to work on the old Baker place for his sister." The arches of her pale eyebrows merged. "I told you the Bakers finally sold the place, didn't I? After Jenny married Doctor Reid?

"Anyway," she hurried on, sounding as if she didn't want to sidetrack herself as she turned back to the man quietly watching her strangely silent daughter, "Kelsey is helping out through the holiday, like I told you." Holding her casted arm protectively at her waist, she set a napkin and utensils on the counter for him. "I don't know what I'd have done if she hadn't been able to make it. It's just us locals and a few low-landers on vacation out at the lakes right now, but give it two days and that road out there will be bumper-to-bumper with folk coming to celebrate the Fourth of July. They're all going to be hungry, too."

He had big hands. Kelsey noticed that as he wrapped one around his mug. He had a nice smile, too. A little reserved. Kind of sexy.

He was smiling at her. Feeling an odd jolt join her panic, she jerked her attention to the older man pouring more maple syrup over the melted butter on his pancakes.

"Good thing you had her to call on, Dora," Amos informed her mom. "You'd have been up a creek with Betsy being gone like she is. You thinkin' to hire somebody to help her when she gets back?" He aimed his fork at her cast. "Leastwise until you get rid of that thing?"

Not by a hair did her mom's tight bun budge as she adamantly shook her head. "Betsy will take her shifts and I'll take mine," she insisted, speaking of her part-time cook, and new grandmother of twins. The birth of those babies had required Betsy Parker's presence in Burlington to help her daughter and son-in-law—right through the busiest week of summer.

"I just need to get used to this thing," Dora muttered, frowning stubbornly at her encumbrance. "Once the crowds are gone this weekend I'll be fine. In the meantime, I'll have Kelsey freeze me up a bunch of pies and such in case Betsy needs more time with those babies."

The frown melted as she glanced back at Sam. "You used to come in here when Kelsey was in high school," she reminded him, returning to what she'd rather talk about. "When she wasn't in the kitchen, she waited tables for me. You might remember having seen her back then."

Kelsey knew her mom was just being her usual chatty self. As far as the older woman was concerned, her little diner was her home and her guests were treated with the same hospitality she would have offered had they been in her living room—which, technically, they were. The entire first floor of the old two-story house Kelsey had been raised in had been converted into the diner after her father passed away twenty years ago. She and her mom had lived in the rooms upstairs. Her mom still did.

Since Dora was just being her gregarious self, Kelsey ordinarily wouldn't have thought anything of her mom's casual comments. But having her mom prod Sam's memory was the last thing she wanted her to do—until she realized he seemed to have no memory of her at all.

"Sure," he said, in that vague way people did when they didn't want to be rude and say they had little or no recollection of a person. "Your mom said that you live in Scottsdale now. You're a chef?"

"Pastry chef," she explained, because it was all she could think to say.

A hint of a smile tugged at his mouth again. "I'm an apple pie man myself. Will you make any of those while you're here?"

"Probably."

Watching her over the steam rising over the rim of his mug, he arched one dark eyebrow. "Are you any good at pancakes?"

She was having trouble maintaining eye contact with him. She couldn't remember specifics, but she was pretty certain that many of the entries in that diary had do with his beautifully muscled body. Those muscles looked as hard as the granite mined from the quarry outside of town and radiated a fine sort of tension that made him seem more restive than relaxed.

The fact that he was making her feel the same way wasn't lost on her, either. "I can manage."

"He always has a full stack, four eggs over medium, wheat toast and two sides of bacon," her mom rattled off, moving from behind the counter to wait on a couple of tourists who'd wandered in with their two offspring. "Sit anywhere you'd like," she told them, then glanced over her shoulder at Sam. "You want buttermilk or blueberry?"

That reserved smile surfaced again. Looking at Kelsey, he said, "She can surprise me."

Realizing she was staring at his mouth, praying he hadn't noticed, Kelsey spun away. She used to practice kissing that beautifully carved mouth on her bedroom mirror.

With a mental groan at the memory, she snatched up a clean stainless steel bowl. With the last batch of pancake batter gone, she needed to mix another.

She couldn't believe how totally flustered she felt. She was twenty-nine years old. Not sixteen. In the eleven years since she'd left Maple Mountain for culinary school, she'd worked her way from a line chef in Boston to master pastry chef in four-star restaurants in San Diego and Scottsdale. She had managed to survive the artistic temperaments of male executive chefs who considered themselves God's gift to man, woman and culinary creativity, and placed in the top three of every dessert competition she'd entered in the last five years. Until two minutes ago—three minutes were she to count from the moment she'd heard Sam's name—her biggest concern had been the terrible timing of her mom's need for her to come home.

She had just been offered the position of executive pastry chef where she worked at the Regis-Carlton resort in Scottsdale. She had also been offered the same position with a high-end new restaurant by Doug Westland, one of the most respected and innovative restaurateurs on the West Coast, along with the opportunity to become his business— and bed—partner. She had huge issues with the latter part of that arrangement. But that wasn't the problem at the moment. Or the point. The point was that she was highly organized, disciplined, creative in her own right and that she was not easily unsettled. Normally.

Scooping a cup of the flour, baking powder and salt she'd premeasured earlier, she folded it into the eggs and buttermilk, gently so as not to make the batter heavy. She felt decidedly unsettled now.

That circumstance no doubt explained why she didn't feel at all slighted to know that Sam apparently hadn't even noticed her existence the summer he'd occupied her nearly every waking thought. Realizing he barely remembered her was actually a relief. A huge one. So was the thought that nothing about his manner indicated that he'd discovered her daring and imaginative writings, much less read them. To the best of her knowledge, she was the only Kelsey in Maple

Mountain. With her name on the diary's cover, it seemed that had he found it, she would have at least rated a raised eyebrow when her mom mentioned her name.

She spread two rashers of bacon on the griddle, cracked four eggs beside them. He probably needed the huge breakfast to fuel all that muscle, she supposed, only to deliberately change the direction of her thoughts. Thinking about the admittedly magnificent body that had inspired the current reason for her anxiety wasn't getting her anywhere. Since it seemed he hadn't found the diary, she needed to get to it before he did. She just needed to figure out how.

She was praying for inspiration when she set the three plates of food that could have comfortably fed two in the window for her mom to serve. With a smile for Amos when he gave her a surreptitious wink to let her know she'd done well, she turned to make the omelets the tourists had ordered.

Sam noticed that wink. Digging into his own meal, he might have mentioned how good his breakfast was, too, had she given him any hint that she was at all interested in anything he had to say. Instead he took another bite of heaven on a fork and frowned at himself while the two old guys next to him suggested he stop by for a game of checkers on the porch of the general store, providing he had time later that afternoon, of course.

Sam liked the two old guys. There were times when he couldn't get a word out of either of them other than a thoughtful and considered "Yup" or "Nope." Then, there were days when they seemed more than willing to share whatever they knew, especially if they figured they could help a person out. It seemed, too, that once they got going, they could reminisce forever about what they considered the good old days—which was pretty much any year before 1955. According to both men, not much of anything was made the way it had been before then, and neither had much use for anything that hadn't existed by the middle of the past century.

He wasn't much for games, except maybe the occasional hand of poker. Still, he told them he'd be glad to join them later, since he was looking for as many ways as possible to fill in his time there, and went back to his meal. He wasn't doing anything but biding his time in Maple Mountain. Any diversion was welcome.

He still didn't think the time off the force was necessary. He had adamantly argued the need for the leave of absence his department psychologist had insisted he take three weeks ago. He would argue it now, if given the chance. Yet, as he frowned into his coffee, he would concede that the shrink may have had one small point.

He'd suspected himself that he had lost the edge on his social skills in polite society. He just hadn't been prepared to truly admit that loss until now. He hadn't been able to get so much as a smile out of the attractive blonde he could see coming and going from the long window above the service counter, much less get any sort of conversation started with her.

He only vaguely remembered the delicate-looking woman Dora had mentioned a couple of days ago. Since he'd eaten only occasionally at the diner all those years ago, he knew he hadn't seen Kelsey often. But the more he thought about her now, the more he remembered that there had been a cute, long-legged blonde he'd looked for when he had come in. He also recalled that she'd been jail bait.

She definitely hadn't possessed the presence or style she'd acquired since then, either.

She had her mother's pale wheat-colored hair, only hers was woven with shades of champagne and platinum and caught in a low ponytail with a black clip at her nape. The rest was covered with a short, white pleated chef's hat that ended below her brow line and revealed the white pearl studs in her ears. Her lovely eyes were as dark as the rich coffee in his mug, her features delicate, her skin flawless and she had a mouth that made his water just thinking about how soft it might be.

Wearing the high-necked white chef's jacket he figured she'd brought with her, since he'd never seen Dora wear anything more sophisticated than the hairnet and white bib apron she wore now, Kelsey Schaeffer looked polished, professional. She also seemed as familiar with the patrons she fed as she did the kitchen she moved through with such ease.

He just couldn't figure out why she would smile and talk with everyone else, but barely converse with him. Drawing out people was his strong suit. Among a certain, corrupt and incorrigible element, anyway. And cons and criminals were usually an even tougher sell.

Deciding it wasn't worth worrying about, he polished off his breakfast, had Dora bag two giant blueberry muffins from the case for later and headed for his truck and the trailer he was temporarily calling home. He had more on his mind than his apparently forgotten ability to flirt with a respectable woman. The department shrink had said he'd grown out of touch with normalcy, whatever that was supposed to mean, and that if he didn't get back in touch with it, he could eventually lose his sense of perspective and his usefulness to the department.

The department was his home, and as much his family as those he was related to by blood. Failing it would be like failing himself. He would do what he needed to do to keep that from happening. He wouldn't like it, but he'd do it.

It had been three weeks since he'd come off a case that had kept him undercover for over a year. The need to stay under had even caused him to miss his brother-in-law's funeral after a road-rage incident left his sister a widow and his young nephews without a dad. He had been ordered to take three months to decompress by doing normal things. He was to reacquaint himself with his family, find creative outlets, wind down. Helping his sister by refurbishing the dilapidated old house so she could raise her sons in the country seemed as good a way as any to him to keep from going stir-crazy while he accomplished that goal. Then, after he put in his time, he could get back to the work that had become his way of life.

There was just one problem. Having spent ten years working his way down the humanity scale from neighborhood beat cop to vice detective to spending the past fourteen months living in the underbelly of New York with crack heads, drug dealers, pimps and prostitutes to break a major drug ring, he wasn't exactly sure he knew what constituted normal anymore.

He felt fairly certain, however, that "normal" wasn't having the pretty blonde who had all but ignored him at the diner show up that afternoon with the smile he hadn't been able to get out of her before and a freshly baked apple pie.

Chapter Two

Kelsey figured she had two options. She could try to get upstairs alone and, depending on how much wall Sam had torn out, get the diary and sneak it out in her purse. Or, she could look around to see how far he was with his demolition and go back when he wasn't there.

The nerves in her stomach were jumping as she watched him walk toward her.

With her oversize handbag dangling from one shoulder, and carrying a pink pastry box with both hands, she left the compact sedan she'd rented at the airport and moved past the construction debris to meet him. Old cupboards, carpeting and a rusted sink formed a pile at the end of the gravel driveway that cut into the deep and wooded lot. Stacks of new lumber nearly blocked the sagging front porch, waiting to be used inside.

She'd heard that he was living in the long white trailer

parked near the curve of the stream that meandered through the back of the property. According to her mom, the leveling of that trailer had been the local event of the day. Charlie and Amos said they'd helped supervise. Lorna Bagley, who took turns with her sister, Marian, waiting tables for her mom, told her she'd packed up a picnic and her kids and headed out to watch—though mostly, the single mother of two had confessed, she had watched Sam. They didn't get many men as easy on the eyes as that one, she'd confided. Certainly, none as intriguing.

Since news and gossip were shared freely among the locals, and since nothing pleased some of the them more than to bring someone who'd been away up to date, Kelsey had also learned that Sam had been a detective for years, and divorced for nearly as long. No one seemed to know what had caused the demise of his marriage. No one knew exactly what sort of "detecting" it was that he did, either. Some thought he solved murder cases like the detectives on television. But no one knew for sure. He apparently didn't say much about his work.

As unusual and fascinating as his occupation was to certain citizens of Maple Mountain, as far as most of them were concerned what he did in the city was no real concern of theirs. Sam was just Tom and Janelle Collier's nephew and he'd come to help out a member of his family. Helping family and neighbors was something they were all familiar with. When there was a need, it was simply what people in Maple Mountain did.

He stopped six feet in front of her, as tall and solid as an oak. Even as he spoke, she had the unsettling feeling she'd been appraised from neck to knee without his glance ever leaving her face.

"I'd ask if you're lost, but I figure you know your way around here a whole lot better than I do."

It was as clear as the gray of his eyes that he remembered their meeting that morning. Specifically, that she'd barely spoken to him—which obviously would make him wonder what she was doing there now.

"I hope I'm not interrupting," she replied, hoping she hadn't offended him too badly.

"I'm not doing anything that can't wait."

Desperate not to appear as anxious as she felt, she held out the box containing one of the pies she'd baked between the breakfast and lunch that morning.

"You said you like apple," she reminded him.

Curiosity slashed the carved lines of his face as he lifted the box from her hands. "What's this for?"

"A chance to look around?" Looking past the impressive shoulders and muscular arms she'd once fantasized about, she glanced toward the old two-story house behind him. "I heard you're tearing out walls in there. If you don't mind, I'd like to see the house before it changes too much." She hesitated, trying to act only casually curious. "How far along are you? With tearing them out, I mean."

She thought he still looked skeptical of her presence. Or, maybe, it was interest in the contents of the box she saw in his expression as he pried up the front of the pink cardboard lid.

"I still have half the upstairs to go." Distracted, he lifted the box to his nose and sniffed. "You use cinnamon."

"It's just your basic apple pie."

"I'm a basic sort of guy."

There was that smile again.

"So." She swallowed, wondering if he had any idea how appealing it was to a woman to see a grown man grin like a boy at her baking. "May I go look around? I used to hang out here with my girlfriend when we were in high school.

This was her grandma's house," she explained. "We'd come out in the summer and spend nights with her. Sometimes in the winter, too, when we'd skate on the pond.

"It's a nostalgia thing," she justified when his only response was the faint pinch of his brow. "I never thought anything about this town would change," she hurried to admit, because that much was true. If finding that damnable diary hadn't been so necessary, revisiting the memories honestly would have been important to her. Some of the best times of her life had been spent in and around the buildings beyond him. "As much as this house meant to me growing up, I'd really like to see it before what I remembered doesn't exist anymore. I don't know if you have any places like that from your childhood. Old hangouts, I mean. But this is really important to me."

Nerves had her rambling. Realizing that, she shut herself up before she could betray just how uneasy she felt with what she'd written about him, and how totally lousy she was at being less than up-front and honest. She really had loved being in this charming old place. But the abandoned gristmill across the stream had been far more important to her. She had spent hours poking around the mill's dim interior, wondering what life had been like for the miller who'd lived there a century ago. She'd spent even more time by its slowly moving waterwheel dreaming of her future, writing those dreams and plans in the diary she needed to find before Sam discovered just how large a part he'd played in her mental musings.

Apparently she hadn't silenced herself soon enough. The curiosity in Sam's expression changed to scrutiny as his eyes narrowed on hers.

Feeling exposed, not quite sure what to say, her glance fell to the ground. She figured she'd be better off to stay silent. Being a detective, he could probably spot a con at ten paces.

Sam was actually far better than that. He could spot a fraud a mile away and the woman now avoiding his eyes clearly had something more on her mind than revisiting memories of old times. She wanted into the house. Rather badly, he concluded, considering that she was willing to bribe him to get there.

Intrigued, his glance drifted from the rapid and betraying blink of her dark lashes and down her long-legged frame. Certain her motive was something other than what she'd claimed, his mind should have leapt to questions, possibilities, objectives. But a heavy dose of pure male interest had joined his more analytical instincts. Indulging it, he found himself fascinated as much by her as with discovering her purpose for being there.

Kelsey Schaeffer was the antithesis of the women he'd encountered day after day living undercover. Women who blatantly advertised what she seemed to deliberately underplay. But, then, when sex was for sale, a little advertising was simply good business. Those "ladies" wore their blouses cut to their navels, if the fabric reached that far, and their skirts or pants were inevitably spandex or leather and fit like skin. Their exotic makeup wasn't used to enhance so much as it was to hide the ravages of drugs, poor nutrition and bruises from their pimps or their boyfriends. Then, there were the women who were so strung-out they didn't bother to take care of themselves at all.

Sam pulled back his thoughts as his glance drifted over the sky-blue pullover Kelsey wore with her white capris. Everything about her was subtle. Her understated clothes. The natural shades of her makeup. Her quiet sensuality. She was the first woman to draw his interest in longer than he cared to remember, but he could only imagine the shape of her small breasts and the curve of her waist under her loose, boat-necked top. And those legs. Even covered to midcalf, they seemed to go on forever.

Something hot gathered low in his gut. With the scents of warm cinnamon and apples taunting an equally basic sort of hunger, he conceded that, in this particular instance, he could be bought.

"It won't look like what you remember," he warned her. "It's pretty torn up in there."

She still wore her sun-streaked hair back and clipped at her nape. Brushing at a strand that had escaped its confines, she offered a quick smile. "That's okay." She motioned toward the pie. "I'll just peek inside while you put that away."

"I'll take you in. Like I said, there's stuff everywhere."

"I don't want to keep you from what you were doing."

"It's not a problem."

Kelsey opened her mouth, fully prepared to insist that she was fine on her own.

The slow arch of his eyebrow stopped her. It seemed as if he were waiting for her protest. Or, maybe, he was just waiting for her to move ahead of him. As thoughts of protest collapsed to a quiet, "An escort would be great," she couldn't really tell.

All she knew for certain as she headed along the walkway cutting through the weed-choked grass to the porch was that she wanted to be upstairs alone. She wanted to get in, get what she'd come for and get out. She couldn't let Sam think it mattered one way or another if he was with her, though. Watching him set the box on the only sturdy-looking section of porch railing, she also realized she couldn't appear to be in too much of a rush to get upstairs.

The sagging steps groaned beneath his weight. Skirting the pile of new lumber on the porch, he pulled open the screen door and motioned her ahead of him.

With a murmured, "Thanks," she stepped past him and into an echoing and empty space. The cozy living room of cabbage rose-print wall paper, Victorian-style furniture and lace doilies was long gone. What little paper hadn't been stripped from the walls had grayed and peeled with age. The carved wood molding that had edged the floors and ceiling lay in neat rows on the bare hardwood floor.

"Take your time."

Kelsey swore she could feel Sam's eyes on her back as she pulled her glance from the narrow door near the end of the room. That open door led to the stairway and the second floor.

"We used to spend a lot of time in the kitchen."

He lifted his hand to his left.

With a smile that felt fainter than she would have liked, she slipped past his scrutiny and into another room that had been stripped to its bones.

"You said this was your friend's grandmother's house?"

"My friend Michelle. Baker," she expanded, wondering if he sounded skeptical or if her conscience only made her hear suspicion in his tone. "It's Michelle Hansen now. She moved to Maine."

"My sister said Mrs. Baker's granddaughter married the local doctor and lives here."

"That would be Jenny. Michelle's younger sister. And she did. And does."

Kelsey turned a slow circle in the middle of the room that no longer looked familiar at all. The old cabinets had all been torn out and the floor stripped of linoleum. The old-fashioned cookstove and rounded refrigerator were gone, too. The only thing that seemed familiar was the mint green paint where the cabinets had been. The rest of the room had at some point been painted a warm Tuscan yellow. From the looks of the large white spackled patches on the walls, that golden color would be painted over soon.

From the corner of her eye, she saw Sam leaning against the door frame. With his hands in the pockets of his worn jeans, his faded NYPD T-shirt stretching across his chest, he didn't seem to be watching her so much as he seemed to be…evaluating.

Doing a little evaluating of her own, she felt a twinge of disappointment. The old woodstove was also gone.

"You said you came here often?" he asked.

"Michelle's grandma was a widow so someone from her family was always checking up on her." She looked into the pantry, quietly closed the door when she found the shelves missing. "I'd come by after school with Michelle sometimes. On weekends, some of us would come out to skate on the mill pond and come over to say hi." She motioned to the empty corner and the now-covered hole in the wall that had once vented a chimney. "We used to warm our hands on the wood-stove that was over there while Grandma B made us cocoa."

"Grandma B?"

"Grandma Baker. She said we were all like granddaughters to her, so that's what we called her. It's like that around here," she mused, thinking how sweet the elderly woman had been to her and her friends. "Neighbors are like family."

She moved toward the back porch, stuck her head out the kitchen door to see what had changed out there. The door had already been replaced. So had the wood-framed windows. They were aluminum now, like the other new ones crated and waiting to replace those on the second floor. The broad steps she and her friends used to sit on were still there, but their lumber was now new.

What she'd just remembered had her turning back into the room.

"The best part about coming here was the slumber parties in the summer. Carrie Rogers and I would come out with Michelle. We'd pick berries in the woods and swim in the pond, then sit on the porch eating popcorn and talking until her grandma chased us up to bed. We wouldn't go to sleep until the sun started to come up."

Conquering the night they'd called it, she remembered, shaking her head at the silliness of what had seemed like such a big deal to them back then. If she stayed up all night now, it was because she was preparing for an event, wrestling with an administrative budget or personnel problem or, lately, she thought, turning away to run her hand along the new window sill, questioning the sudden developments in her career.

Propped against the door frame, Sam watched her check out his handiwork. He had no idea how something as inconsequential as a childhood memory could put such warmth in a person's eyes, but that warmth had definitely been there in the moments before she'd turned away. It had lit her face, her eyes, curved the fullness of her mouth. He could barely recall his own childhood. It hadn't been a bad one. He just never thought about it. Certainly he never thought about the innocence she had just so easily recalled of her own.

Swimming and skating on a mill pond sounded like something straight out of a Currier and Ives painting to him. Practical to a fault, cynical, distrustful and more hardened than he would admit out loud, he couldn't begin to imagine something so idyllic.

He dismissed his failure as totally inconsequential. Distrust and doubt had saved his hide on more than one occasion. Doing what he did for a living, he'd come to regard the traits as skills. He wasn't at all anxious to be rid of them.

She turned back, now studying the new plywood underlayment for the kitchen floor. "Do you mind if I go upstairs?"

Still curious about what she was up to, enjoying the distraction, he pushed himself from the door frame and idly motioned for her to proceed.

Seeing her smile in the general direction of his chin, he watched her slip past him and into the dim living room. The faint scents of cinnamon and something impossibly fresh drifted behind her. Her shampoo, maybe. Or her soap.

She headed for the door at the far end of the room, only to stop as she reached the fireplace a few feet from the stairs. Looking as if she might be remembering something about the fireplace, too, she slowly ran her hand along the carved wood mantel.

It had taken him an entire day to sand the mantel down and repair the cracked corbels. All he needed to do now was stain it the dark cherry his sister had picked out and apply a few coats of varnish.

"You're doing all of this yourself?" she asked.

"My uncle helped me tear out the kitchen and bathroom. And he or one of his workers will help me install the new cabinets when they arrive next week. But other than that…yeah. Pretty much."

"This feels like satin." The tips of her fingers caressed the smooth surface, her brow knitting as if she were savoring the velvety feel of the grain. Or, maybe, marveling at it. "I thought you were a detective."

"I am."

She glanced toward him. "Then, how do you know how to do all this?"

He gave a dismissing shrug. "Where I grew up, nobody called a carpenter unless he was a relative. Same went for a plumber or an electrician. Dad did the repairs around the house and I watched."

"And helped," she concluded, stroking the wood again. "A lot."

That was true, he thought, though he'd all but forgotten the hours he'd spent watching his dad turn wood scraps into picture frames or the little tables and chairs he gave away to his cousins and the kids in the neighborhood. Pete MacInnes was a cop, too. Nearing retirement now. But carpentry always had been his escape and he'd seemed to enjoy sharing it with his son. He had never said as much. His father had never been big on words. He still wasn't. But he was a patient man. He'd been a good teacher. And a slap on the back was still high praise.

"Yeah," he finally murmured, pulling his thoughts back in. He didn't want to think about his dad. Specifically, he didn't want to think about what his dad had said about taking more leave than had been recommended.

Take a little more time, son. Think about supervising. Or working internal affairs. Your mom worries about you when you're undercover.

He knew his mom worried. But his mom worried about everything. As for moving up the chain of command, the last thing he wanted was to sit behind a desk supervising a sting. He needed to be in the heart of it.

"You do beautiful work."

As she spoke, Kelsey dropped her hand from the perfectly prepared wood. She'd had no idea all those years ago that they'd had so much in common. Years of watching and assisting her mom tend whatever had broken or malfunctioned around the diner had left her with a few eclectic skills of her own. She was probably the only student to graduate from the Boston Culinary Arts Academy who'd taken apart and reassembled a sink drain her first week of sauce class because another student's engagement ring had been rinsed down the drain with her burned beurre blanc.

She might have told Sam that, too, had she not noticed the small white scar under the hard line of his jaw. Another peeked above the band of his T-shirt near his collarbone. The thin silvery line widened, looking slightly pink where it disappeared beneath the worn fabric.

Realizing she was staring, her glance jerked up.

He was waiting for her to move.

Her purpose for being there had her starting for the stairs. But she'd barely taken a step before his hand clamped around her arm.

"Be careful," he told her. "The third and fifth steps are loose."

Sam's fingers circled her biceps. Beneath the thin fabric of her sleeve, the heat of his broad palm seeped into her flesh. The sensation unnerved her. More unnerving still was the way that heat slowly moved through the rest of her body.

Doing her best to ignore the disturbing effect, she murmured a quiet, "Okay."

"Watch where you're going when you get up there, too."

Her response this time was only a nod. Yet, it satisfied him enough to let her go. Even then, the heat of his touch lingered, distracting her, making her even more aware of the feel of his eyes on her back as she started up the stairs, and carefully climbed past the boxes of nails and odd-looking metal brackets. The handrails had been removed, the steps were trailed with sawdust and most of those that weren't loose creaked. But she was mostly conscious of the big man moving behind her—and the way he watched her when they reached the top and she stopped to glance around.

Many of the interior walls had already been removed. Piles of old lumber and sheets of knotty pine paneling were stacked everywhere. With little left to divide it, the area was mostly a series of upright studs and dangling wires.

With her back to him, Kelsey looked past a pair of saw-horses and a table saw with a long orange cord that ran to an electrical outlet beneath an open window. The glass globes had been removed from the overhead light fixtures. Bare bulbs and afternoon sunlight illuminated the varying degrees of destruction. In some places, the ceiling was missing.

The only room she was concerned with, however, was the one at the end with most if its paneling still intact. She could see into it through the row of studs that had once been the hallway wall. The wall separating it from what had been Grandma B's sewing room was still there.

Sam lifted a board angled across what remained of a door-way. It landed with a clatter and a puff of dust on the stack behind him. "There's not much left up here to see."

Hugging her purse to her side, growing more uncomfortable by the second standing between him and her fantasies, she skimmed a glance past the open window. The window in Michelle's old room was open, too.

Before he could catch her calculating, she glanced around once more.

"It feels different in here without the furniture and the walls. It's sort of…"

"Unfinished?" he suggested.

"I was thinking more like…lonely."

There always had been so much laughter there. Reminding herself there would be again once his little nephews moved in, she nonchalantly nodded toward the room that had been Michelle's. In the middle of the wall jutting toward her, presumably resting on the floor, was the object she had no hope of reclaiming at the moment.

"Is that room going to stay the same size, or are you going to take out that wall, too?"

"It's coming out."

Her heart jerked. "Oh?"

"My sister wants more space for the kids up here." He motioned behind her. "This will all open up to a playroom and study."

Hoping to appear as if she were merely showing neighborly interest, she edged to where he'd left a tool belt draped over one of the sawhorses. With the hallway part of the wall already gone, she wondered if she could see between the panels. "Is that what you were working on when I interrupted?" she asked, taking another step back.

She could have sworn she felt his glance narrow on her.

"Actually I was tearing apart the door frame you're about to back into. That whole wall is going."

She drew herself to a halt before he could do it for her.

Still aware of the warmth on her arm where he'd grabbed her before, telling herself she was only imagining she still felt his heat, she took a more careful step toward the stairs. If she was rattled by anything, it was what she was doing. Casing a place, or whatever it was called, wasn't exactly her area of expertise.

"Then, I should let you get back to it," she told him. "I need to get back myself before Mom thinks I abandoned her." The floor creaked as she edged toward the stairwell, slowly, though what she really wanted to do was bolt. "I really appreciate you letting me look around."

He dipped his dark head, his eyes on hers, his tone as casual as she was trying to be. "Anytime."

"Thanks." With the promise of escape only seconds away, she turned toward the stairs, only to turn right back. "Don't forget your pie."

"Not a chance."

His claim drew a faint smile an instant before she started down the stairs. Watching her go, Sam stayed where he was and wondered at the betraying tightness he'd seen at the corners of her mouth. That strain hadn't been there when he'd seen her smile at the diner's regulars that morning. Or in the brief moments she'd recalled bits of her childhood.

Standing in the midst of his demolition, he heard the last step creak and the quickness of her footsteps across the living room floor. She wasn't running, but she wasn't wasting any time getting out of there, either.

Moments later, rusted hinges gave an arthritic groan when she pushed the screen door open.

It was only when he heard it bang shut that he headed down the stairs and to the door himself.

From the seclusion of the interior's dim shadows, he watched her hurry along the cracked concrete path and climb into the car she'd parked under the sweeping branches of the maple tree shading the driveway.

She didn't stop anywhere along the way, though he did see her glance toward the house before she climbed into the car and drive out to the narrow main road leading into town.

He could practically feel a frown settle between his eyebrows as he stepped onto the porch and watched her car disappear across the expanse of meadowlike front lawn. He would have bet his badge that there was something more going on with her than she was letting on. Her body language alone had practically screamed that she wasn't being entirely up-front with him. At least, it seemed to him that it had.

Still, as he headed back inside, he couldn't help wonder if maybe the department psychologist hadn't been right—that he did need the break. From the way Kelsey had breezed in and out of there, it seemed she really had just wanted to look around the place—and that he'd seen intrigue where there was none at all.

* * *

Kelsey could hardly believe what she was doing. It was two o'clock in the morning, she was dressed like a cat burglar in a dark stocking cap she'd found in her old ski bag and a long-sleeved navy T-shirt and jeans, and she was climbing through a second-story window of a house that did not belong to her.

Ten minutes ago, she'd parked her car at the old mill, taken the bridge across the stream and the path through the woods, and quietly made her way to the back of the house. She'd nearly stopped breathing every time the snap of a twig beneath her feet broke through the cacophony of crickets, croaking frogs and the hammering of her heart. She felt as if she were barely breathing now.

In the light of the half moon, Sam's darkened trailer had seemed to glow like snow on a winter's night. His truck sat parked like a shadow near its door.

Mercifully the back corner of the house wasn't visible from the trailer. That had made it relatively easy to get the ladder she'd seen earlier on the back porch and carry it to the window next to Michelle's old bedroom. When she'd been there before, both windows had been open. Both were now closed, but she'd also noticed that the locking lever on the window by the table saw had been missing.

Two stories up, desperately hoping she wouldn't do what her mom had done and slip off the ladder, she balanced on the third rung from the top and tried to lever open the window.

It didn't want to give up without a struggle. The frame had rotted in places and layers of old paint made the wood stick. There was also no handle or lever on the outside to lift with. It was only by laying her palms flat against the glass and pressing in and up that she was able to get any leverage and move it enough to get her fingers between the frame and the sill. Once she'd managed that, she was able to work it open the rest of the way.

She'd never make it as a thief, she decided, wiping bits of old paint onto her pants while clinging to the ladder for balance. She had just left impressions of her palms on the glass, and all ten of her fingerprints.

The inside of the house was dark. Poking her head in, she raised one leg and stuck it through. Hugely relieved that she hadn't fallen, she pulled in the other behind her and cautiously eased her feet to the floor. The moonlight penetrated only far enough for her to see the outline of the lumber she'd nearly stepped on.

She couldn't go any farther without her flashlight.

It had taken her forever to find one. Her mom, who, thankfully, still slept like the dead, had always kept one in their tiny upstairs kitchen. She'd kept another in the utility room for the inevitable power failures that came with winter storms. The one in the kitchen had a dead battery. The one in the utility room had been replaced with something the size of her car's headlamp. It would have lit up the entire house and drawn far too much attention to anyone who might have noticed the light moving inside. Not that there was anyone around. No one other than Sam, anyway. The nearest neighbor lived a half a mile away, and the road itself rarely saw any traffic at all past ten at night.

She'd found the eight-inch long yellow flashlight she now pulled from the waistband of her jeans in the diner's storage room. Clicking it on, she trained the beam on the floor to see where she was going and headed for the sawhorses. That was where she'd seen Sam's toolbox and tool belt.

Her plan was simple. She would pry away the piece of paneling concealing the diary with one of his hammers or screwdrivers, get what she'd come for, then wedge the panel back in place as best she could. She wasn't about to risk waking Sam by nailing it. The board would be loose, but if he thought anything about it when he went to tear it out, he'd have no idea it was loose because of her.

She made it halfway across the creaking floor before she turned the beam toward the wall separating the room she was in from Michelle's—and found the beam illuminating a spot at the end of the house.

The wall wasn't there.

Her heart gave a sick little jerk as she swept the circle of light everywhere the wall should have been. The paneling had been ripped away. All that remained of the wall and her hiding place were the upright studs that ran ceiling to floor a foot and a half apart, and a few horizontal pieces of a two-by-four that had been hammered between them for stability. The one in the center was undoubtedly the little ledge Michelle had told her was there. The one her diary had slid straight past.

Feeling a nightmare coming on, she started toward where it would have landed, only to stop at the squeak of wood behind her. The sound stopped when she did. Infinitely more concerned with where her diary might be, she ignored what she assumed where only the creaks and groans typical of old houses settling in at night and raised the flashlight to see more clearly into the room beyond the studs.

The instant she did, the hairs at the back of her neck rose. The sensation had barely registered before something hard clamped around her wrist. A gasp caught in her chest as her cap was yanked from her head. The sting of her hair being yanked with it hadn't even registered before she was spun like a rag doll, her back slammed into the stud behind her and her air cut off by what felt like a bar of steel across her throat.

Somewhere in that startling split second, the flashlight had been snatched from her hand. Its beam was aimed straight at her face, leaving her totally blinded—and so frightened as she struggled for oxygen that she couldn't even scream.

Chapter Three

Sam didn't know what had wakened him. After spending fourteen months sleeping with one ear open because he never knew when his identity would be discovered and he'd find himself seconds from being dead, it could have been anything. He still woke a dozen times a night. Every night. And when he did, his first thought was that he'd blown his cover and that someone had identified him as an undercover cop.

Logic would eventually remind him that he was no longer playing the role of a down on his luck bartender and working nights in a dive in the seediest area of the city. Members of the gang he'd sought to bust were either no longer among the living, or in jail awaiting trial and a trip to prison. He was in Maple Mountain. Quiet, peaceful, boringly uneventful Maple Mountain. Yet, the thought that he was as safe here as he could be anywhere failed to form.

Logic tonight told him someone was out there.

In the dark, trusting nothing, pure instinct took over. That instinct had him easing open a window of his trailer. The faint sound of metal bumping wood had been all he'd needed to hear before he'd jerked on his pants, shoved the gun he'd kept under his pillow into the back of his jeans and slipped as quiet as a breath into the night.

Years of living on a blade-thin edge, of knowing how desperate and vengeful people could be, allowed his mind to work only one way. He always assumed the worst. To do anything less left him open and vulnerable to whatever mayhem he might face. If a threat proved minimal, he could always back down. It was infinitely more difficult, and more dangerous, to walk into a scenario expecting minimal conflict and have to gear up under assault. It was how every cop he knew survived.

He'd been locked in that mindset when he'd crept around the house to see a dark figure slip through the second-story window. In his mind, the intruder could only want one of two things. Tools to fence for drugs, or payback. He never discounted the possibility that he had been ID'd by a suspect who'd escaped a bust, and that someone he'd helped put in jail might look to get even by having a buddy nail him.

Now, primed for survival, his only thought as the intruder's identity registered in the beam of the blinding light was that he was crushing Kelsey's windpipe.

She looked terrified.

He was hurting her. The knowledge that he was a hair-breadth from hurting her more shot a sharp, totally unfamiliar pang of fear through his rigid, adrenaline-charged body.

He swore even as he jerked away his arm. The gun in his hand glinted dully as it passed through the beam.

He swore again, adrenaline still surging as he swung the light from her eyes.

"God Almighty, Kelsey." His voice held fury, his words as close to a prayer as he'd been in years. He could have snapped her neck. "What in the hell are you doing here?"

Blinking to clear her vision, she sagged in relief against the post when she recognized Sam's voice. She couldn't see him. All she could see were spots as she lifted her shaking hand to her throat. "I'm…"

"Do you have any idea what I could have done to you?" He was nowhere near ready to hear from her just yet. Furious with her for jerking around with his adrenaline, equally upset with the thought of the force he'd used on her, he slammed the end of the flashlight down on the sawhorse beside him. As it rocked on its base, its light formed a wavering circle on the ceiling. "You should *never* sneak around a cop. *Ever.* Do you understand me? What in the hell were you thinking?"

Kelsey's heart beat furiously against her ribs. She wished he'd stop swearing at her. She wished he'd stop yelling. Mostly she wished he'd move. He'd only backed up a couple of feet. As near as he stood, it seemed she could actually feel the tension radiating from his body. That tension roped around her, making it hard to breathe even without his arm jammed against her neck.

"I wasn't sneaking around you." She forced insistence into her voice, along with a bravado she truly did not feel. What she did feel was a little sick from an adrenaline rush of her own. Her knees were shaking. Locking them, her chin edged up another notch and she focused through the fading spots. "You were the one who snuck up on me."

"You were breaking and entering—"

"I didn't break anything! The window wasn't locked."

"It's a term." He growled the words as he jammed his hands onto his hips, his stance now even more imposing as the he glared down at her. "You're trespassing on private property in the middle of night. You climbed through a second-story window to get in here. That's called breaking and entering," he informed her, clearly familiar with the technicalities. "What you haven't said is why."

She would rather avoid that.

Ignoring the sore place on the back of her head where it had bumped the stud now supporting her, she dropped her glance to the cleft in his chin. The night-time stubble shadowing his face made the carved angles look as inflexible as granite. His voice sounded as hard as tempered steel. "I was just looking for something that I'd left here."

"This afternoon?"

"Before that."

In the dim glow of the flashlight, he abruptly turned away. A few frantic heartbeats later, she saw him flip on the overhead light—a single bulb waiting for a new cover—and head back to where she remained rooted in the sawdust.

He had been easier to take without the harsher light. Then, he'd been a huge, menacing shadow with eyes that seemed to penetrate the dark. As he walked toward her now, she could clearly see the rugged, unyielding lines of his face, his broad—and naked—shoulders and chest, and the silver-white scar that slashed at an angle from his collarbone to the rippled muscles six inches below one flat male nipple.

Her glance slid down, only to dart back up when it reached the patch of dark hair that arrowed below the band of his unsnapped jeans. A quarter-size circle of puckered flesh showed faintly pink above his left biceps. The sight of all that cut, carved and scarred muscle was disturbing enough. The glimpse she'd caught of the handgun he tucked into his waistband below the small of his back was even more so. It was only then that she realized he'd had it drawn.

She jerked her glance from the six-pack of muscle forming his abdomen to the disconcerting light in his eyes. It was clear he no longer regarded her as any sort of a threat. It seemed equally obvious that he was in the process of calming himself down. His fury had subsided to something more like controlled irritation, aggravation or whatever it was that had his jaw working as he jammed his hands back onto his hips.

"What is it?"

Shaken beyond belief, she shook her head. "What is… what?"

"What you left here."

The nature of her distress abruptly changed quality. "It's just something that's…mine."

"If it's yours, what is it doing here?"

"It wasn't always here," she explained, the faint ache at the back of her head making her rub there, anyway. "I'd kept it at the gristmill until I heard that some of the boys from school had started hanging out there, too. I was afraid they'd find it, so Michelle let me put it in the hiding place in her room."

She let her hand fall, brushing back her hair on the way, and crossed her arms protectively around herself. "I'd only meant to leave it there for a while. But it fell past the ledge she'd said was in there and we couldn't get it back out."

For a moment, Sam said nothing. He just stood with his eyes narrowed on her decidedly pale features. The knot of hair she'd wound near the top of her head had loosened when he ripped off the cap laying on the floor. Strands of that flaxen silk fell against her cheeks. One lock tumbled over her shoulder.

Not trusting himself to touch her to push it back, not sure if he wanted to ease the disquiet in her eyes or shake her, he stepped back instead. He couldn't believe the trouble she'd gone to to retrieve something she could have simply asked him for.

Feeling as if he'd wound up in Oz, he moved to where he'd left the book he'd found that afternoon. The thing had been between the walls dividing the rooms, along with a tube of dried up lipstick and a pile of candy bar wrappers. The only reason he hadn't tossed it along with everything else was because of the name on its pale pink cover. *Kelsey* had been written out in hot pink glitter. Much of the glitter was gone, but the looping outline of the name remained visible enough.

More concerned at the time with how he was going to reroute the electrical wiring in the wall, he hadn't considered much about his little discovery. The only thought he'd given it was to mention it to the Kelsey, who'd brought him the pie that was now nearly gone, in case it belonged to her, since she'd known the Bakers, or some relative of theirs who shared her name.

"Is this what you're looking for?"

Kelsey's eyes widened on what he held.

"That's it," she confirmed, and was halfway to him when she lifted her arm to grab it from his hand.

"Not so fast." Remaining by a pile of panels he'd salvaged, he held the diary up out of her reach. "I want to know what's so important about this that you'd do what you did to get it."

The nightmare Kelsey had felt coming on began to materialize.

"It's just a diary I kept in high school," she insisted, minimizing drastically as she tried again to reach for it.

He held it higher.

She was inches from his bare chest. Looking past the hair shadowing his armpit and the sculpted muscles along the underside of his arm, she breathed in the scents of soap and something warm, vaguely spicy and totally, undeniably disturbing. He'd showered before he'd gone to bed.

Not sure if the heat she felt radiated from him or from a purely primitive female awareness of his big body, she swallowed hard and backed away.

"It's nothing. Really. It's just…sentimental stuff."

"A lie detector would be wasted on you."

Kelsey opened her mouth, only to close it because she couldn't decide if she should beg or just try again to snatch for what he'd just lowered. He had an easy six inches on her, and a decidedly longer reach. Even if he hadn't been so much taller, and bigger, the thought of getting up close and personal with the rock wall of his chest definitely gave her pause. It also added a new element to the anxiety clawing at her when he stepped back, took a small piece of wire from the toolbox and deftly popped the lock guarding the pages between their faux-leather covers.

A new form of panic surged. "What are you doing?"

"I don't believe it's 'nothing,'" he said simply. "There's something in here. Since you just took ten years off my life breaking in to get it, I want to know what it is."

"No!"

A sense of impending humiliation made her grab for the book again. He promptly stuck it back in the air. Already in motion, she raised on tiptoe, stretching her arm the length of his, getting far closer than she would have intended had she felt she had any choice. With her breasts pressed to his chest, she reached over him, her stomach flattening against abdomen and his zipper as he edged the book farther back.

Catching her glance, one dark eyebrow slowly arched. Something dark glittered in his quicksilver eyes.

Her breath went thin. Their bodies were molded from chest to thigh. Something liquid gathered low in her belly.

Totally disconcerted by the way his heat moved into her, she lowered her heels and jerked back.

Looking totally unfazed by their contact, and her desperation, he stepped back himself to move beneath the lightbulb. Opening the paperback-size book, he flipped through the pages of small, looping script.

When Sam had found the little volume, it had simply looked like a girl-thing to him. Preoccupied with his project and the constant and nagging knowledge that he had weeks to go before he could leave, it had been of no real interest at all where he was concerned.

Aware of how uneasily Kelsey watched him, he conceded that he was definitely interested now. On a number of levels. The feel of her tempting little body arched against his had seared itself into his brain. As conscious of her effect on his long-neglected libido as he was the pages themselves, he started reading a page toward the front. The date was April 23.

The math test was awful, she'd written. *I think I passed it, but I was so not ready for cosigns. Tommy M kept trying to look over my shoulder. He's such a jerk. I helped Mom in the diner before homework. Bertie Buell came in to have another slice of mom's coconut pie. Mom says Bertie is trying to figure out her recipe and is all bent because she won't give it to her. I told her Mrs. Buell is always bent. I overheard Carrie's mom say its because she's never had sex.*

Seeing nothing incriminating there, he flipped to the middle.

I'm at the mill. Carrie is grounded. She sneaked off to see Rob again. Shell has to baby-sit her sister. I wish I could live here. I could fix up the old miller's quarters and plant flowers in the window boxes. The building seems sad sitting here with nothing to do. It's like it's just sleeping and waiting for someone to wake it up and put it back to work.

He'd never thought of a building being sad. And just that afternoon, she'd said the house they were in seemed lonely. He had no idea what made her think such things about inanimate objects, but other than a bent toward sentiment he couldn't begin to relate to, nothing he read accounted for why she looked as if she were holding her breath.

Or so he was thinking when he skipped forward a few more pages.

His own name stared back at him, written in a half dozen ways.

Sam. Sam MacInnes. Samuel MacInnes. KES + S?M. Mr. and Mrs. Sam MacInnes. Kelsey MacInnes.

Frowning, he turned the diary toward her. It was out of her reach, but still close enough for her to see.

"What's this all about?"

Heat moved up Kelsey's neck. "It's just something teenage girls do. It doesn't mean a thing," she insisted, reaching for the diary again.

He immediately lifted it away, leaving her to back off once more as he flipped ahead a few pages.

"'I dreamed about Sam again,'" he began aloud, only to pause, glance up, then start reading more slowly. "'It was just like on *The Tame and the Torrid* when Jack kissed Angela's neck and backed her into her bedroom. My heart was pounding when I woke up and my stomach felt weird. Just like when I'm around him. I'd give anything if he'd kiss me. Really kiss me. The way Jack did Angela.'"

Thinking this was definitely getting better, he turned back a few pages to see what he'd missed, skimmed over an entry that began with *I haven't seen Sam for four days,* then began again when he noticed his name once more. "'Carrie asked what I like best about Sam,'" he read. "'I didn't know where to start. I like his smile and the way he twists his mouth when he seems to be thinking about something. And I like his eyes and how big his shoulders are—'"

Kelsey heard him cut himself off as he read the rest of the line to himself. A moment later, he looked at her with a grin that would have stopped her heart had she not been so busy being mortified.

"You thought I had a great butt?"

He watched her press her fingertips to her forehead, and slowly shake her head as she lowered it. Her cheeks had turned a telling shade of pink. If he had to guess, he'd bet she was burning with embarrassment from the inside out.

He should put her out of her misery, he thought, and give her back her diary. It would be the decent thing to do, given how uncomfortable she clearly was. She really did look pretty thoroughly humiliated. But he wasn't ready yet. He honestly couldn't have imagined anything that would have so completely diverted his focus from what he'd nearly done to her.

He also couldn't remember the last time anything had made him genuinely feel like smiling. Especially after his perusal of a few more pages revealed him to be the subject of a few more rather specific fantasies. Very specific, actually.

"I can see why you wanted this back."

Kelsey was dying inside. "May I have it now? Please?"

She couldn't remember exactly what else she'd written. All she knew for certain was that whatever she'd felt toward him had been fueled by a huge romantic streak—and that whatever he was now reading must be fairly provocative. His eyebrows had risen just before his mouth formed a thoughtful upside down U and he gave what looked very much like an approving nod.

She noticed, too, that the tension had left his face, allowing his smile to reach his eyes when he finally looked to where she stood wishing she could evaporate.

"Do you still have erotic fantasies?"

"No," she insisted, not about to give him any more insights than he already had. "That's nothing but the imaginings of a teenager who used to watch a lot of soap operas." And read a lot of romances, she thought. She and her girlfriends had devoured them. Sam had been every hero she'd ever fallen in love with. No doubt she'd written something about that in there, too.

"You mean you're repressed now?" he asked, still grinning.

Her tone went heavy with forbearance. "I am not repressed."

"Then, you do still have fantasies?"

He was having entirely too good a time at her expense. Even the rich tones of his voice held a smile. "Of course, I do. Right now, I'm fantasizing about a hole opening up under my feet. Or yours."

"Hey, I wasn't the one who wrote this stuff."

"It was meant to be private."

"I don't mind that you shared."

"I didn't share. You picked the lock."

"A technicality," he murmured and, still grinning he finally, mercifully, held out the diary.

She practically snatched it away.

"Thank you," she muttered, so relieved to have the incriminating little volume back in her possession that she didn't bother wondering what else he'd read. All she wanted now was to leave. Better yet, to get on a plane back to Phoenix and forget she'd even come to Maple Mountain.

She wasn't at all inclined to give Sam points for sensitivity. Yet, he actually seemed to take pity on her rather desperate need to escape.

The floor creaked beneath his weight as he walked over

CHRISTINE FLYNN   53

and closed the window she'd opened. "You might as well go
out the door," he said, nodding toward the stairs on his way
back. "No need to risk your neck on the ladder." He flipped
on the stairwell light, turned off the one overhead.

"Thank you," she murmured again, and was down the
stairs and halfway across the living room before he stopped
her.

"The back door is open. You can go that way."

She changed direction as the beam of a light arrowed over
her shoulder. "Don't forget these." Coming up behind her,
undoubtedly still grinning, he handed her the flashlight she'd
borrowed from her mom's and the stocking cap he'd tossed
to the floor.

She didn't bother to thank him this time. Taking them, she
clutched the cap in her hand with the diary and followed the
flashlight's beam through the kitchen to the back door. She'd
made it across the porch and down the steps when his deep
voice stopped her again.

"Where's your car?"

From a dozen feet away, she turned to see him close the
door and descend the steps. Bathed in the pale moonlight,
his body gleamed like hammered bronze. Broad shouldered,
bare-chested, scarred, he looked like a warrior to her. Heaven
knew he'd had the training of one.

"It's at the mill." Not sure if she was compelled by the
thought or disconcerted by it, she motioned behind her. "I
walked over from there."

"It's dark. I'll walk you to it."

The offer caught her off guard, the chivalry behind it. A
warrior and a gentleman. The combination held a certain lethal quality of its own. "You don't have to do that. Really,"
she insisted, backing up. "I know the way."

For a moment, Sam said nothing. He simply watched as

she kept going, glancing behind her so she wouldn't trip over a tree root or a stray piece of lumber. She clearly wanted nothing other than escape. The thought that it was him she wanted to get away from kept him right where he was.

"Be careful then," he finally allowed.

"I will," she assured him, and turned, her movements as quick and silent as a deer's as she headed for the trees.

Sam watched her disappear in the direction of the foot-bridge, but he stayed where he was until he heard the distant sound of her car engine when she started it up. Only then did he move the ladder from where she'd propped it beneath the window, shaking his head at the thought of her wrestling its cumbersome weight in the dark, and return, smiling, to the trailer and bed.

Kelsey buried the diary in the bottom of her travel bag the moment she slipped back into her room, locked the bag and dropped the key into her purse. Any relief she felt having it back in her possession was pretty much buried beneath the embarrassment she'd suffered listening to Sam read from it.

She didn't know how long she lay with her head under her pillow after she'd crawled into her old twin bed trying to block the inescapable feeling. But the tenacious sensation was still there when her mom knocked on her door a little before 5:00 a.m. and started loudly humming "Oh What a Beautiful Morning," which had always been her way of telling Kelsey it was time to wake up. That awful discomfort remained, unbudging, as she threw together batches of blueberry and carrot raisin muffins, fired up the griddle and made herself smile at the morning's first customers, all the while dreading the moment Sam would walk through the diner's door.

From what she'd learned yesterday, he ate there every morning. Usually around seven-thirty.

The Fates apparently decided to toy with her a little more. Seven-thirty came and went, which left her feeling that much more anxious each time the door opened because each time it did, she thought it was him. There was something a tad distressing about facing a man who knew she'd once obsessed about him. Especially since he now knew that what she'd wanted was for him to get up close and very personal. But that had been a lifetime ago, back when she'd been all imagination and no action. Not that she was into action that much now. Or ever had been, actually.

She could honestly say that no man had ever consumed her thoughts the way Sam once had. She could also swear on every bible the Gideons had ever printed that she had not written down her thoughts about a man since her last entry in that diary, whatever it had been. She hadn't looked. As rattled as she'd been, still was for that matter, she'd been in no hurry to read what else she had written and further embarrass herself.

By ten o'clock, Sam still hadn't shown up. Desperately hoping he'd chosen to avoid her, and finding a certain humiliation in that, too, she busied herself peeling apples for pies since the breakfast rush was over while her mom scurried past to answer the ringing telephone. Within seconds of her mom picking up the dated instrument on the wall by the stainless steel fridge, Kelsey's agitation was joined by an entirely different sort of distress.

"It's for you," her mom announced, leaving the receiver dangling by its black cord. "It's Doug Westland."

Doug wanted a decision. Unfortunately she was no closer to making one now than she'd been when she'd left the day before yesterday. Because Sam and that damnable diary had totally occupied her, she'd thought of little else. "Tell him I'll call him back, will you?"

Her mom's forehead pinched as tightly as the coil of her intricate bun. "This is the second time he's called since you've been here. He sounds very nice, dear. You should talk to him."

She had talked to him. Yesterday afternoon, she'd returned the call he'd made while she'd been at the Baker place. He'd wanted to make sure she hadn't yet accepted the offer from the Regis-Carlton so he could overnight the contract and offer they'd talked about rather than wait for her to return. She'd told her mom that. What she hadn't mentioned was how he'd assured her again that he knew they would work well together and repeated what he'd maintained before, that they would make a great team, a great partnership.

You have no idea how passionate I can be about what I want, Kelsey. And what I want right now is you.

He'd first informed her of that in the beautifully appointed bar of his most successful restaurant to date, the restaurant he and all the critics predicted soon would be surpassed by the endeavor he'd invited her to join. It had been midmorning, the restaurant wasn't yet open and he'd made the offer over coffee and pie-charts illustrating parts of his proposal at the long granite bar.

It had been strictly a business meeting. In her mind, anyway. Yet, the way he'd looked at her, the way he'd sounded, had made it clear that his words could be taken however she chose. There had been times in her meetings with him since then, too, when he'd subtly let her know he was interested in more than business. She would concede that she cleaned up fairly well when she bothered with heels and a skirt rather than the comfortable baggy pastry chef shirt and clogs she worked in. But the man was a hugely successful entrepreneur. He was smart. He was wealthy. He oozed charm. He had gorgeous single women on his staff and hanging around his establishments. He could easily have the pick of any one he wanted.

He was a player. She was not.

At the moment, however, all she cared about was not being pushed. When her mother's refusal to pass on her message resulted in her having to take his call, she told him that, too. Nicely, because the professional opportunity he'd offered was incredible and it was entirely possible that her own insecurities were playing with her head. As she stood at the back of the room, holding the phone to her ear with one hand and rubbing at the little knot at the back of her head with the other, she told him she wasn't signing anything with anyone until she returned to Arizona. She also assured him when he asked that she wasn't stalling as a ploy for a larger salary or bigger percentage of the partnership. And that, yes, she was enjoying her visit with her mom.

It seemed like a good news/bad news sort of morning to her. The good news was that she would only be in Maple Mountain for less than a week, which meant she only had less than a week to go before she never saw Sam MacInnes again. The bad news was that at the end of that time, she really did need to make a decision about her future employment. She just didn't know which position was the better move for her career. Or her personal life.

Listening to Doug—who sounded as if her coming on board was a done deal—and thinking of how the Regis-Carlton's manager assumed the same about her accepting the promotion, she could feel a headache brewing. With a silent sigh, she pulled off the chef's cap covering her hair and rubbed once more at the little knot on her skull.

From where he'd just sat down at the counter, Sam

caught the pinch of Kelsey's brow and the tentative motion of her hand.

He had arrived late on purpose. He wanted to talk to Kelsey. He just didn't want to do it with the regulars around. He knew how nosey the locals could be. Proof of that had been evident less than two hours ago when Charlie had stopped by to see why he hadn't been at the diner that morning. Amos had driven by two minutes later and stopped when he'd seen Charlie's pickup.

When Amos had asked why he hadn't shown up for breakfast, Sam had told him the same thing he'd invented on the spot for Charlie. That he just hadn't felt all that hungry when he woke up. The explanation seemed inconsequential enough, until Charlie proceeded to confide that the last time he'd lost his appetite, he'd been coming down with a summer cold. According to him, the best remedy for that particular ailment was lemonade spiked with whiskey and honey. Heavy on the whiskey.

Amos swore by chicken soup. Homemade. Not store bought.

Sam promised to keep the prescriptions in mind simply because both men had bothered to be concerned. He'd also made sure they both understood that he really felt just fine. He knew how the grapevine worked in Maple Mountain. If he hadn't declared himself healthy, it wouldn't have been long before word of him being ill made it out to his aunt and she or one of her friends showed up with broth and a poultice. Concern seemed to run as deep as the granite mines in people's veins around there.

He was feeling an uncomfortable dose of concern himself as he sat at his usual spot at the counter.

"I didn't know if we'd be seein' you or not this mornin'." Sounding as friendly as always, Dora automatically filled a mug with coffee and set it in front of him. "Charlie stopped by on the way back from your place and said you might be coming down with a cold. You should get extra vitamin C," she insisted. "How about some orange juice?"

"The juice would be great, but I'm feeling fine. Honest." So much for preempting that little rumor. "I'm just late this morning," he explained, sticking closer to the truth than he had earlier. "There's nothing wrong with me that food won't cure."

"In that case, I'll go start your breakfast myself." Holding her injured arm protectively at her waist, she glanced over her shoulder into the kitchen, then back at him. "Kelsey's on an important call. She might be a while."

As usual, she asked if he wanted buttermilk pancakes or blueberry with his bacon and eggs, then disappeared through the swinging door before she reappeared again inside walking past the service window.

His focus, however, was on Kelsey. He could see her at the back of the kitchen, pacing as far as the six-foot phone cord would allow.

She'd been the last thing on his mind last night, and the first that morning.

He couldn't begin to deny how it intrigued him to know that she had once fantasized about him. With the memory of her scent and the feel of her long, taut body fused into his brain, he couldn't deny the temptation to invent a few fantasies about her of his own, either. But entertaining such thoughts, interesting as they were, would have to wait. He had slammed her pretty hard against that stud.

He had never in his career come as close as he had last night to harming an innocent person. And she was an innocent. Despite the way she'd been sneaking around, she was definitely not the hard-core type he'd grown so accustomed to dealing with.

He picked up his coffee, watching her over its rim. He'd come to make sure she was all right, but his initial assessment was that she was not. She rubbed the back of her head as if it might be sore. From what he could see of her profile, she also seemed to be struggling over something, or someone, as she hung up the phone.

She stood with her hand on the receiver, clearly lost in thought, in the moments before her mom noticed she was no longer occupied.

"Grab the eggs for me, will you?" he heard Dora call to her.

Without a word, Kelsey turned to the refrigerator beside her, yanked open the door and pulled out a large gray cardboard flat.

"Sam's here," Dora continued, her tone utterly conversational. "He wants his usual. That means four. Best bring more bacon, too."

Kelsey's preoccupation fled. Sam watched, fascinated, as she jerked her head toward where he observed her through the window. As she did, her eyes met his, her arm bumped into the door and the eggs hit the floor.

"Oh, Kelsey, no." Dora practically moaned the words. "That's the last of the eggs till Edna delivers more tomorrow. Are there any that didn't break?"

Kelsey sank to her knees. "One," she murmured, as fifteen others oozed from their shells.

"Why didn't you just take out what we needed?"

She hadn't taken out what they'd needed because the instant she'd heard Sam's name her thoughts had scrambled. She was not, however, about to admit that to her mother. "I'll run up to the store and get more."

"I'll do it. You clean that up." Already working her apron loose with one hand, her mom headed for the back door.

"There's nobody else out front except Claire and her cousin from Montpelier. I just refilled their coffee so they'll be fine until I get back. Sam has a fresh cup."

Flustered, hating it because it made her feel so out of control, Kelsey grabbed a roll of paper towels and was back on her knees as the screen door banged shut. The sound coincided roughly with the ominous beat of rather large work boots coming through the swinging door.

Sam's knees creaked as he crouched in front of her and reached for the towels himself.

Her glance made it from the denim stretched over his powerful thighs to the scar on the underside of his chin before it fell back to the mess on the beige linoleum. "You don't need to help."

"I'm the reason you dropped part of my breakfast. The least I can do is help you clean it up."

Feeling flustered was bad enough. Knowing he knew he was the reason for that circumstance magnified her discomfort level by ten. She hadn't behaved like her normally calm and collected self since yesterday when she'd first heard his name.

With their heads nearly bumping, she picked up a paper towel full of the slippery mess, shells and all, and dumped it on the cardboard flat between them.

Paper ripped as he separated a towel from the roll. "I wanted to talk to you anyway."

A hint of the raw tension she'd felt in him last night surrounded her once more. Even banked as it was, there was no mistaking that quiet intensity, that edge of complete and utter control. It surrounded him like a force field, invisible, invincible and emitting a kind of restive energy that taunted every nerve in her body.

She now understood completely why that edge was there.

She'd had no idea that a man his size could move so quietly or so fast. But she didn't care to imagine what he'd dealt with that had honed his skills to such a degree, and instilled such lethal instincts. What she had encountered last night told her all she cared to know. The man did not do his work from behind a desk.

That edge lurked beneath his quiet perusal even now.

"I could have hurt you last night." He hesitated, his deep voice dropping as he ducked his head to catch her eyes. "Are you okay?"

There was no mistaking his concern, or the guilt that tightened his jaw. Caught off guard by both, she quietly murmured, "I'm fine."

"Then why were you rubbing the back of your head?"

"It's just a little bump," she conceded, taking the towel he held to take another swipe at the floor. "It's nothing."

"That's what you said about the diary."

She didn't get a chance to tell him she wished he'd never laid eyes on the blasted thing. With her head bent, she could only see his spread knees, but she caught the motion of his hands an instant before she felt them on the sides of her head.

"Let me see," he insisted, and skimmed his fingers toward the back of her hair.

Sam was accustomed to relying on his own assessments, making his own judgments. Thinking she might be minimizing to get him to go away, he wanted to determine the size of the bump for himself.

Crouched in front of her, remembering where he'd seen her rub, he slipped his fingers over the strands of shining wheat and flax. He didn't doubt for a moment that she was still embarrassed. That was evident enough from the way she'd barely met his eyes. But he was more concerned with the harm he might have caused her than with her discomfort with him. With her hair restrained by the clip at her nape, he couldn't get down to her skin, but he could feel the knot under the baby-fine strands. It was small, just as she'd said. Barely the size of a quarter. He'd already noticed that her dark pupils were equal and reactive. Tipping her head up to double check, he saw no visible sign of concussion. Other than for the wariness in their lovely brown depths, her eyes looked fine.

His clinical assessment suddenly stopped there.

He had her head cradled in his hands. With his palms cupping her cheeks, he became aware of the velvet softness of her skin, the delicate feel of her bones. Each breath he drew brought the clean scent of her into his lungs, the subtle vibrancy of it, the lightness. It was like breathing sunshine.

He couldn't remember the last time he'd experienced a woman's softness. He knew only that it had been long before his last assignment. He couldn't remember the last time he'd had his hands on a woman he'd wanted to touch, either. One he'd wanted to taste. To explore. The majority of those he'd encountered in the past year had either been addicts, had charged for their services, or both. And of interest to him only because he'd needed to learn where they'd scored their drugs.

Touching Kelsey was like touching something fragile. Something…fresh.

His glance drifted to her mouth. Lush and inviting, her unadorned lips parted as she drew a deep, shuddery breath.

Kelsey felt something squeeze at her heart as his thumb brushed the corner of her mouth. She wasn't even sure what it was she saw in the carved lines of his face. Desolation maybe. Or need. Soul deep and weary. She knew only that no man had ever looked at her the way Sam did in the moments before he frowned at what he was doing and lowered his hands.

Reaching for two broken shells by her foot, he picked them up and tossed them onto the tray.

"How's your neck?"

He wasn't at all comfortable with whatever it was he'd felt. She was dead certain of that. He also seemed fully prepared to ignore it.

Feeling even more unsettled herself, she followed his lead and tried to ignore it, too. "My neck?"

"Here." Lifting his hand again, he touched above the hollow of her throat. "Do you feel bruised?"

Beneath his fingers, she felt her pulse jump. "Only a little."

His dark eyebrows formed a single slash as he pulled back once more. "Maybe you should get over to the Doc's and get yourself checked out."

"And tell him what?" Her voice lowered to nearly a whisper. "That I was going for a midnight stroll in the old Baker place and you attacked me?"

His voice fairly dripped with patience. "We could explain what happened."

"We're not explaining anything. I'm fine," she insisted, because aside from a slight case of mortification, she really was. "But as long as we're discussing last night, there's something I need you to know." Picking up eggshells herself, a quiet plea entered her tone. "Despite what you read, I wasn't the town wild child. I'm not even a wild adult. No one but you knows what's in that diary."

As involved as she tended to get with other people, few realized that she was a rather private person herself. She always had been. That was why she'd recorded her dreams in a diary rather than share them with anyone else. No one had known how drawn she'd been to the old mill, or that she'd once wanted to live there. And no one, not even her best friends, had known how she'd let her imagination run wild with Sam.

She would really rather it stayed that way.

"I'd appreciate it if you would just forget what you read."

"Even if I wanted to, I'm not sure I could."

His blunt admission made her go still.

With her eyes trained on the toe of his boot, she quickly reached for the towels. "You could if you didn't think about it."

"It's not just that," he told her, handing her the roll. "I can still see what you wrote."

Pure skepticism had her glancing up.

"I have a photographic memory," he explained with a shrug.

"Right," she muttered.

"I'm serious. What I see tends to stay stuck. If you don't believe me, I can tell you exactly what you wrote on the pages I saw. Do you want to hear July twelfth?"

She had no idea of the specifics she'd written that particular day. She was quite certain from the glint in his eyes, however, that she did not want to hear him quote it to her.

She was about to tell him that when the door to the dining room swung open.

Claire McGraw poked her curly red head into the kitchen.

In the time it took the mayor's gregarious wife to smile, she had taken in their positions across from each other and what was left of the mess between them on the floor. It was as clear as the curiosity burning in her eyes that she wanted to know what Sam was doing in there.

"I left money for my bill next to the coffeemaker, Kelsey." Her curious glance bouncing between them, she stepped inside the door. There wasn't a shade of pink she wouldn't wear. Today's ensemble reminded Kelsey of an antacid. "Tell your mom the chicken dinner committee meeting will run late tonight, so to stop by if she can after she closes."

Enormously grateful that the woman hadn't walked in while Sam had been checking her head, Kelsey handed the roll of towels back to him. "I'll do that, Claire," she said, rising to dump the cardboard container in the trash. "Do you or your sister want more coffee? I'd be happy to get you some."

"Thank you, Kelsey, but we need to be going. I do have a question, though." The woman's smile never faltered as it shifted to Sam. It simply changed quality as she watched him rise, too.

"You know Sam," she began, checking out the breadth of his shoulders the way a farmer might check out the potential strength of a workhorse, "I was just telling my cousin we could use a little more muscle out at the lake in a few days. Setting up bleachers for the fireworks," she explained, looking as if she might be mentally calculating just how much he could heft. "I know you're working on your sister's house, but you'll be here until September. Surely you can spare a little time to help us out. The third at four in the afternoon? It won't take long."

Sam eyed the matronly woman eyeing his chest.

Anything to kill time, he thought. "Be glad to," he told her.

"I hoped you say that." Curls bobbing, she gave him a nod, smiled again at Kelsey and seeing nothing of interest going on, backed out, leaving the door swinging behind her.

Kelsey was already back on her knees. "You were wise to agree," she murmured. "If you hadn't, she'd have nagged you until you did."

He crouched again himself. "I have the time."

"It wouldn't have mattered if you didn't. Claire has headed every Fourth of July festival in Maple Mountain for twenty years. She prides herself on getting everyone involved. That's one of the things I love about this place," she confided. "It's so predictable."

Conscious of him watching her mouth, remembering how he'd touched it, she returned her attention to what was left of the mess on the floor. "Is September when your sister is moving up from New Jersey?"

"It's when I'm due back on the force."

Mention of his work gave her pause. There was little she really knew about him anymore. So much she'd never known. Years ago, he'd been as much fantasy as reality to her. She had no idea what drove him, what passions had compelled him to choose his career or the choices he'd made that had affected its direction. Faced with choices of her own, she couldn't help but wonder if he'd ever felt he'd chosen the wrong course, or regretted decisions he'd made along the way.

Regret. Maybe that was what she'd seen in him when he'd touched her, she thought. There were scars hidden beneath those she had seen on his body. She didn't doubt that for an instant. And the visible ones alone spoke volumes. Some of them had definitely looked older than others. He'd clearly been in more than one accident. Or incident.

"Are you looking forward to going back?"

He was counting the days, Sam thought. "I am," he replied, picking up the last of the shells while she wiped up the rest. He didn't fit in Maple Mountain any more than the woman looking at him so earnestly would fit tattooed, pierced and working a sting. The town wasn't a bad place to be for a break, he supposed. It was just that what Kelsey seemed to like about the little community would have had him climbing walls if he'd had to stay any longer than he did.

He thrived on change, on adrenaline and on the challenge of not quite knowing what to expect.

Since his arrival there, Kelsey had been the only surprise he'd encountered.

"I can't imagine what I'd do if I didn't go back," he finally admitted as he rose to head for the sink. "It's home. It's where I work."

His response had Kelsey feeling a strange twinge of envy. He clearly suffered none of the doubts plaguing her about where she belonged. Doubts she wanted to believe were nothing more than just professional cold feet now that everything she had worked toward was finally happening.

"Do you ever have any misgivings about your career? About what you chose to do for a living?"

He looked as certain as he sounded as he washed off his hands at the sink. "I never considered being anything other than a cop. Gramps was a cop. My dad still is. So is my Uncle Paul."

"Uncle Paul?"

"My dad's brother." He shrugged. "It's just what the MacInnes men are."

"So you chose it because it was expected of you."

Her conclusion threw him a little. So did her vaguely sympathetic tone. He did a lot of things because they were expected of him, but there was little time for him to consider that no one expected more or pushed him harder than he pushed himself. As he took the paper towel she handed him and dried off his hands, the back screen door opened with a squeak and closed with a bang.

Her mom was back. Now that he knew Kelsey was all right, it was time for him to leave her alone anyway.

Wadding the towel into a ball, aware of how consciously Kelsey stepped back from him, he tossed it past her into the trash. "I better get out of your way."

"I'll get started on your breakfast."

"Thanks. Hey, Dora," he said to her mom and walked out, wondering why the older woman was staring at her daughter with such a knowing look in her eyes.

Chapter Four

Kelsey would have bet her favorite French rolling pin that her mother was about to question what Sam had been doing in her kitchen. The efficient little space was her domain, after all, and customers seldom entered beyond the doorway. She also would have thought she'd look a little more puzzled about his presence. Or, at least, a little more curious than she did as she set her grocery sack on a stool by the work island and reached into it. Her mom, however, didn't seem the least bit surprised to have seen him there.

"Men from the city certainly move faster than the menfolk around here," she muttered, shaking her head at the phenomenon. "I had the feeling he was interested in you the minute he walked in the door."

As puzzled as her mother was certain, Kelsey moved to help unload the bag. "What are you talking about?"

"Sam, of course. He couldn't keep his eyes off you when

he came in." Her voice low, she handed over the first of the four dozen eggs she'd bought so Kelsey could start cooking. "The man is truly smitten."

Kelsey blinked at the side of her mother's silvering head. The woman didn't just leap to conclusions. She vaulted headlong. Sam had been concerned about what he'd done to her. And, maybe, a little curious because of what she'd written about him. But her mother couldn't possibly have known that. Sam was also definitely not the sort of man to be "smitten."

Her voice dropped to a murmur, too. "I seriously doubt it."

"No need to doubt it, honey. That man hasn't paid anything more than polite notice to Marian or Lorna," she pointed out, speaking of the two single sisters who waited tables for her. Since Kelsey had arrived, she had them working only lunch and dinner. Knowing how much overtime they would put in over the weekend and wanting to keep her expenses down, Dora had taken the breakfast shift herself. "Those two have done everything short of slicin' his meat tryin' to get his attention. You must have been too busy to notice, but that man was flat out flirtin' with you yesterday." One eyebrow arched. "What was it he wanted just now?"

"He came in to help me clean up the floor."

"See?" As if her assessment had somehow just been confirmed, she gave her a quick little nod. "Now," she continued, opening the fridge to put away the rest of her purchases, "you get his breakfast and I'll tend to his coffee. Then, you can tell me about your phone call. I want to hear all about Doug," she informed her, clearly more interested in Kelsey's career than in the man whose attentions she'd just completely dismissed. "I want to know what you think about his offer compared to what the Regis-Carlton is offering you. I can't imagine anything more prestigious than that promotion, but if this Westland fellow is as big as you say, maybe that's the way you should go." Letting the refrigerator door swing closed, she headed for her apron. "Whatever you decide, I'm sure you'll do the right thing. You always do." She smiled to herself. "That's what's always made me so proud of you."

Kelsey wasn't sure what to make of the squeezing sensation she felt in her chest just then. It could have been gratitude for her mom's unfailing belief in her. It might have been a hint of panic. Trying to ignore whatever it was, she simply smiled weakly at the woman who had actually accomplished so much herself, and turned her attention to Sam's meal.

In many ways, her mom had been her role model ever since her dad had died of a heart attack when she was nine years old. She didn't remember much about her father. Stew Schaeffer had been a farrier who'd trimmed cow and horse hoofs on farms all over New England, so he'd been gone much of the time. Her mom had been a housewife who'd won blue ribbons with her pies every year at the state and county fairs. Kelsey had been their sole offspring. She had also been her mom's biggest concern when they'd suddenly been left with no means of support.

It seemed to Kelsey that after her father had passed on, her mom had simply stifled her tears, taken a deep breath and plowed ahead as best she could. She'd had only one marketable skill and a daughter whose life she refused to upend by moving them from their home. So within months, she'd taken the small life insurance check she received and thrown her grief and her energy into converting her only other asset, her house, into the diner.

That diner, and Kelsey, had been her life ever since.

That was one of the reasons Kelsey hadn't hesitated to return home when her mom had called. Her mom had always been there for her, wanted what was best for her, and done her best to see that she got it. Kelsey had always been grateful for that, too. Unfortunately what her mother wanted for her now didn't necessarily coincide with what Kelsey wanted for herself.

She hadn't realized how often that had been the case, however, until that evening when she dug the diary from the bottom of her suitcase.

Kelsey's travel clock sat on her old white nightstand next to a pink ceramic lamp. The sleek, efficient chrome timepiece looked as hugely out of place in the frilly girlish room as the expensive caramel-colored leather travel bag sitting open on a chair. She wasn't paying attention to the contrasts, though. Or the time. Propped in her narrow twin bed, covered with the pink blanket and chenille bedspread that matched the rosebud print wallpaper, she slowly flipped through the pages she'd written so long ago.

An entry in May reminded her that she'd been barely halfway through high school when she'd started daydreaming about living at the mill and grinding grain there to bake breads. Even then she'd loved to bake. Her mom, however, had pointed out that no one needed a mill to grind grain since flour was plentiful enough at the store, that even if it weren't, the mill was a wreck and that Maple Mountain was too small to support a bakery. With that idea thoroughly trounced, Kelsey had never mentioned it again.

She had always been happiest in the kitchen. That was why, daydreams aside, she had assumed all through high school that she would stay in Maple Mountain after she graduated and help her mom by doing all the baking for the diner. Her mom, however, had insisted that she needed to be where she would be exposed to more opportunities than she was likely to find in such a small place and suggested cooking school. She'd also pointed out that she needed to set herself apart with her talents if she were to succeed anywhere away from there, and to do that, she had to learn from the best. Ultimately her mother had convinced her to go to Boston. The move had opened a world of possibilities Kelsey had never imagined, and led to a life far different from what she'd rather reluctantly left behind.

"It's what's best for you," she remembered her mom had said as, slowly turning pages, she came upon an entry she'd made on her birthday.

It had been her sixteenth and she'd written about a sunshine-yellow sweater she'd seen in a JC Penny catalog. She'd wanted it for her birthday because all her friends were wearing the color. Her mom had ordered the sweater and given it her, but in blue because she'd thought the color flattered her more.

Kelsey had poured out her disappointment on the page, but she knew she hadn't let on to her mom. It had been a gift, after all, and it would have hurt her mom's feelings to tell her she really didn't care that the color was better for her. Yellow was what she'd hoped for.

An old feeling of powerlessness came out of nowhere. Her mom had always done so much for her. But what she'd done was always what she considered best, not what Kelsey had wanted for herself.

Stifling the tug of resentment that came with the thought, feeling guilty for feeling less than grateful for the sacrifices her mom had made, she flipped ahead a month in her diary—and winced.

The page staring back at her was filled with Sam's name in various forms and stages of embellishment. And her own, with his last name. It was the page he'd asked her about.

Not wanting to think about that, either, she made another quick turn.

SAM SMILED AT ME!

The large capital letters fairly leapt off the page.

He came into the diner today, she'd written. *He'd gone to St. J for his uncle and ordered a cheeseburger with everything, two orders of fries and apple pie and ice cream. I was so nervous I didn't remember to tell Mom the fries were a double order and when I brought him his food I remembered and apologized and told him I'd get his other fries right away. He's SO nice. He smiled and said it was okay because he forgets stuff sometimes, too, and he didn't need the fries because it was just a snack and he needed to save room for dinner.*

From the next date entered, she'd apparently had nothing else specific to write about for nearly a week. Prompted as much by curiosity as an apparently masochistic need to know what else he'd read, she leafed ahead, catching bits and pieces of how she'd been afraid he'd gone home because no one had seen him for a while, and how excited she'd been when he'd shown up at church with his aunt and uncle.

Much of what she'd written had her groaning at the teen-age angst she'd poured onto the yellowed pages. Some had her shaking her head at her innocence as she agonized and fantasized about whether or not he would be at the Fourth of July celebration. The entry for July twelfth, however, had her holding her breath. It was the entry Sam had offered to quote to her.

She'd seen him again. At the feed store this time, helping his uncle load sacks of grain. He'd apparently taken off his shirt because it was so warm and inspired thoughts that were utterly shameless.

He has to be the strongest, most amazing man in the

world. His body looks so big and so hard. I wonder if his skin feels rough or soft. I wonder what it would feel like next to mine. I wish I knew. I wish we could be here in the moon-light and that he would kiss me and unbutton my shirt and put his hands on me. I want him to be the first to touch me. I want him to be the first to show me everything...

Kelsey drew a deep breath. She didn't know if the know-ing smile she'd seen in Sam's eyes when he'd offered to quote that particular passage had been there because she'd called him incredible and amazing, or because she'd been so willing to give up her innocence to him. Or so she'd so boldly claimed. Heaven only knew what she'd have done had he ever really touched her.

She actually hadn't been skin to skin with a guy until she'd turned twenty and fallen head over challah with a young chef from Milan she'd met in advanced breads and baking. Their relationship had lasted until it came time for him to go home and he'd told her it was time for her to move on with-out him. Just like that. He hadn't even given her the chance to decide for herself whether or not she wanted to go with him. He'd made the choice for her, and was gone.

In the years since, moving on—and up—had taken prior-ity in her own life. She'd had a couple of almost-serious re-lationships along the way, and lots of friendships, but no man had ever inspired anything like the early and undying pas-sion she'd apparently felt for Sam.

Remembering his concern for her that morning and the way he'd looked at her when he'd cradled her head, she couldn't deny being drawn to him in some ways even now. Ways that weren't particularly wise and would have dis-turbed her greatly had she not known she was leaving in a matter of days.

Thoughts of the mysterious and compelling man he had

become gave way to feelings of chagrin, nostalgia and a strange hint of melancholy as she started reading about her dreams for restoring the mill and living there with him. After they were married, of course. She'd even planned out the wedding. And named their children.

She didn't think Sam had read that far back in the diary. Not being certain, all she could do was hope that he hadn't seen those particular entries. Not that it mattered, she supposed. The man already knew she'd been crazy about him. He knew she'd lusted after his body. Still, she hoped he hadn't realized how totally she'd once built her dreams around him. It would be nice to have at least a little dignity left where he was concerned.

She was still hoping for that when he showed up for breakfast right on time the next morning.

The diner was full by 7:00 a.m., mostly with neighbors who had come from outlying areas to set up and stock their craft booths for the start of the festival tomorrow, and with tourists getting a head start on the weekend. Busy in the kitchen, Kelsey had barely noticed who'd come and gone. She could have sworn she felt it when Sam walked in, though. Or, maybe, what she felt was the pull of his eyes when she looked up from where she'd just set two filled plates on the ledge. His glance pinned her through the window, making her heart give an odd little jerk as he took his seat by Charlie.

Over the sizzle of hash browns, breakfast meats and four orders of eggs waiting to be turned, she heard the older man greet him. She was more aware, though, of the way Sam's glance drifted to her mouth, lingering long enough to remind her of how he'd touched his thumb to its corner before his focus settled on his friend.

"Hey, Charlie," she heard him say. "Where's Amos?"

"Avoidin'," came Charlie's laconic reply. "He don't care much for crowds."

Far more conscious than she wanted to be of Sam's presence, she pulled her attention back to her tasks as her mom turned from the other side of the window. "We won't be seein' much of him till Tuesday or so," her mom informed him. "Hang on a sec, Sam, and I'll get your coffee. Marian," she said to the dark-haired woman slipping behind her to retrieve the steaming plates. "Bring out more cinnamon rolls your next trip to the kitchen, will you?"

Marian Bagley's response was to deepen her dimples at the man who'd just joined them. "Sure, Dora," she murmured, obviously conscious of him, too.

"I could really get spoiled having Kelsey around." Looking as if she were enjoying the rush, her mom slipped her hand under the large pink pastry box in the service window and balanced the side of it with her casted arm. "I never have time to make cinnamon rolls except in the winter."

"So why don't you keep her here?" Hanna Talbot, whose family ran the Maple Mountain Motor Inn, posed the query from behind Charlie. She'd come for the rolls Dora was donating to the crew setting up tables in the community center. Reaching for the box over Charlie's head, she aimed her smile into the kitchen. "Would you be interested in stayin' here, Kelsey? It would be good to have you back."

Kelsey heard the friendly question. She just didn't get a chance to answer it, or to tell the thirtysomething woman she'd known all her life that there were times when she thought it would be good to be back, too.

"Can't see her wantin' to do that," her mom concluded flatly. "This very minute she has people waiting for her to decide whether she wants to be the executive pastry chef at the resort where she's working now, or take the same position in a restaurant being opened out there. The fellow wantin' her for that wants her for a business partner, too.

"I don't know if she's right or not to take the offer at that new restaurant," she confided, sounding as concerned as she looked. "Like I told her, I think there'd be a lot more prestige stayin' at the Regis. And her future would certainly be more secure with a company that's been around for years over somethin' that's just openin' up. On the other hand, going with someone who gets lots of publicity himself might help her get into *Bon Appétit* like she did last year. Only this time maybe she could be featured in her own article rather than being part of one about up-and-coming pastry chefs."

Kelsey didn't know if she groaned out loud at what her mother was saying, or if the sound was merely mental. She knew her mom loved to talk. She also knew that her mom was proud of her. She just didn't feel that her personal affairs needed to be served up for her customer's consumption along with their breakfasts.

"Mom?" she calmly called over the chatter and clink of silverware. Setting another steaming plate in the window, she managed a wan smile in the general direction of Hanna, Charlie and Sam. Hanna and Amos smiled back. Sam, his expression inscrutable, simply watched her. "Would you come in here, please?"

With a glance over her shoulder, her mom offered a quick, "Sure, hon. I'll be there in just a minute.

"Anyway," she continued to Hanna, speeding up so she could finish what she was saying, "this fellow is so anxious to have her sign on that he's called her every day since she arrived."

"Mom?"

Her mother's voice dropped a notch. "From the way he

asks how I am and how she's doing when I answer the phone, I think he's interested in her more personally, too. From what I gather from Kelsey, he'd be quite a catch."

All Kelsey had said about Doug was that he was a well-known and highly successful restaurateur, and when her mom had asked, that, yes, he was single. Her mother had drawn her other assumptions completely on her own. Truly wishing the oblivious woman with the blond bun wouldn't be so free with the conclusions she so hastily drew, Kelsey took a deep breath and tried once more. "Mother?"

"In a second…"

"Hey, Dora." With a smile for the dark-haired waitress who'd just poured him his coffee, Sam nudged his cup. "Can I get some cream?"

Dora had been fully prepared to continue. Now, interrupted, her forehead furrowed. "You always drink your coffee black."

He shrugged. "This morning I'm drinking it with cream."

Beside him Charlie gave a sage nod. "I like a change once in a while, too. Good for a person. Keeps him from stagnatin'."

Since Charlie fought change with the fervor of a religious zealot, his claim sent Dora's pale eyebrows flying upward. "Why Charlie Moorehouse. How long did it take you to get that hip of yours replaced? And how long did you have that old truck before the fenders rusted off and you had to get another one?"

Charlie muttered something about ten years on the hip and proceeded to inform them all in defense of his truck that there was no good reason to trade in something that could still get him where he needed to go just because it was held together with a little bailing wire.

Having provided the interruption he was looking for, Sam

listened to Charlie defend himself as Kelsey disappeared from the service window. It had been as clear to him as the unease in her eyes that she was no more comfortable than he would have been having his personal business so openly discussed. He had the feeling, too, that she wasn't nearly as enthralled as her mom seemed to be about either one, or both, of the offers her mom had just broadcast.

As Dora handed him a small pitcher of cream and headed into the kitchen, he couldn't help wonder if the call that had left her looking so preoccupied yesterday had been from the man her mom had sounded so enthused about, and just how involved she was with the guy. It was none of his business, but it gave him something more interesting to think about than Charlie's muttering about how they just didn't make bailing wire the way they used to.

Sam had come to her rescue.

Kelsey didn't know if anyone else noticed what he had so deliberately done. Since conversations in the diner tended to drift from one subject to another and interruptions were frequent anyway, she rather doubted that anyone had. She had no opportunity to thank him, though. The best she could do was offer him a small smile before her mom bustled in wanting to know what she needed seconds before Lorna clipped two more orders to the order wheel and a party of four came in to take the only vacant table.

From that moment on, the diner had remained packed. As usual, many of the regulars stayed away for the weekend, as they tended to do when visitors overran their haunts. The town's seasonal festivals were a major source of income for the little community, helping provide everything from the new roof on the community center to football uniforms for the Maple Mountain Maroons. Being a practical lot, those who lived there wanted to give everyone else space to spend their money and beef up the community coffers. Even Sam didn't come into town over the weekend, though she didn't know if that was because he knew his friends wouldn't be there or if he wanted to avoid the crowds himself.

Her mom always closed the diner on the Fourth. That was the morning everyone converged on the community center for the town-sponsored pancake breakfast. Outside the sprawling white building, the short road leading to it was lined with bunting-draped booths that would later sell hamburgers and homemade sausages. Other stands, decked out in that same patriotic red-white-and-blue, offered ears of buttered corn, watermelon, ice-cream cones and strawberry shortcakes. People came for miles for the dinners at the center where the church ladies served fried chicken, biscuits and slices of the blueberry and apple pies made with fruit from their own backyards.

Kelsey usually adored everything about the festivals. She'd loved the preparations, the anticipation, the sense of belonging. When she'd lived in Maple Mountain, she'd been right in the heart of everything, working at the kid's face-painting booth, serving at the dinner. In between, she'd wandered with her friends through the displays of hand-crafted quilts, locally made pottery, maple syrup, jams, jellies and wines from the vineyards lowlanders were only now discovering. When the high school band led the parade of decorated farm equipment and bicycles down Main Street, she'd been on the sidelines waving to the costumed participants with everyone else before heading for the old-fashioned fiddle competition at the school football field a few blocks away.

That morning, she avoided it all.

By eight o'clock her mom had already left for the community center. She hadn't pressed Kelsey to come help, something that had surprised Kelsey a little, given that her mom could be as persuasive as Claire when it came to recruiting. Apparently feeling she'd worked her hard enough, she'd simply stuck her head into Kelsey's bedroom, suggested she use the day to visit with her old friends and said she'd see her later.

Though Kelsey had spent the majority of her waking hours working in the diner's kitchen, she'd spent a lot of that time socializing through the window while she worked. Carrie Rogers, now Carrie Higgins, had stopped by with her three young children as soon as she'd heard Kelsey was back. So had Michelle's sister, Jenny, and Sally McNeff, who'd sat behind her in English and History class and now ran her mom's bookstore. She enjoyed seeing them all and had thought to catch up with those she'd missed. Yet, as she showered and dressed in her favorite old jeans and a cropped white, sleeveless blouse, she was feeling an old and familiar need for a little time and space to herself.

She'd always felt that need when she had things to think about, to sort through. Or, for that matter, when there were things she didn't want to think about and needed to escape. The problem just then was that she didn't know whether she wanted to sit down and weigh her options, or simply forget for now, that she had a choice she needed to make.

It wasn't like her to be so indecisive. It wasn't like her to avoid a decision, either. Those failings only compounded the odd sense of uncertainty that had plagued her for the past week.

That was why, with Main Street clogged with more traffic than it had seen since the Maple Sugar Festival last March, she climbed into her rental car and headed toward the mill. She had one stop to make before she got there, though.

Two miles out of town, her windows down and loose hair

flying, she sailed past the lane to the mill and rounded the curve of the narrow road. Thick stands of lush birch and maple trees gave way to a meadowlike front yard as the Baker house came into view.

She didn't know if Sam would be there or not. It was entirely possible that he was spending the day with his aunt and uncle on their farm, or that he'd gone into town to meet them at the breakfast. But whether she saw him or not didn't matter. She had something she needed to leave for him. A half dozen of the blueberry muffins she knew he liked and a note she'd taped to the top of the pink box that simply said, "Thanks for the rescue."

She wanted him to know she'd appreciated what he'd done. She also hoped the gesture would make him remember something about her other than what he'd read in her diary. From the way she'd noticed him watching her the other day, she had the distinct feeling he hadn't forgotten a thing she'd written.

The disquieting thought gave her pause. So did the realization that he was there. She could see his shiny black truck parked by the trailer as she turned onto the house's long driveway. She could hear him, too. As she bounced over the ruts and pulled to a stop beside the house, the sharp beats of hammering pierced the reverberating base from a boom box. The instrument shattering the normal peace of the place couldn't possibly have been a radio. Maple Mountain only received one radio station and its programming leaned heavily toward elevator music and farm reports.

She knew for a fact it did not play rap.

Picking up the box from the seat, she slid from her car. She'd thought to leave it on his trailer step if he hadn't been there. Since he was, she would simply hand it to him.

She found him near the house's back porch, working beside a pair of saw horses. Across them lay a long piece of wood he was apparently trying to salvage by pounding out its old nails. A gray T-shirt stretched across his broad shoulders. Over his jeans, a chamois-colored carpenter's apron was slung like a gun belt around his lean hips.

Seeing her, he set his hammer aside and moved to the silver box vibrating on a back porch step.

The sudden quiet seemed as loud as the music had been when he turned to where she stopped ten feet away. Beneath the dark hair falling over his forehead, his keen gray eyes skimmed her face.

Conscious of his curiosity, more conscious of the quiet power in his bunched and sculpted muscles, she nodded toward the porch.

"I didn't figure you for the rap type."

"I got used to it on my last assignment. If I don't know the lingo, I'm too easy to identify."

She hesitated. "To identify?"

"As a cop," he replied, tossing a bent nail toward the debris pile by the saw horses. "If someone figures it out while I'm working, it could be bad for my health."

He spoke easily, his manner and tone so offhand she might not have realized how serious he was had it not been for their encounter the other night.

She had yet to shake the image of him towering over her. All that raw, vibrating strength. The hair-trigger tension. And the scars. The only ones she could see now were the inch long streak under his jaw and the tip of the one that crept above his collar. The World's Best Uncle T-shirt he wore effectively hid the rest.

Were she meeting him for the first time just then, her impression would be of a man who had nieces or nephews who thought him a pretty great guy, and who had a definite tendency to mess with a woman's heart rate when he smiled.

"So," she murmured, pulling her glance from where the older-looking wound, the puckered disk of flesh on his shoulder, was hidden. She was as grateful as the next person for those who were willing to protect and defend ordinary, law-abiding citizens. And she thought his calling terribly noble. She just couldn't help but wonder if all those injuries had been inflicted in the line of duty, or imagine the danger he'd been in if they had. "Why aren't you in town enjoying the holiday?"

Beneath soft cotton, his broad shoulders lifted in a dismissive shrug. "I work through them."

"All of them?" The sudden and disturbing thought that he might well be attracted to that danger succumbed to hesitation. "Even Thanksgiving and Christmas?"

"Even them."

"Why?"

"Because the job usually requires it."

"But you're not on your job now," she pointed out, lost by his logic.

He struck her as a man prepared for anything. Yet, she had the feeling her challenge had caught him completely off guard when a muscle in his jaw jumped.

"My aunt and uncle invited me out for a barbecue. My sister and her boys are there for the weekend, so I might go out later," he said, as if to end that particular line of questioning. "What about you?" The quick tension in his jaw gave way to his deceptively easy smile as his glance shifted to the box in her hands. "What are you doing out here?"

Wondering at the invisible wall she'd just run into, she set the box on the top porch step. "I brought you some muffins. To thank you for cutting off my mom the other day," she explained, wondering, too, if he didn't find the whole sack-race and cakewalk thing a little quaint for his tastes. She'd always loved that simple, uncomplicated atmosphere. But he was undoubtedly accustomed to far more excitement than he was likely to find anywhere around there.

Straightening, Kelsey snagged back her windblown hair. "I didn't realize it was so obvious I was uncomfortable with what she was saying."

The caution in her fragile features had told Sam the moment he'd seen her that her uneasiness with him had yet to go away. At the moment, however, he was more aware of how the motion of her arm as she pushed back her hair drew her blouse taut across her breasts and lifted the hem of her shirt. The glimpse of bare skin above the low waist of her jeans was gone in the time it took her hand to fall, but there was no mistaking its effect on him.

All he had to do was look at her and he could feel the tightening low in his gut. On the other hand, all he had to do was think of the plea in her eyes when she'd asked him to forget what he'd read about them to know her basic discomfort with him wasn't going to go away easily.

"It wasn't."

"Then how did you know I didn't really need her in the kitchen?"

"By your eyes."

Her dark lashes flicked with an uncomprehending blink. "My eyes?"

"Yours are a dead giveaway." The lingering disquiet in her expression shifted to curiosity as she nudged her hair back once more. He liked that she'd left it down. Swept back behind her ears, the tousled strands of pale ash and wheat looked to him as if she might have left the window down on her car. He liked that, too, the thought of her driving along, the wind whipping her hair and the radio blasting.

"When a person is under emotional stress, she blinks more. We see it all the time when we interrogate suspects. Or interview witnesses." Or when you're trying to mask how uptight you are around me, he thought. "You were pretty insistent about interrupting her, too."

"How did you know I didn't have a problem with something else?"

"Did you?"

A row of small white buttons bisected the front of her blouse. Closing her fingers around the top one, she rubbed it like a talisman. "No," she conceded, looking as if she found his ability to read her so easily a little unfair. "I just wanted her to be quiet. Everyone here knows everyone else, so everyone pretty much knows everyone else's business. There's actually a certain security in that," she hurried to defend. "If someone needs help, someone else is there to offer it. But Mom just doesn't get how intrusive talking like that can be sometimes."

"So ask her to be a little less generous with your personal life."

"Have you ever had a conversation with a brick wall?"

"She can't be that dense."

Kelsey eyed him evenly. "Asking my mother to keep anything to herself is pointless. Telling her it bothers me is useless, too," she insisted, in case he was about to suggest it. "You can't make a person understand how you feel when they simply don't get why something bothers you in the first place. It's like trying to make someone who doesn't like chocolate understand why you crave fudge."

When she had finally found a minute the other day to talk to her mom, she had told her, politely, that she would truly appreciate it if she would keep what she'd confided in her to herself. In all innocence, her mother had replied that she'd always shared news about her with her friends and neighbors, so she saw no reason why she shouldn't talk about how sought after she was now.

The same frustration she'd felt then tugged at her once more. Trying to shake it off before her agitation could fully surface, she drew a deep breath, blew it out. She had more important things to think about than a minor annoyance with her mother. Her career for one thing. She was pretty sure, too, that Sam had better things to do than listen to her complain.

"Sorry," she murmured. "I came to thank you, not dump my little problems in your lap." She didn't doubt for a moment that they did seem insignificant to him, too, considering the situations he probably dealt with. "I should let you get back to what you were doing."

With a self-deprecating smile, she started to take a step back.

"Just out of curiosity," he said before she could, "I hear you're leaning toward the restaurant. Is that the job you're going to take?"

Frustration with her mom prodded harder.

"Where did you hear that?"

"Over at the general store."

The town grapevine was obviously still alive and as tangled as ever. "I honestly don't know which I'm taking," she admitted, certain not knowing was part of the reason for her exasperation. "And just for the record, if you hear rumors about me being involved with the man Mom was talking about, they're not true."

"So, you're not almost engaged to the guy?" he asked mildly.

"I've never even dated Doug," she insisted, as exasperation surfaced anyway. "I'm not personally involved with him at all."

A hint of color had risen in her cheeks. It wasn't embarrassment this time, though Sam had seen her color with that, too. This time it was pure annoyance.

As he leaned against the porch railing and crossed his arms over his chest, what he noticed most was that her frustration with her mother and the rumor mill had overshadowed her discomfort with him.

"Your mom seems to think he wants you to be."

"If he does," she confided, crossing her arms herself, "it's probably only to keep me from going to work for the competition."

"Nice guy."

"Actually he is. He's very nice."

"So what makes you think he's only manipulating you?"

Her tone went as flat as her first soufflé. "He's a forty-year-old bachelor who can have any woman he wants. He dates models. He's friends with entertainers and politicians and people who know people. I can't imagine he's really interested in me beyond what I can do for his business."

She looked as matter of fact as she sounded, and utterly convinced of her conclusions. Sam just didn't know if she realized what she had just admitted, or how surprising that admission was.

As outwardly self-assured and outgoing as she seemed, and as polished as she looked even wearing jeans and a shirt that would take a man forever to get off her, he never would have suspected she doubted her appeal. The woman had the face of an angel, the body of a showgirl and a smile that radiated like the sun. That combination of innocence and seduction had snagged his attention in seconds. Having become privy to her old fantasies, that hold had become merciless.

"So how do you feel about working with him?"

A thoughtful frown knitted the delicate arches of her eyebrows.

"Being in on the ground floor of one of his restaurants would be an incredible opportunity." Kelsey offered the admission quietly, considering her words even as she spoke. She wasn't all that comfortable with the beautiful people and their groupies who frequented his establishments, but she could definitely hold her own in the back of the house. "Especially if I could eventually bring out a line of cakes and tortes that we could market outside the restaurant. The way Wolfgang did with his pizzas."

"Wolfgang?"

"Puck. Spago?" she prodded, mentioning the famous chef's most well-known restaurant. "In Los Angeles? Anyway," she continued, when his only response was an uncomprehending shake of his head, "I wouldn't be able to do that working for the hotel. Their corporate philosophy doesn't allow for marketing outside their own properties. But the position at the hotel has a lot going for it, too."

She turned away, turned back. Frowning, pondering, she started to pace. "Some of the events we host are huge. We really go over the top with our desserts and wedding cakes and there's always a major event to plan. As executive pastry chef, I'd be in charge of creativity, the budget, the staff. Everything."

She was one step from that responsibility now. She didn't even blink at the thought of managing a line of sous-chefs to turn out five hundred mousse-filled chocolate tulips plated with sauces of raspberry and white chocolate for a charity gala while preparing tortes, tarts and brûlées for the regular menu. As executive, though, she'd have the creative control she lacked now.

"So why don't you see this decision as the opportunity your mom does?"

His quiet question brought her head up. "I never said I didn't."

"At the diner the other morning," he reminded her, "your mom said you were on an important call. By the time you hung up, it was pretty clear you weren't happy with whatever that call was about. It was right after that when you asked if I'd ever had any doubts about my career. It just made me think you might be doubting something about yours.

"So what is it you're really having trouble with?" Despite the faint challenge in the way he arched one dark eyebrow, his tone remained as casual as his manner. "Which job to choose, or what you're doing in general?"

There had been a time when Kelsey would have totally dismissed the latter part of his question. It was a fair indication of how confused she'd become that it now didn't even strike her as odd.

Prodded as much by his subtle coaxing as the need to answer that question herself, she returned to her pacing. "I know I should see this the way she does. I know I should be happy to even have these choices. I've worked hard and it's finally paying off," she insisted, as frustrated with herself as she was with the situation. Working hard was how she was happiest. When she had time on her hands, she inevitably felt as if something were missing. Or, maybe, what she felt was that she would miss an opportunity. As confused as she'd become since receiving the offers and returning home, she honestly didn't know.

"I never thought I'd have one offer like this, much less have two. But I don't feel nearly as certain about my career as you do yours." She paced away, paced back. He'd said he'd never considered being anything other than what he was. She couldn't even pretend to understand what he got out of the work he did. She just knew she wasn't getting what she needed out of hers. "You're very lucky. I hope you know that," she said in all sincerity. She didn't have to understand why he wanted to do what he did. What was important was that he was apparently happy doing it. "You want the life you were expected to lead."

His voice went flat with conclusion. "And you don't want yours."

There were parts she definitely didn't want. She could handle the work. She just hated the politics, the competition, the arguing that went on behind the scenes when egos clashed. She balked at the size of the businesses themselves. The push was always to be bigger, to be more lavish. She wanted the simplicity of a small operation. In her heart, that was all she'd ever really wanted.

"What I'm doing is Mom's dream. Not mine."

The unexpected admission brought her to a halt. She had never acknowledged just how much her own dreams had been buried. Not until a few nights ago when she'd been reading her diary. She wasn't at all certain how she felt having verbalized that long buried suspicion, either.

Dragging her fingers through her hair, she felt an entirely new sort of uneasiness wash over her. "I'm not sure why I told you any of that."

He didn't seem to think what she'd done at all extraordinary as he pushed himself from the post. "Sometimes it's easier to tell a stranger what's bothering you than it is someone you know. That's why bartenders hear so much."

"That's not it," she replied flatly. "For one thing, you're not a stranger. You're part of the community." She'd always thought him so, anyway. "It's probably more that you're just good at what you do. The interrogation thing, I mean.

"I should let you get back to work," she concluded, not at all certain how he'd homed in on her need to talk. It seemed the man was destined to know all her secrets. Best she leave before he learned any more. Not, she thought, that she had any left. "I didn't mean to keep you. I was just on my way to the mill." Apology softened her smile as she backed up. "I always visit it when I come home."

It wasn't often that Sam found himself disarmed. Yet, at that moment, he was. Completely. He had no idea what to make of her unquestioned acceptance of him, or of her peculiar fondness for the places in her past. As she had of the house, she'd spoken of the mill as if the place had a soul.

"Is going to the mill one of those nostalgia things?"

It seemed he hadn't forgotten the excuse she'd offered the last time she'd shown up bearing baked goods.

"This time, yes. It really is. And there's nothing wrong with a little nostalgia," she defended. "There are probably things or places you're sentimental about, too."

His gray eyes steady on hers, he slowly shook his head. "I can't think of a one."

His certainty gave her pause. "Everyone has a soft spot for something that once mattered to him," she insisted. More curious than she wanted to be about what might matter to him, she tipped her head, studying him back. "You can't think of anything that makes you long a little for what once was?"

"I can't afford to be sentimental. I'm a cop."

He made his occupation sound like an excuse. "You weren't always one. And just because that's what you are doesn't mean you're nothing else," she replied, wondering why he wanted to cheat himself out of all the other roles that defined him. "You're a son, and a brother, and an uncle. And a friend," she added, thinking of Charlie and Amos.

"I'm pretty sure that if you think about it, you'll remember something that was once important to you. A pet. Or a place." She hesitated. "A car," she suggested, her tone helpful now. "A guy's first car can be as important as his first love. Or so I've heard."

Sam wasn't quite sure how she had done it, but in less than a minute, the woman smiling at him in the sunshine had managed to target a hefty portion of nearly everything he seldom considered about himself—along with much of what he had chosen to bury. Her comment about how lucky he was still bothered him. But her question about longing for what had once been had him ruthlessly dismissing any further possibility of discussion.

"I guess you heard wrong. As I said, I can't think of a thing."

Like a flame in a draft, her smile flickered and died.

The unease that replaced it made him feel like a louse.

He hadn't meant to be so curt with her, or sound so defensive. Thinking this must be one of those social skills the shrink had referred to, he tried to think of how to soften his response, only to find her already backing up.

Walking backward, she motioned to the box she'd left for him. "I think I'd better get out of your way. Don't forget your muffins."

"Kelsey, wait a minute."

"It's okay," she said, as if she knew he was about to apologize and wanted to save him the trouble. Offering a ghost of her gracious smile, she took another step back. "You're busy and I really did just want to drop those off."

Every time he saw her alone, it seemed she was hurrying away from him. She'd done it the day she'd shown up with the pie. She'd done it the night he'd found her in the house. She hadn't done it the other day in the diner's kitchen, but that was only one out of four.

Jamming his hands onto his hips, he watched her as she turned away now, his focus on her long legs, the heart-shaped curve of her backside, the swing of her hair.

He wasn't thinking of her taut and taunting body,

though—something he would have found rather surprising had he bothered to consider the oversight. At the moment, he was actually more interested in her mind.

He had become a master at avoiding what he didn't want to think about. In the time it had taken him to realize how easily she'd cracked the door to his past, he'd slammed it shut again. He was equally proficient when it came to focusing his energies when the pieces of a puzzle didn't fit.

He loved the challenge of finding clues, discarding what wasn't important, homing in on what was. That was what he missed about his work. Not having something to resolve. He also hated leaving a puzzle unsolved. And Kelsey Schaeffer definitely puzzled him.

The woman was clearly intelligent, independent and ambitious. She obviously had no aversion to responsibility, and he didn't doubt for a minute that she had worked hard to earn the accolades her mother prided herself in passing along. Considering what he knew of her, it made no sense to him that she hadn't already changed her path if the one she was on wasn't taking her where she wanted to go.

Two minutes later, too edgy to let it rest, he'd put the muffins she'd brought inside the trailer so the deer or the ants wouldn't get them, and headed through the woods for the bridge that led to the mill.

Chapter Five

It seemed to Kelsey that the mill never changed. The two stories of gray rock, parts of it covered with moss and ivy, stood as strong as a medieval fortress beside the babbling stream. A huge waterwheel that had once powered the grinding stones inside turned lazily with the steady flow of water spilling over the dam that created the pond beyond.

With the change of seasons, the surrounding sugar maples and sycamores would turn from lush green to gold to bare. The wide meadow that stretched to the forest would transform itself from a carpet of wildflowers to dry weeds and finally to a pristine snowfield before spring started the cycle all over again. But the little mill itself never looked any different to her.

With her hands in her pockets, she walked through the summer grass and wildflowers that had long ago overtaken the dirt road. Her glance drifted up, as it always did, to the row of small timber-framed windows below the pitched roof line. The rooms there were where the millers had lived with their families. In the hundred and fifty years since the mill had been built, four generations of the Harding family had passed it from father to son, working the great grinding wheel inside, turning wheat into flour for the farmers and residents of the area. Then, the big flour mills had gone into production, the farmers had made more money selling their grain to them, commercially milled flour became relatively inexpensive and the business had died.

For nearly seven decades the mill had sat silent. With their livelihood gone, the mill had fallen into foreclosure and the Hardings had moved on.

Kelsey waded through the grass to the larger of the two lower doors. Breathing in the rich smell of good earth and vegetation, she remembered how much she'd missed the clear, clean sweetness of the air in the hills. And the peace. She'd missed that, too.

The chirp of birds melded with the murmur of the creek as she reached for the door's big iron latch. That peace was what she had always missed most about the place. It was also the first thing she sought to find whenever she moved to a new city.

In Boston, she'd found a little patch of that tranquility in a lovely commons on the Charles River. Her refuge in San Francisco had been in the wooded park beneath the bay bridge. In Scottsdale, she'd settled for a tree-lined patch of lawn and a man-made lake on the resort's property. She could have hiked the preserves and gotten her nature-fix there, but cactus and spare desert vegetation, beautiful in their own stark way, didn't hold the same appeal for her as deep meadows and trees that rustled in the breeze.

A forged iron handle barred the heavy wood door. Tugging on its latch, she wondered where Sam went when he felt the need to regroup. Or if he somehow possessed the enviable ability to simply find peace within himself. He didn't strike her as a man who would know what to do with stillness or calm, though. He even chose to work on holidays.

Not sure why that bothered her, bothered just as much by the feeling that she'd definitely overstepped herself with him, she gave the door another tug. It moved six inches before it became solidly stuck in a deep tangle of leaves, grass and pine needles. It had been so long since the door had been opened that rains, wind and snows had compacted the vegetation into a door stop.

She'd had to clear the overgrowth away to get in when she'd last been there. And the time before that. With no owner to care for it and as hidden as it was in the trees, only nature seemed to remember the building was there.

"Need help?"

At the distant sound of Sam's voice, she turned to see him crossing the meadow toward her.

The other night in the moonlight, he had reminded her of a battle-scarred warrior. A few minutes ago, wearing the tool belt he'd now left behind, she'd had the impression of a lawman of days gone by. The images intensified as she watched him now. With his long strides carrying him toward her, aware of the power in his big body, she realized that a warrior might well be who he was. Considering how he'd either blocked or dismissed the things that might have once mattered to him, she just couldn't help wondering how many of the battles he fought were within himself, and whether peace was something he knew at all.

"It's just overgrown," she called back, too aware of her own restlessness to wonder why he was there.

He gave no indication at all as he walked up to where she

stood and checked out the problem himself. With the heel of his boot, he cleared the accumulation of pine needles at the base of the door, then hauled back on the handle. Hinges groaned as heavy wood slipped over the thick grass and stopped. He'd opened it two feet. Giving another yank, he gained two more feet and stepped back from the gap that was now wide enough to walk through.

She would have pulled the grass to get the door open. He'd simply applied a little brute force.

"I came over to check this place out when I first got here," he admitted, sounding very much like a man who preferred to know what surrounded him, "but I never went inside. Since you seem so interested in it, I thought I'd come see what the appeal is in here."

"I thought you were going out to your aunt and uncle's."

"If I go, it won't be until later. Give me a tour?" he asked, looking as if he'd pretty much expected her reluctance.

That reluctance was definitely there. But not because of how totally he'd shut her out a while ago. Not exactly. It was there because she didn't believe for a moment that she could make him see the mill the way she did. He was entitled to his cynicism. He'd probably earned it. But as unsettled as she felt about her life just then, the last thing she wanted was for a man without an ounce of sentiment in his body to question what she could possibly have found so interesting about the old place, or to have him laugh at her haven.

She'd wanted to be here alone. She'd wanted to quietly poke around the old building, to experience even for a few moments, the sense of hopefulness and potential she'd felt when she'd come there as a young girl. She was growing desperate to shake the feeling that she had come up against a huge wall in her career and that she didn't know which way to go to get around it. She might be living her mother's dream, but she had been the one who'd made the choice to follow it.

"There really isn't much to see," she warned.

"Then just show me what there is."

She told herself to be quiet, to just give him a quick tour before he picked up on her hesitation and her unwillingness only increased his interest.

"I'm not hiding anything in here, if that's what you're thinking."

"I never said I thought you were."

Feeling trapped, or maybe it was exposed, she slipped past him and into the dim interior. In the beams of light shafting through the broken-out windows, dust flickered and danced. Above their heads, the twigs of birds' nests poked from the ledges of the high windowsills. Cobwebs dangled from the beams supporting the second floor.

Hearing his footfall behind her on the stone floor, she crossed the large, empty space to another door, this one opening to the inside. Grabbing its handle with both hands, she hauled it open with the groan of protesting hinges. Fresh air rushed in, along with enough light to chase away the gloom.

"This is where the farmers used to pick up their flour." Absently wiping her hands on her jeans, she motioned behind her. "They would bring their grain for the miller to grind and dump it in a hopper out there."

She glanced to the huge flat circular disks taking up the center of the room. A thick wood shaft ran through the wall, connecting them through a series of pulleys to the waterwheel outside.

The stones, what was left of the wood casing surrounding them, and some old pallets, boxes and moldy burlap bags piled in a far corner were all that was left of the old operation. Gone was the wood hopper, the flour spout and the stacks of flour sacks she'd seen in sepia-toned pictures hanging in the community's small library. Gone, too, were the saw blades and chains that had converted the building to a sawmill each spring before the harvests came in. The bank had sold off everything of value years ago. The only reason the grooved, thousand-pound stones hadn't been carted off and sold or scavenged was because the building had been built around them and no one could get them out. Or so she'd learned when the mill had been her subject for a local history paper in high school.

She told Sam all that, then admitted that was pretty much all she knew about the place before she saw him glance to the open stairway at the back of the room.

"What's up there?"

"Just the miller's quarters."

Arching one eyebrow, he lifted his hand for her to go first.

It seemed to Sam that Kelsey looked even more reluctant than she had outside in the moments before she headed up the thick and surprisingly solid slabs of rough wood. He wasn't interested so much in the history of the building as he was in what drew her to it. But he saw nothing to explain her fascination with the place. Certainly he found nothing worth an emotional attachment, if that was what she felt for it. To him, the mill simply felt like what it was. Empty. Abandoned. Forgotten.

Unable to imagine what he was missing, he followed her up and into a space filled with light and the distant chirping of birds. He could hear the sound of the creek, too. Many of the windows here had suffered the same fate as those downstairs and were broken or missing completely. Those that did remain were rain-stained and cracked. Yet, Kelsey didn't seem aware of the dinginess and disrepair as she glanced around the open space. While he regarded the dilapidated interior with abject skepticism, she simply looked as if she were reacquainting herself with it as she touched a gray slate counter that had once held a sink, then moved to a window with the little bench built into its narrow recess.

The bead board on the front of the box bench was broken. The window itself overlooked the pond and the woods.

"Mrs. Farber's geese are loose again."

Sam had thought he'd heard squawking on occasion. Coming up beside her, he looked down to see three white fowl with beaks as orange as their feet waddling along the bank.

It was Kelsey's expression that had his attention, though. Her smile was soft, the look in her eyes distant.

There was a pensiveness about her here that he hadn't seen before. He'd caught a hint of it when he'd come upon her outside, seen her mask it before she'd hurried through the mill's history downstairs. As she reached to brush away a cobweb from above the bench, she seemed even more distracted to him, her thoughts even farther away.

His glance drifted over the long line of her body while she batted away the web's wispy strings. He was a little distracted himself. He always was when he was around her.

Wanting to believe distraction was all he was after, he reached above her to knock away the last of the dangling web himself.

"Do you still think about living here?"

Something vulnerable slipped into her expression. He caught it in her profile even before she glanced up.

"It was in your diary," he reminded her, since she looked as if she couldn't recall having mentioned that. "You wrote that you were sitting in the window." He hesitated. "Was that this one?"

With a nod, she looked away.

"You wrote about how you wanted to live here and make the building useful again."

She had wanted a lot of things back then, Kelsey thought, bracing herself to hear how implausible her old dream had been. She knew he thought the place a wreck. That had been apparent enough in the dubious way he'd eyed every surface in the place.

Her glance fell from his broad chest to the seat beneath the window. That worn wooden bench with its storage spaces beneath and broken front panel were where she'd recorded much of what she'd dreamed about. It hadn't mattered back then that her mother had dismissed the idea. In her mind, Kelsey had painted and scrubbed and filled the space with curtains and cozy furniture. She'd daydreamed of baking bread in the kitchen, made of grain she'd somehow grown and ground herself. As naive and idealistic as her thinking had once been, she doubted she'd given a single thought to the fact that she knew nothing about the mechanics of a mill. She doubted she'd even noticed that the only source of heat upstairs was a stone fireplace, that the plumbing rattled or that the window frames in the stone walls had rotted. As a young girl, she knew she hadn't been terribly practical. Practicality ruined fantasies.

"Living here was never possible."

"That's not what I asked. I asked if you ever think about living here now."

"Not really," she murmured. *Sometimes,* she admitted to herself. She did think about being here. Only not the way Sam meant. This was the place she escaped to in her mind when she'd lie in bed at night trying not to think about whatever it was keeping her from sleeping. It was her escape. The safe place she could come to flee the awful feeling that she was madly treading water in an ocean that was getting bigger by the moment. It felt sometimes as if the shore were getting farther away with each stroke and that the only way to reach it was to swim harder, faster, but the harder she tried the farther the shore receded.

It was hard to remember that she'd once loved to swim.

"I really wish you'd forget what you read in that diary. Please," she asked. Nothing in there mattered anymore. Not the way it had all those years ago.

Or so she wanted to believe in the moments before he reached over and tipped up her chin.

"Which part?"

Seconds ago she'd been prepared for his skepticism or, at worst, his disbelief at what she'd wanted. She'd also battled the awful feeling that the senses of hope and optimism she'd come here to find no longer existed. She'd once felt tranquility here, but she'd also felt anticipation, eagerness and a passion for what she'd let herself dream. It was the passion she hadn't felt in longer that she dared remember. For anything. For anyone.

With his fingers under her chin, his thumb moving slowly toward the corner of her mouth, anticipation suddenly surfaced.

Her pulse skipped. "All of them."

Sam met the vulnerability in her eyes as he slowly shook his head. Her fresh scent drifted toward him, hooking him, drawing him closer. He hadn't realized how badly he'd wanted to touch her until he found it impossible to keep his hands to himself. He could still recall the incredible softness of her skin, her hair. He could still imagine the feel of her lithe, supple body pressed to his. He had imagined it, too, late at night when he should have been sleeping, only to find himself restlessly pacing the floor instead, trying to find something, anything, to do to take his mind off of her.

"I'd really like to accommodate you," he admitted, letting his thumb skim the fullness of her lower lip, "but June is still stuck in my mind."

"June?"

"The Tame and the Tempted. You wanted me to kiss you the way some guy named Jack kissed someone named Angela before he carried her off to bed. You just didn't say exactly what way that was."

She felt her heart bump as his fingers drifted down her throat. "The Torrid." Her voice went a little thin. "It was the Tame and the Torrid. It was a soap opera."

He'd read that entry out loud. If she lived to be a hundred, she would never forget the embarrassment she'd felt at that moment. She should have felt it now, too. And she probably did. But she was aware mostly of the thoughtful way he watched her, and that he held her there with nothing more than his touch.

"I figured as much." His glance drifted to the buttons on her shirt, skimmed the gentle swells of her breasts. "Then, there's July twelfth." The slivers of silver in the gray of his eyes seemed to glint when he glanced back up. "Do you remember what you wrote?"

The blunt tips of his fingers had settled on the hollow of her throat. Beneath them, her heartbeat jerked. "I read it the other night."

She had wanted him to kiss her. She had wanted him to slip off her shirt so she could feel his skin against hers. She didn't know which disturbed her more just then. Knowing he knew that. Or the thought of being held by him, of being skin to skin with the hard muscles of his chest and surrounded by all that strength. He caused her knees to feel weak doing nothing more than brushing her mouth with his thumb.

"Then you know how it starts," he murmured, trailing his fingers back up. "And it really would be a shame to let a perfectly good fantasy go to waste."

Meeting the intent darkening his eyes, her pulse scrambled all over again. "Don't you think fantasies are overrated?"

"Probably," he agreed, his head inching lower. "But there's only one way to find out for sure."

She didn't know what she had imagined years ago. Considering how naive she'd been, it was entirely possible she'd thought he would kiss her, then literally sweep her off her feet and into his arms. She knew for a fact that she couldn't have imagined the warmth she felt at the touch of his mouth to hers, or the way that heat slowly gathered low in her belly at that experimental contact.

It was a kiss designed to test, to satisfy curiosity. She had the feeling that was all he really wanted. Yet, a shiver shimmered through her at that teasing contact, causing her lips to part with her quiet intake of breath. At that small invitation, his tongue touched hers, toying, teasing. The heat pooled lower.

She didn't know which one of them moved first. It might have been her because her knees suddenly felt weaker and she needed to lean on him for balance. It might have been him, because even as her palms flattened against the hard wall of his chest she felt his hand at the small of her back and its gentle pressure pulling her closer. All she knew for certain as he drew her deeper was that the reality of Sam infinitely exceeded anything she might have once imagined about him. She wasn't prepared for all the sensations he coaxed from deep within her. Every nerve in her body felt as if they were coming alive as he aligned her curves to his harder angles. Every cell seemed to awaken at his touch.

She had wanted him to show her…everything.

Sam nearly groaned at the thought.

He'd been curious. He would have admitted that in a heartbeat. Any man would have been after reading what a woman had so explicitly written about him. Especially when that woman still seemed to want his touch. He just hadn't expected the hunger. He was a man who allowed nothing and no one control over him. Yet, the moment she'd sagged against him, wildfire had ripped through him, threatening to turn restraint to ash and his blood to steam. The woman in his arms tasted like honey, felt like heaven and he would have had no desire at all to pull back had it not been for the inexplicable need he felt to not let her pull back first.

She'd all but run from him too many times. The last thing he wanted just then was for her to withdraw from him now.

Easing his hand from the silk of her hair, he lifted his head far enough to see her face.

Her mouth was damp with his moisture. Her eyes, when they flicked to his, held a heavy hint of the caution he was feeling himself.

With the edge of his thumb, he wiped the moisture from her bottom lip. The temptation to draw her back into his arms was strong. The desire to keep her from pulling away felt even stronger.

"As fantasies go," he murmured, "that one definitely holds potential." He smoothed back her hair, using the time to slow the rate of his heart. "Now, what about the rest?"

Having no idea which date he had in mind now, and shaken to the core by her response to him, Kelsey looked up in confusion. "The rest?"

"Of what you wrote about. The mill for instance. What would you do if it were suddenly yours?"

Kelsey didn't know which threw her more. The way he

seemed to accept what she'd once wanted as something plausible, or the question itself. She felt a little confused by his touch, too, as he smoothed back the hair he had tangled. His hands had excited before. Now, they seemed to soothe.

Her palms had flattened against his chest. Beneath one, she could feel the strong beat of his heart. She had never experienced the phenomenon before, and she wasn't at all sure what to make of it, but with that connection she could almost feel her own heart slowing to match its steady rhythm.

"The things I've thought about doing with it are totally impractical."

"Forget practical. What would you do?" he asked, tucking a lock of hair behind her ear. "Gut it and turn it into a house?"

Her glance flew up from where she'd covered the U on his shirt. "I'd never do that. Gut it, I mean. It's a mill."

Indulgence colored his tone. "It's a building. It can be anything a person turns it into."

"I thought this was my fantasy."

"It is. Absolutely," he insisted, though he liked his idea better. In the right hands, the mill could be a great house. The place had good bones. As solidly as the stone walls were built, the thing would outlast the pyramids. "But you said yourself the big companies killed its business. About all it would be good for is a museum."

"It needs to be a working mill. So, if it were mine," she insisted, tracing the U with her finger, "that's what I would want it to be. It would just have to produce something unique."

"Such as?"

"Something like artisan flours, I guess. I use them whenever I can for my baking," she explained, remembering how often she'd thought of this place over the years when she'd placed her orders. As unbelievable as it would seem, she would now never think of it again without remembering how she'd stood there in his arms. "Always for my breads. And always the best quality available. They're more expensive, but there are grinds and types of flours that consumers can only get in specialty stores or by mail order. There just aren't that many places that make them."

"Where would you get the wheat?"

Light entered her eyes. In her self-contained little dream, she'd turned the meadow into a wheat field and grown it herself. "From local farms." Even dreams could evolve. "And I'd grind corn and barley. And oats," she added, toying with his shirt as she tried to remember what else the farmers around there grew. "We have organic farmers in the area, too. There aren't many of them," she recalled, only to cut herself off as further inspiration quietly, suddenly struck.

"That's it." Her fingers stilled against his chest. "That's what I'd do. I'd start a line of organic products."

She honestly hadn't thought of it until just then. But the market for organic products was huge. It was also one that would be perfect for a small mill given that organic farms tended to be small themselves. More often than not, those farms were labors of commitment rather than labors for profit. And doing anything with the mill would be a labor of love for her.

"I would blend mixes, too. For breads and rolls. And muffins," she decided, turning to pace as the ideas flowed, "like for the blueberry kind you like. And the pumpkin pancakes Mom always makes in the fall. Only I'd make them all organic." Her mind leapt ahead, envisioning product boxes and bags. Natural brown in color. Orange print maybe. Tied with raffia. "I would even sell the pumpkin mixes with the local maple syrup. I know distributors. I have connections in the industry. I'd eventually have to hire a couple of people, but I would have my own little cottage industry right here."

Every word she spoke was pure hypothecation. Still, Kelsey could feel herself smiling. It didn't matter that the root of her blossoming idea would go back into dormancy in a matter of minutes. It didn't even matter that her current concept had more holes in it than a good Swiss cheese. It simply felt good to be enthused about something. To run with possibilities. To think about something that *felt* right, whether implementing it was possible or not.

Wanting to savor the unexpected moment, thinking she could have gladly hugged Sam for it, she tried to overlook the niggling thought that this was the enthusiasm she'd wanted to feel for one or the other of the positions she'd been offered. Neither one even came close.

"Anything else?" Sam asked.

Meeting the speculation in his eyes, she shook her head. "That's all I can think of offhand. But thank you."

"For what?"

"For not laughing at the idea," she admitted, still smiling, "and telling me how impractical it is. Or pointing out all the reasons it would never work."

Shooting her down was the last thing he wanted to do. He couldn't believe how her excitement transformed her. That enthusiasm had started with a flicker of light in her eyes that had grown until she practically glowed with energy. Each new thought had put more passion into her voice. Each possibility had broadened her smile. He couldn't remember the last time he'd seen anyone look or sound so enthusiastic. No one over the age of ten, anyway. He knew for certain he'd long ago stopped feeling anything resembling it himself.

"Would you take that idea over what you've been offered?"

She didn't even hesitate. "In a heartbeat."

"Then, why don't you?"

Excitement turned to hesitation. "Turn this into an organic mill?"

"Why not?"

"Because it *is* impractical." It was one thing to have someone else poke holes in a vision. It was another entirely to be realistic about it herself. "I know absolutely nothing about restoring a mill. Since I don't know a thing about running one, either, I would lose every penny I've saved on this place. Then, there's my mother," she continued, that final reality killing the light. "She encouraged and paid for my schooling and I'm sure she'd feel I was wasting her investment if I didn't pursue my career."

Taking a deep breath, Kelsey shook off the last thoughts of the best idea she'd ever had for the place. As she did, she tried desperately to shift the enthusiasm she'd felt in a more practical direction. "I have a really good job," she insisted. "The promotion they're offering me and the offer from Doug are as far up the ladder as I can go working for someone else. With Doug I could even have share of the ownership," she pointed out, because that was a huge draw for her. "No matter which position I take, I finally get to make the creative decisions, not just implement someone else's. What more could I want?"

She was trying hard to convince herself to be happy with what she had. Sam could see that as clearly as he had the eagerness that had slowly slipped from her face.

He didn't know if she realized what she had just admitted in her undeniably practical arguments. But it didn't sound as if it was a particular job or a position or prestige she wanted. It seemed that what she wanted most was to make her own decisions rather than live with someone else's, and to move in her own direction no matter how impractical others thought her goals.

Relating to anyone or anything other than on a professional or superficial level wasn't like him at all. Empathy felt utterly foreign to him. Yet, he knew exactly how that need felt.

"How about your own dream?" he suggested, when speaking of dreams wasn't like him at all.

He looked from the sudden hesitation in her face to the condition of the worn wood floor and the ivy encroaching along the rotted sill. He couldn't believe how drawn he'd been by what he'd seen in her. He had no idea what to make of the unfamiliar energy she had him feeling, either. But it felt as if something dying inside him had just caught a breath of oxygen, and he wasn't at all inclined to let it go.

"I could get you started on the construction," he told her, reaching past her shoulder to rap his knuckles on the stone wall. "I'd just need to know how authentic you want the place to be so I can start looking around for materials. My uncle still has wood from the old barn they tore down a few years ago. It would be easier if you wanted to renovate and modernize rather than restore. But I suppose," he concluded, aware of her blinking blankly at him, "you could do a little of both."

"You would do that?"

"I have over two months before I can go back on the force. Since I'll be finished with my sister's place in half that time, I can use the project." He'd go stir-crazy without something definite to do. Getting this place into shape for her would be an excellent way to fill the rest of the time. "As for your mom," he warned, "you'll have to handle her yourself."

He had no advice to offer her there. When it came to family, he tended to cut a fairly wide swath around certain matters himself.

The thought brought a frown, along with the reminder that he'd been invited out to the farm. He really hadn't planned to go. He'd thought he'd work for a while then take his fishing pole downstream to try the new lure Charlie swore by. But he really didn't feel like being alone. He felt even less like letting Kelsey and her fantasies go.

"Look," he said, before she recovered enough from his suggestion to say anything herself. "I'm supposed to be at my aunt and uncle's in an hour. If you want to come with me, we can talk about what needs to be done on the way. I'd be grateful if you would come," he admitted, refusing to worry about the pull he felt toward her. She would be gone in a matter of days. Even if she wasn't, he soon would be gone himself. "If you're there, Aunt Janelle and my female cousins won't drop their usual dozen hints about me finding myself a woman. They've been on that mission for years."

Kelsey had no business entertaining the idea of refurbishing the mill. She knew that. She also didn't believe for a moment that anything would come of their discussion about marketing her imaginary products. She was only fantasizing about possibilities, something she'd obviously once been rather good at and feared she'd almost forgotten how to do. Fantasizing with Sam rather than about him was a new twist, but as she accompanied him across the bridge to his truck and they ultimately headed along the winding mountain road to the Colliers' farm, she didn't let minor details get in the way.

Given what Sam had read in her diary, he already knew more about her old dreams than any man ever had. The way he'd encouraged those thoughts rather than finding fault with them meant more to her than it probably should have, but there was another reason she'd accepted his invitation.

She'd suspected before that he kept much of himself hidden, that she saw only what he wanted people to see. There were parts of himself that he simply didn't share, that he'd shut away. Or shut down. She'd never been so conscious of that as she had since he'd said it would be a month after he finished his sister's house before he could return to the force. *Before I can return,* he'd said, as if his leave wasn't as voluntary as everyone thought.

"May I ask you something?"

He sat behind the wheel of his truck, one hand resting atop it, his dark hair fluttering over his forehead in the breeze from the open window. His only concession to the fact that they were about to be someone's company had been to change into a blue chambray shirt that did amazing things for his shoulders.

"This leave you're on," she began, pulling her glance from the sleeves he'd rolled to below his elbows to brush at the worn knee of her jeans. There wasn't a hole there. But the fabric was worn enough that she'd been concerned about being dressed inappropriately for the occasion.

He hadn't even looked at her as he'd pushed the comb she'd borrowed into the back pocket of his own jeans. As if he were already aware of exactly what she wore, he'd said she was fine, told her it was just a picnic, and headed off to change his shirt.

Typical male, she'd thought at the time. But that was where her comparison had ended. She suspected now there was little typical about him at all.

"Are you having to take it because of an incident like those I've read about in the paper?" she continued. "The kind where you're put on probation or whatever it's called because something went wrong when you were arresting someone?"

His glance slid to where she sat watching him. "What makes you think I'm not taking time off on my own?"

"Are you?" she asked.

Sam had always kept much about his work to himself. Or, at least, he'd kept it within the ranks. Mostly because he'd learned that only another detective could understand another officer's mindset. But partly, too, because much of what he did or learned was classified.

Then, there were the nightmarish things he'd seen and dealt with that he simply didn't want to relive by relating them. They haunted him enough without having to drag up the gory details.

That odd empathy he'd felt for her hit again as he conceded a quiet, "No." In the kitchen at the diner, she'd told him she needed him to know she wasn't as wild as her writings might have led him to believe. He didn't know if it was his admittedly healthy ego or something more forgivable prodding him just then, but just as she hadn't wanted him to have the wrong idea about her, he didn't want her to have the wrong idea about him, either.

"I've definitely screwed up before," he acknowledged, thinking of how close he'd come to official reprimands on occasion. He wasn't a lose cannon. He had too much control for that. But he had been known for not always waiting for backup when seconds made the difference between catching a suspect and letting him escape. "Just not this time."

Her glance moved over his shoulder, his chest, then fixed on the underside of his carved jaw. "Were you injured?" *Again,* she might as well have asked.

She'd seen his scars. He'd forgotten about that.

"I was just undercover longer than usual," he told her, not caring to think about how he'd earned the badges of honor slashing his chest and puckering the skin on his arm. He wasn't supposed to be thinking about work, anyway. "I'm supposed to be doing normal stuff."

"Normal stuff?"

"They called it 'decompressing.'"

"You make it sound as if you had the bends."

He thought her amazingly astute. That had been the analogy the department shrink had used. "It is something like that," he admitted. A diver who descended below a certain point in the ocean had to rise slowly to avoid the effects of the water pressure on his body. If he came up too quickly, or without benefit of a decompression chamber, nitrogen bubbles formed in his blood, turning it into a sort of plasma-and-cellular soda pop that brought on the bends. The resulting internal damage could be deadly.

He was certainly in no physical danger, but he'd come out from deep cover as quickly as a diver racing for the surface. It was his psychological health his bosses were interested in. But he'd tuned out the psychobabble. As far as he was concerned, his only problem was that he hadn't been willing to allow himself time to readjust.

"I'd been on a job that ran fourteen months. Some people in the department thought I should take a vacation."

"You were undercover all that time?"

"I had to be," he told her, when he would have much preferred to talk about how to get the old waterwheel hooked up to the grinding stone. They'd discussed replacing the shaft, since it was split, but they hadn't gotten any farther. "It was the only way to gain the credibility I needed for us to make the operation work."

There wasn't much else he could say. Even less that he really wanted, too.

"What did you do all that time?"

That, he could tell her. "I lived and worked as a bartender

in an area you truly wouldn't want to be in. It was the only way to make the contacts we needed."

"Can you say what kind of operation it was?"

"Drugs."

"And you weren't injured?" she repeated, as if wanting to be sure.

Anyone else would have asked about his alias, or what it was like pretending to be something he wasn't day after day. All she seemed to care about was that he hadn't been hurt.

"Not that time. Honest," he said, when she looked as if she wasn't sure she believed him. "The sting went perfectly. The only people who got hurt were the bad guys. I'm on leave only because I was under for so long, and everything was over so fast. I guess it takes time to readjust."

Or so he'd been told. He'd never been under that long before. One month. Six, max. He'd had no trouble moving on from those assignments. He'd had no reason to think this time would be any different.

Except for the inability to sleep without waking a couple dozen times a night, and the restlessness he felt to get back to work, it really hadn't been.

"How long ago was this?"

"Three weeks."

It had actually been a little longer than that now. By a few days, anyway. Yet, he could still envision how it had all gone down. He needed to remember those details even though he'd written everything down in case the D.A. wouldn't take a plea bargain and he was called upon to testify. All he told Kelsey, though, was that one minute he'd been Rick, a bartender, playing the role of an intermediary for a buyer and getting ready to trade a hefty chunk of change in marked bills for a briefcase full of cocaine. The next, the surveillance team listening to the transaction from a van on the street had sent in the SWAT team that had been set in place and all hell had broken lose.

Within the hour, the parties to the transaction who hadn't been present had been picked up. Two hours after that, he'd been back at the station, filling out his report and pacing like a caged panther because the adrenaline was still flowing.

He'd reported at the precinct the next morning to tie up any loose ends on the case and get his next assignment. It was then that his supervisor, who also happened to be a friend of his dad, had reminded him that his sister had lost her husband six months ago and that he might want to take some time for family. He'd agreed to a couple of days and gone to see his sister in Jersey for the weekend. When he'd returned, the fact that he hadn't wanted any more time off had apparently sent up some sort of red flag. He'd been sent to see the department psychologist and a couple of days off had turned into three months.

Kelsey listened quietly as they drove through deep woods, past the lake and farms lush with wheat and corn. It amazed her how easily he'd described his role, and how much annoyance slipped into his tone when he'd mentioned his forced break.

She couldn't begin to imagine how he immersed himself in such a dark and unfamiliar world, or what he must have seen or done over the years. More than anything else, she couldn't imagine how he could stand to be so disconnected from his family for such long periods of time, or what it was that pushed him to avoid everything she and everyone she knew would consider normal—such as a job that didn't involve getting himself into situations most sane people would avoid, and a home and family of his own.

According to his comment about his relatives' quest to get him married again, he'd been avoiding the latter for years.

"I can see why they thought you might need a leave," she confided.

A muscle in his jaw jerked. "I'd have been fine going back to work."

Aware of the quick tension she sensed in him, she started to ask why he was so anxious to go back. But he turned just then from the blacktopped lane they'd taken to an even narrower road of ruts and gravel. With the ride turning bumpy, she looked out the front window and promptly swallowed her question.

They'd reached the farmhouse.

His aunt was already on the front porch, waving for them to come in.

Chapter Six

Ted and Janelle Collier's dairy farm sat among hills as green as the hay in the fields and the forest of trees surrounding it. A gleaming aluminum silo stood guard near a cherry-red barn and a half a dozen smaller outbuildings. Miles of fencing surrounded livestock grazing acres of pasture. In the middle of it all rose a white dormered house that had been added onto with abandon over the years.

It was the sort of bucolic setting Kelsey had grown up taking for granted, and tended to forget existed, living as she did with freeways and shopping malls. It was also the sort of place that would have tugged harder at the totally impractical longing she felt for her home had it not been for the man walking with her from his truck.

I'd have been fine going back.

There'd been no mistaking Sam's certainty when he'd claimed that, or the displeasure he felt with the leave he'd been forced to take. She just had no idea why that displeasure should be there. After fourteen months without a vacation, any sane person would be begging for time off, no matter what it was they did for a living.

Or so it seemed to her as his quiet tension brushed over her nerves and she considered that she should have given a little more thought to coming with him.

This was his family's gathering. Kelsey knew many of the Colliers, but she hadn't seen any of them in well over ten years. Because their farm was so far out of town, their paths simply hadn't crossed on her visits home. And she'd never met Sam's sister before at all. She knew from talk at the diner that Megan's husband had been killed in a road-rage incident in New Jersey, and that the young widow was anxious to move her sons to a safer, quieter environment. But that minimal knowledge only added to the sense that she would be encroaching on family time. She'd just been so caught up in the little daydream Sam had encouraged—and in him—that she hadn't considered much else.

"Oh, Sam. I'm so glad you're here!"

Janelle Collier's salt-and-pepper bob bounced against her rounded cheeks as she crossed the long porch with its overflowing pots of petunias and wicker rocking chairs. Dressed in denims and a red T-shirt embellished with a waving flag, Sam's fiftysomething aunt bounded down the stairs with the energy of a twenty-year-old.

Lines earned by worry and laughter crinkled as she offered a smile as wide as the stretch of her arms.

"I thought for sure you'd cancel on us," she announced, wrapping him in a quick hug.

His deceptively easy smile once more in place, Sam hugged her back. As big as he was, the small, squat woman practically disappeared in his arms.

"And Kelsey!" She stepped back, little flag earrings dangling from her ears. Curiosity fairly danced in her eyes. "What a nice surprise. I'd heard you'd come to help your mom, but I didn't know I'd get a chance to see you."

"I hope you don't mind me coming along, Mrs. Collier." Aware of Sam restively shoving his hands into the pockets of his jeans, her uncertainty compounded itself. "I didn't think to ask Sam to see if you'd mind an extra guest…"

"Of course I don't mind." Looking as if she couldn't imagine why she'd think she would—neighbors were neighbors, after all—she motioned her to follow her up the steps. "Sam's sister and the boys are out back shucking corn. Come on and I'll introduce you.

"Sam," she called, still smiling as she opened the screen door. "Your uncle wants you in the barn. He can use some help changing the clutch on the tractor. Tell him you have someone with you and he won't keep you down there all day."

From the way Sam hung back, Kelsey thought for certain he was about to abandon her and head for the barn. Or for his truck. Moments ago, she'd thought his displeasure had been with the leave he hadn't wanted to take. Now, considering his aunt's comment about having expected him to cancel, she wondered if he wasn't balking because he didn't want to be there at all.

She was leaning heavily toward the latter when he started up the steps.

"I'll say hi to sis and the boys first." He hesitated, something that looked like concern battling unmistakable reluctance. "How's she doing? I only saw her for a while yesterday."

"I think she's doing better since she bought that house and you started working on it for her. It gives her something positive to focus on." Mrs. Collier glanced over her shoulder, her tone at once sympathetic and good-natured. "She didn't really think you'd come today, either," she admitted blithely, leading them through the comfortable living room with its slip-covered furniture and family photographs. "She'll be glad you did. "

Sam's only response was the almost imperceptible jerk of his jaw. Kelsey caught it an instant before she heard a door slam open in the kitchen. They had barely stepped into the bright room itself when two towheaded boys in the three-foot-tall range barreled across the shiny floor in a blur of red, white and blue and into the arms of the man who'd just crouched like a baseball player to catch them.

She had no idea how Sam kept himself from landing flat on his back.

The boys, both blue-eyed future heartbreakers, were grinning as he easily scooped up the weight that would have had most people straining, and rose with one on each arm.

"Mom!" the older one hollered, his little hand on Sam's broad shoulder. "Uncle Sam's here!"

A slender young woman with a dark ponytail and eyes as gray as her brother's appeared in the doorway. Their Aunt Janelle was apparently responsible for the boy's patriotic dress. Sam's sister looked as if she couldn't have cared less what day it was. She wore no makeup and had dressed in a short black T-shirt and low-riding, gray sweatpants. She was also positively stunning.

"I see that," she replied, affection in her tired-looking smile. Her glance shifted to Kelsey. "Hi," she murmured. "I'm the monsters' mother. They've been into the cupcakes we made this morning."

Kelsey smiled, partly at the woman's friendliness, partly at the relaxing effect her exuberant offspring had on her brother. "Sugar high?"

"Stratospheric."

"Megan, this is Kelsey." Sam's dark head dipped toward his sister. "Kelsey. Megan."

The curiosity in Megan's expression mirrored that of the older woman whose glance kept bouncing between the two of them. Both clearly wanted to know why she was with the man neither had expected to show up. Or, more specifically, what their relationship was for him to have shown up with her. Whatever Megan started to say to hint in that direction, however, was overridden by the chatter of her sons.

"Did you build it, Uncle Sam?"

"Yeah, Uncle Sam." The smaller of the two boys gave a little bounce. "Did you?"

"You said you would." The older of the boys, the one who looked about six, wriggled from his uncle's arm and slipped to the floor. The instant his miniature sneakers hit the polished pine, he cranked back his head to look up. "You promised."

"Build what, Trevor?" asked his Great-Aunt Janelle.

"A trap for the monster. He told Tyler and me he'd make one so we can catch it if it follows us here."

"Hey, have a little patience." Teasing, Sam, ruffled the boy's hair. "I haven't had time yet." Lowering the smaller child beside his brother, he crouched to bring himself to the boys' eye level. "It'll be ready by the time you move in."

"And you'll give us a key so we can lock it in?" Trevor asked.

"Absolutely. I really don't think it's going to come here, though."

Tyler's little brow furrowed. "How come?"

"Will you arrest him?" Trevor wanted to know.

Sam's expression went as solemn as the child's. "You know, buddy, I would if I could. But I really don't think you'll see him once you move here. He's a New Jersey monster," he explained, sounding every bit as serious as he looked. "It's going to be too cold for him in Vermont. It freezes and snows here. A lot."

"Oh, yeah," the sober little boy mumbled, as if he'd forgotten what the adults in his life had told him he had to look forward to with the move. Apparently remembering, his eyes widened, his fears temporarily sidetracked. "That means we get to go sledding and everything!"

"Yeah! And everything!" his younger brother echoed. Swiping back the fine hair brushing his forehead, Tyler grew even more animated. "Can you teach us how?"

"Come on, boys." Darting a look of concern toward her niece, Mrs. Collier motioned one work-chapped hand toward the door. "Let's get back to our project. Your second cousins and all the kids will be here in an hour or so," she told them, speaking of her own offspring and grandchildren, "and your uncle needs to go help his uncle in the barn." She glanced to Sam. "Grandma and Grandpa Collier are coming, too. And I think your Aunt Mary," referring to her in-laws, who also happened to be his grandparents and an aunt on his mother's side. "She was going to work the festival for a while and come out later."

Looking more than willing to spare the boys the deluge of relatives, or more likely spare himself, he touched a protective hand to the boy's heads. "Why don't I take them down to the barn with me?"

His sister's voice went flat. "Because they'll get dirty again."

"No, we won't!" Trevor insisted.

"Nuh-huh," Tyler agreed with a vigorous shake of his head.

"Tell you what," said Sam. "If they get too dirty, I'll just turn a hose on them. What do you say, boys? Do you want to stay and shuck corn, or learn how to fix a clutch?"

Both boys grabbed their uncle's hands and hauled him toward the door. Neither one of them seemed to have a clue what they were doing, but if their uncle was doing it, they clearly wanted to do it, too.

"What's a clutch?" the older one wanted to know.

"It's something that helps shift gears."

"What's a gear?" voiced the younger one.

Pushing open the screen, Megan stepped aside to avoid getting trampled.

"Keep them away from anything pointed or sharp," she called as the trio squeezed through the doorway. "And no more sugar!"

"They'll be fine," Sam called back. "Hey, listen. If you guys need any pies baked, let Kelsey do it." His glance caught hers, something like apology, or maybe it was guilt, in his quick smile.

Until that moment, Kelsey wasn't sure he'd even realized she was there. Watching his sister glance to where she remained by the magnet-and-crayon drawing-covered fridge, she also realized she'd just been abandoned. With his uncle having rescued him from the women, he apparently didn't need her as a buffer.

Without him with her, she felt much as she had outside—as if she might well be intruding. Lines of worry deepened in Mrs. Collier's forehead as she searched her niece's face.

"What's this about a monster trap, Megan?"

The weariness Kelsey had noticed in Sam's sister's smile moved into her eyes as she turned from the door.

"We've been having a little problem with nightmares." She spoke quietly, her tone as matter-of-fact as Sam's had been when he'd related what he had about his last assignment. "Ever since Rob died, the boys have had to sleep with the lights on. Or with me," she explained, bending to pick up the bits of grass that had come off the boys' shoes. "Their pediatrician says it's not abnormal for a child who's lost a parent to suffer insecurity. Especially when it's the father, since he's usually regarded as the protector." Crossing the room, she dropped the grass in the trash under the sink and turned with another smile in place. This one apologetic.

"I'm sorry," she said to Kelsey. "Bummer subject to walk in on, huh? Anyway," she continued to her aunt, "when we were out at the house yesterday, Trevor asked Sam where the closets would be so he'd know where the monster would hide. After I told Sam what was going on, he came up with the idea of the trap. The boys were talking about it last night. I think knowing they'll have some control might actually help."

"Well, I like that he told them he didn't think it would come here at all. He's a good uncle."

"Yeah. He is. I just wish he was around more." Her voice dropped to a mutter. "What I really wish is that he'd quit that damn unit, but we all know that's not going to happen." Taking a deep breath, she blew it out.

"So, Kelsey," she said, sounding truly anxious to change the subject. "At the risk of being totally rude, how about helping me make coleslaw while you tell us how long you've known my brother?"

The feeling that she shouldn't have accepted Sam's invitation faded somewhere between admitting that she'd first met Sam thirteen years ago and learning that Mrs. Collier had never known or suspected that he'd stopped at the diner on his way back from running errands for his uncle. According to his aunt, during the summers he and his sister had spent with them, he'd always been ravenous come suppertime. Ac-

PLAY THE
Lucky Key Game

and you can get

FREE BOOKS
and a FREE GIFT!

Do You Have the LUCKY KEY?

Scratch the gold areas with a coin. Then check below to see the books and gift you can get!

YES! I have scratched off the gold areas. Please send me the 2 FREE BOOKS and GIFT for which I qualify. I understand I am under no obligation to purchase any books, as explained on the back of this card.

335 SDL D7X2   235 SDL D7Y3

FIRST NAME   LAST NAME

ADDRESS

APT.#   CITY

STATE/PROV.   ZIP/POSTAL CODE

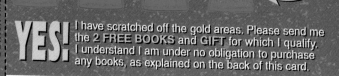

2 free books plus a free gift   1 free book

2 free books   Try Again!

cording to his sister, who'd remembered the diner but had never been in it back then, he must have been impressed with more than the food there now to have brought her with him.

"You're the first woman he's brought around family since his divorce." With a speculative smile, she reached into the fridge. "That's what, Aunt Janelle? Ten years now?"

"About that," the older woman replied, clearly speculating herself.

Megan turned, held out a head of cabbage. Taking it, Kelsey refused to find any importance at all to what he'd done. He'd brought her as his cover to avoid having his relatives poke around his personal life the way they were doing now. That was all.

"That doesn't mean anything," she insisted. "We've really only known each other for a few days. It's not like we're dating." *Or anything,* she might have added. But that wouldn't have been quite true. They had her old fantasies between them—such as the one that had started with a kiss that had slowly melted her insides and left him looking more than willing to explore the rest of her imaginings.

"This isn't a date?"

"We're just…friends."

Unable to think of a better way to describe whatever their relationship was, she added an apologetic smile for Mrs. Collier. The woman looked truly disappointed.

Megan ignored the claim.

"Our mom met Dad working at a diner. It was a coffee shop, actually," she corrected, unceremoniously spooning mayonnaise into a bowl. "At Stowe. Mom worked at the lodge there after high school. She said it was as far from this house as Grandpa would let her go."

"She lived here?"

"Until she was twenty," Megan replied. "Uncle Ted's her

brother. He took over the farm when he married Aunt Janelle. Anyway, Dad was a rookie cop and he'd gone there on a ski vacation."

"Cocky rookie cop," her aunt pronounced, handing Kelsey a cutting board and a knife before she turned to start hulling strawberries.

"From what I understand," Megan continued, still spooning, "Mom didn't want anything to do with him. I guess he showed up every morning that week to ask her out. And every morning, she said no. When his vacation was over, she thought she'd never see him again, but he came back the following weekend and asked her out again."

"Did she go then?"

Megan's dark ponytail swayed as she shook her head. "Mom said she told him she didn't want to date a policeman. She didn't want to move to the city and have to worry about losing her husband in the line of duty. She wanted a nice farm boy.

"He told her he didn't want to date her," she continued. Tipping the jar, she dug at what was left in the bottom. "He said he wanted to marry her. I guess he also told her that if she wanted a man with a safe job, she better look beyond the farm because he'd heard of some pretty nasty accidents with combines and tractors. Then, he promised he wouldn't die on her. He told her he was the third generation of New York's finest and his family had a tradition of staying healthy."

"Cocky," Mrs. Collier repeated.

"'Confident,' he'd say," Megan defended. She glanced toward Kelsey. "Has my brother promised you that?"

Caught tossing the first layer of cabbage leaves toward the garbage disposal, the question nearly made Kelsey miss the sink.

"Megan," her aunt softly chided. "She said they're just

friends. Just because they met in a similar way doesn't mean anything."

"I know my brother, Aunt Janelle. He's very much his father's son when it comes to knowing what he wants." The jar clinked against the counter as she set it down to look at Kelsey. "I already know he must care about you to have brought you here. I guess what I really want to know is how much influence you have with him. He's told you what he does, hasn't he? About the assignments he takes?"

Kelsey hesitated. Sam's sister was nothing if not direct. Her claim about his caring, however, was terribly off course. "He's told me some." Enough to make me wonder why he didn't want this leave, she thought to herself.

"Did he tell you how long he was under last time?"

"Fourteen months."

Looking vindicated, Megan reached for a lemon. "Then you know why we worry about him." She set the citrus on the counter, whacked it in half with a knife. "Mom hates the duty he's pulled the last several years. Even Dad tried to discourage him before he went under this last time. You know it has to be bad for my father to do something like that, too," she insisted. "Dad is as loyal as blood to the corps. And he'll defend Sam every time to the rest of us. But you have to know he's getting concerned himself when he starts trying to talk him into transferring into something else. I overhead him tell Sam right after he came off this last assignment that there's a reason there aren't many fifty-year-old undercover detectives. They either burn out or get shot." Her hand tightened around the knife as she glanced up. "Do you know what Sam said?"

Unable to even venture a guess, Kelsey shook her head.

"He said, 'I've already been shot, so I have fifteen years before I have to worry about the other.'"

As if to make sure her niece hadn't just offered news out of turn, Janelle darted a cautious glance to where Megan pressed half the lemon, hard, onto the juicer. "That might not be something he told her about, dear."

"It's okay." Kelsey offered the assurance quietly. "I knew. That he'd been shot, I mean." She knew none of the details of the incident. But she'd seen the puckered scar, along with enough police shows to suspect what it was. And she'd seen the other scars. The ones that looked like slashes. Watching his sister now, she found herself hoping there weren't others in places his pants had kept her from seeing.

Having no idea how to ask, reluctantly hoping his sister might offer more, she remained silent and returned to her task.

"At least he talks to you," Megan muttered, assuming far more than Kelsey had intended. "We can't talk to him about his work at all. His back goes up the minute any of us says a word about it." Her voice dropped lower. "Maybe you can talk some sense into him."

The assumption that she could be their champion brought Kelsey's motions to a halt.

"I'm sorry, Megan. I really am. But I don't have any influence over Sam at all." She'd never met anyone less susceptible to another's influence, either. His very need to rely on himself, his skills, his judgment made him very much his own man, insular in ways she couldn't begin to comprehend. "I can't imagine that he's not the absolute best at what he does, though. He has good instincts." She encountered some of them herself. "He knows how to protect himself."

Even as she spoke, she knew how weak her assurance had to sound. Megan had grown up in a family of policemen. Her brother had already been injured in the line of duty. She knew what the risks were.

"That's what I tell myself, too." Defiance fought helplessness. "It's what everyone who loves a cop does. I love my brother and I love my dad, but I was like Mom. I didn't want to live with the uncertainty that came with being married to one.

"My husband was an accountant. You don't find a job much safer than that," she said quietly. "He was my best friend. He was a good man. A gentle man. But we lost him to the kind of random violence my brother deliberately walks into. I know there are no guarantees," she insisted. "And I know all the arguments about why we need people out there watching out for us. I grew up hearing all of them. I just want somebody else to do it."

She shook her head, blew a breath. "Ignore me," she muttered, tossing the empty lemon rind onto the cabbage leaves. "I quit talking to my brother about this ages ago. I should know by now that no one's going to be able to keep him from doing what he wants to do."

Kelsey considered the young widow squeezing the life out of the other half of the lemon. As much as Sam's sister had already lost, she clearly feared losing more should something happen to her brother. Knowing no possible way she could help herself, Kelsey offered the only idea that might.

"If it's been that long," she suggested softly, "maybe you should say something to him now."

Megan gave her head another shake, wiped back a stray hair with her forearm. "I don't want to wreck the time we'll have with him here. Especially for the boys," she said, as the front door opened and voices drifted in. "I don't know if you've noticed it yet," she said as the voices grew nearer, "but my brother is a master at avoiding people he thinks are going to say what he doesn't want to hear."

"You must be talking about Sam."

That breezy observation came from a younger version of

Mrs. Collier as Cathy, her oldest daughter, walked in with a pie in each hand, a husband bearing a bowl of potato salad and two little girls who promptly wrapped themselves around their grandmother's knees. Seeing Kelsey, Cathy gave a little squeal of recognition and set the pies on the table before throwing open her arms à la her mother to greet the classmate she hadn't seen in years. Her husband, whom Kelsey had never met since he wasn't from around there, sought the security of the barn the minute he was introduced and learned that was where the other males had gone.

For the next hour, talk moved with comfortable ease from the rumors Cathy had heard about Kelsey's job offers, to how work was progressing on Megan's new house, and on to the long-ago summers the cousins, Megan and Cathy, had spent together on the farm with their respective brothers.

As more food was prepared, and the little girls were set on chairs to help, Kelsey began to realize that Sam hadn't just visited the farm outside Maple Mountain on occasion. As a child he'd spent part of nearly every summer there. As he'd grown older, he'd worked entire summers with his uncle. He hadn't worked there in college, though, other than the summer between his junior and senior years. That had obviously been the year her hormones had kicked in and he'd gone to work on her imagination.

She learned, too, that those summer visits to the farm were sacrosanct as far as Megan and Sam's mother was concerned. Since her children were being raised in the city, she had insisted that they have the balance spending time in the country would provide. She'd very much wanted them to know the quieter life she'd grown up with.

As much as Kelsey admired their mother's parenting philosophy, quiet was nowhere to be found as more relatives arrived bearing food and small children. The afternoon breeze soon carried the screams of kids running through sprinklers and the laughter of women visiting while they drank iced tea at the long picnic tables and chased wet offspring. When the men finally showed up needing to wash because they all had grease under their nails, the sounds filling the air were joined with the deeper chuckles of good-natured ribbing and, eventually, the clank of horseshoes being played on the far lawn.

All the while Kelsey found her thoughts drawn to the man who stood a little taller than the rest, whose deep laugh masked deeper secrets and whose occasional smile in her direction had her conscious of the members of his family curiously watching them both.

He said very little to her, though. Other than to sit beside her when they all finally ate with everyone jammed elbow-to-elbow at the heavily laden picnic tables, he spent most of his time with the men and the kids—until the adults started gathering the children to go see the fireworks at the lake.

It wasn't until his aunt had asked Sam if he and Kelsey would be going out to the lake with them that he realized how long he'd been there. It had been in the back of his mind when he and Kelsey arrived to stick around for an hour or so, then head back to the mill. Between helping his uncle, a man he admired as much for his live-and-let live attitude as his ability to repair or rebuild practically anything, and horsing around with his nephews, that hour had turned into the entire afternoon.

Leaving had still been his plan when he'd come up from the barn and seen the women buzzing like bees around the tables outside. That had been when he'd caught sight of Kelsey laughing with his sister and one of his cousins. He didn't know if he hadn't wanted to interrupt because his sister looked as if she were having a good time or because

Kelsey did, but he'd taken his cousin Ed's bet on a game of horseshoes and the rest of the day had disappeared.

Now with everyone piling into their cars to head for the lake and Kelsey waving goodbye to a carload of his relatives from the seat beside him in his truck, he had the feeling he should have stuck to his original plan.

"You wanted to go to the lake, didn't you?"

"It's okay." As if to forgive him for having told everyone he needed to get her back to her car—as if it were her fault they wouldn't be joining them, she flashed him a totally unconvincing smile. "I've seen fireworks before."

"If you want to go, we will. After today," he conceded, "I owe you."

"You don't owe me anything. I had a great time. I did," she insisted, mistaking the reluctance behind his offer for doubt. "It would have helped if you'd warned me, though."

"About what?"

"You didn't just want me there so your aunt wouldn't nag you about finding yourself a woman. You wanted me there so she and your sister wouldn't gang up on you about your job."

Sam kept his expression impassive as he put the truck into gear and pulled out onto the road. He had no idea how she'd handled what she'd heard. He didn't know either if he was sorry she'd been privy to whatever they'd had to say, or sorry that he'd subjected her to it. All he knew for certain was that he could feel his defenses rising like missiles in a silo.

They had no sooner locked into place, however, than he glanced over to see her adjusting the harness of her seat belt. The accusation he'd heard in her tone was there only because he'd sent her into a situation unarmed, not because she had joined ranks. She wasn't saying a word about how dangerous his work was or about how his family worried about him being undercover for so long. Especially this last time.

He also knew that he was guilty as charged. That didn't relax his guard, however, or make him any more inclined to deal with the frustration he inevitably felt having to defend the life he'd made for himself. He thrived on what he did. And as for their worry, while he was doing his job, they had their own, neatly ordered lives. Except for his sister, he mentally qualified. Since she'd lost her husband, her life wasn't so enviable anymore.

"She's having a hard time, isn't she."

There was no question in her tone. All he heard in the simple statement was understanding, and an unspoken agreement to leave his family's objections to his job alone.

"Yeah," he murmured. "I think so." Thoughts of Megan added an even sharper tug of guilt. His sister's presence had been another reason he hadn't been crazy about going to his aunt and uncle's today. He never knew what to say to her. He felt totally helpless when it came to dealing with emotional pain. Especially in a woman. Most especially in a woman he cared about.

"I don't talk to her about anything but the house," he admitted. When he wanted to know how she was coping, he would ask someone else. His mom. His aunt. "So I'm not really sure."

"You talk to her about her sons," she reminded him. "The monster trap?" she coaxed, leaning forward to catch his eyes. "From what she said, I think you've helped ease her mind about the nightmares as much as you did the boys'." A hint of something that sounded almost like admiration softened her tone. "I don't imagine there's anything more important to her than knowing her boys can sleep at night. What you did for them was huge."

Guilt jerked hard. He didn't deserve anyone's appreciation. Had he not been on a forced leave, his sister would have hired a contractor and he wouldn't have been working on the house at all. "I just happened to be there when Tyler asked his mom about the closets."

"Exactly," she agreed. "You were there. And you had a solution that gave them control. I don't think she feels as if she has a whole lot of that right now.

"So," Kelsey murmured, thinking it best to ease away from how much his sister and his nephews might need him. She knew how easily he could withdraw, and there was something she needed to ask.

Dusk was rapidly turning to darkness as they followed the road leading to the lake and to town. Soon fireworks would be visible over the tops of the trees. She wondered if they might see them as they passed, or if they would pass the area before they started and she would miss them completely.

She really would have loved to see the display.

"Is this one of the holidays you don't like?"

In the pale evening light, she watched him glance toward her. "What makes you think I don't like it?"

"You said this morning that you always work holidays. I just wondered if there are some memories that make you want to avoid this one more than others."

Sam didn't mind talking to her about the mill. He certainly didn't mind talking about her diary. He didn't even mind talking with her about his family and that wasn't something he was inclined to do with anyone. But this particular territory lead to a minefield.

"I don't think of any of them any differently than the rest," he admitted, fully intending to skirt that particular piece of his past. He kept his tone nonchalant, his eyes on the darkening ribbon of road. "When I first joined the force, I worked every holiday because I had to. I was a rookie, so I was always assigned the lousy shifts." That circumstance alone had kept him from joining the others at turkey- and ham-laden tables. For the first year, anyway. "What I remember most about the Fourth of July is working crowd control and hauling in drunk drivers."

"But you haven't been a rookie for a long time."

Evading, he reached to turn on the radio. "I guess I just like what I do."

The lively strains of a John Philip Sousa march had barely filled the air before Kelsey reached over and turned the radio back down. "That's not fair."

"What?" he grumbled. "I just want some music."

"What you want is to avoid the subject. You're really very good at that, too, by the way. But you don't have a diary I can pick the lock on," she pointed out, reminding him of how he'd come by her own secrets. "All I'd like to know is why you like your job better than being with your family. Or having one of your own to celebrate with," she added quietly, wondering about the woman he'd been married to so briefly all those years ago. No one had said a word about her. "Your aunt and your sister said you used to love holidays, but this is the first one you've spent with the family in years."

That was only because he'd been put on leave and couldn't work. She didn't doubt for a moment that was why he hadn't stayed away this time, too. What she didn't understand was why he felt the need to keep that not-so-subtle distance in his relationships, or why it mattered so much to her that he did. She just knew she needed to know what had created his aversion to all the things she'd yearned for so deeply. The home and family she'd told herself must wait for the right time, the right place, the right man.

She'd just never been in a place that felt like it could be home. Or met a man that made her feel that anywhere she was with him was where she was supposed to be.

"So this is payback for picking your lock?"

"If that's what you want to call it."

He really needed another assignment, Sam thought, eyeing the woman silently daring him to deny the exchange of information. When he was involved in a case, his mind was too occupied with playing his role and staying alert to trouble to allow room for the old tapes now playing in his head. All of Kelsey's talk that morning about remembering things that had once been important had resurrected memories he could have sworn he'd shoved back. But they were right there again, staring him in the face and avoiding her question wasn't going to make them go away.

"I was thinking of family when I first started working holidays," he finally defended. He would stick to the facts. Considering what she'd not-so-willingly shared with him, it was the best he could do. "Same for when I was working all the overtime I could get. That's why I was never around even after I didn't have to take the rotten shifts. I didn't want to miss the extra pay."

There had been a point in his life when he couldn't have imagined not having a wife and children. He'd truly wanted the life his parents and aunts and uncles had. The life his cousins had now. He wasn't sure, but he might have decided to marry Trish McDonald even before they'd graduated from high school. He'd been that infatuated with her. She'd wanted to teach, have babies. She'd seemed crazy about him, too. And his Mom and Dad had adored her. So had his sister. She'd fit his dream perfectly.

"I'd known Trish forever," was all he cared to admit aloud, though. "We waited until after I'd graduated from college and joined the force to have the big church wedding, then settled down to what had seemed the logical next step. We wanted to buy a house, then start a family. Only I worked so much overtime trying to earn the extra money we needed for a down payment that she got lonely. We'd barely been married a year before she found herself a lover to occupy her time and wound up pregnant. The baby wasn't mine."

His focus remained on the road, his tone matter of fact. "It wasn't too long after the divorce that I went into undercover work. That took up holidays, too," he continued, sounding as if what he'd just revealed was only of secondary importance to defending his failure to appear at family gatherings. "By now, I don't give them much thought one way or the other."

For a moment, Kelsey said nothing. She didn't doubt for an instant that he'd been far more affected than he let on by his flat recitation of his ex-wife's infidelity. His dreams had been shattered. Right along with his trust. And his heart.

The thought that his heart might bear the worst of his scars put a funny little ache in her own.

"I can see why you wouldn't rush back into anything." The magnitude of that betrayal might have destroyed a lesser man. "But what about someday?" He'd already spent years alone. Much of that in a world she couldn't begin to comprehend. "Don't you ever want to marry again?" she asked, thinking of how incredibly lonely he must be at times.

"I don't think I was meant to be married to begin with. I'm good at what I do. And to be good at undercover, you can't be worried about what's going on with a family you're not even living with." In the deep dusk, the lights of an oncoming car illuminated his easy smile. "It's not as bad as you're thinking. Honest. I meet some really interesting people."

She couldn't quite make herself smile back. "Then you really do like what you do."

"I can't imagine doing anything else."

He'd told her that before. Back when she'd thought he'd chosen his work because it had been expected of him. But he wasn't living the life someone else wanted for him. He wanted exactly what he had. She just couldn't shake the feeling that his job had become a sort of cover itself. Something that protected him from having to think about what might have been, about what he would be reminded of not having himself every time he was with his family.

Not wanting him to realize how sad she thought his self-imposed isolation, she looked away from his shadowed profile. He had such a good heart. She'd seen that with his family, with his concern for his sister, his nephews. He'd exposed it when he'd shown up the day after he'd knocked her head into the post to make sure she was all right. There was an undeniable generosity about him, too. It had been there in the way he'd encouraged her dream about the mill. But he'd locked the most vulnerable part of himself away with his own dreams, and buried himself right along with them.

She'd forgotten to look toward the lake when they'd passed it. Now, miles beyond where rockets were illuminating the night sky, she listened to the crunch of gravel beneath the truck's tires as he turned onto the old mill road.

The thought that he was somehow larger in life than he'd ever been in her imagination only compounded the pensiveness she felt when she realized it wouldn't be long before she needed to say good-night. And goodbye.

Chapter Seven

Kelsey didn't want to say goodbye. Not yet. She didn't want Sam to say it, either. Yet, she had the feeling from the way his glance fell to her mouth as he turned off the ignition that he was thinking along those lines himself. A kiss for the road. Then they could both be on their way.

She simply wasn't ready. She wanted more time with him. She also wanted what she'd come for that morning, to try to absorb the peace she usually felt in this place.

Wishing he could feel it, too, she opened the passenger door. "Walk me to my car?" she asked.

The slam of his door echoed hers, then gave way to the chirp of crickets and the brush of field grass and wildflowers against the ankles of her jeans as she moved to the front of his truck. The moon had crested a distant hill. Its pale beam reflected off the mill's stone walls and the water cascading over the pond's little dam. A faint breeze, cool enough to make her shiver, whispered through the trees.

Instead of moving toward her car a few yards away, she turned full circle, slowly taking everything in. She never knew how long it would be before she could come back.

"I really wish I didn't have to leave." It was probably good that she had to, though, she supposed. The more she learned about Sam, the more time she spent with him, the more she realized how capable he was of resurrecting her little fantasies all over again. There was nothing sensible about the pull she felt toward him. Certainly there was nothing logical about entertaining the lovely ideas he'd encouraged for the mill.

His features shadowed, he walked toward her, his gait easy, his eyes glittering in the darkness.

"When are you leaving?"

"The day after tomorrow. I want to make sure Betsy gets back before I go."

Tipping her head when he stopped in front of her, she tried for a lightness she truly didn't feel. She hated to think she actually dreaded going back, yet there was no denying the knot that formed in her stomach at the thought. "As long as you're going to be here for a while, keep an eye on this place for me. Will you?"

"Why don't you come back and keep an eye on it yourself?"

She heard the smile in his voice, matched it with her own. "Because I work a couple of thousand miles away," she reminded him. "And because I wouldn't have a way to support myself if I came back here."

"You don't have to work where you do unless that's what you really want to do," he pointed out, ever so casually. "You don't have to take that other guy's offer, either. And if you came back here, you could do what we talked about and reopen the mill."

"That was just talk." Like the stars that had slipped behind a wisp of cloud, her smile vanished. She didn't want him drawing her any deeper into the idea than he already had. The old longings he'd resurrected tugged hard enough as it was. "It wasn't anything but something fun to think about."

"Your excitement was real enough."

"It would take forever to get it up and running," she insisted, determined to keep her thoughts in perspective. That excitement still felt real. And far more compelling than she should have allowed. "A year at least."

"A year isn't forever," he countered mildly. "And I told you, I'd help you get started."

"But it's not practical," she argued right back, not at all sure why he wouldn't let it go. "Then there's the fact that it's not sensible. Or realistic. Or financially responsible."

"That's three."

She blinked at his maddeningly shadowed features. "What?"

"That's three," he repeated. He stepped closer, blocking the moonlight, making her tip back her head to see his face. "You said fact," he reminded her, his voice hushed as he skimmed his knuckles over her cheek. "That's singular."

He was smiling again. She could hear it as surely as she felt the quickening of her pulse at his touch. He'd reached for her as if he couldn't help it. As if it were something he'd thought about all day.

"I'm trying to make a point."

His knuckles slipped beneath her jaw.

"So am I," Sam said. "You told me I was lucky. But you're the one with the chance to make something you've always wanted actually happen. Some people live their entire lives without an opportunity like that."

In the moonlight, her skin looked as pale as alabaster, as

smooth and perfect as a sculpture. But it was her softness that drew him, along with the respite she'd so unexpectedly offered.

He had wanted to believe that he hadn't thought of the dreams he'd lost until she'd come along and unearthed their ashes. But all she had done was poke at what already had been a little too close to the surface anyway. Being back in the real world the past few weeks and being around his family again, he'd been painfully aware of the gaping void in his life. That void just didn't seem so apparent when he was around the woman so easily allowing his touch. When he was with her, he didn't always feel the restiveness that plagued him nearly every other minute of the day.

Not caring to question why that was, just grateful for it for now, he slipped his fingers into the silk of her hair. He'd learned to live his life in moments, to look behind only to remind himself not to repeat a mistake, and to look no farther ahead than was necessary to survive. He carried no encumbrances, wanted none. Life was simpler that way. For him, anyway. Someone like Kelsey needed far more. He hated to see her cheat herself out of it.

"I was just thinking you shouldn't dismiss something like that," he murmured, lowering his head to kiss the furrows in her brow.

Breathing in the clean scent of her hair, he heard her faint, "Oh."

"I was thinking about what I want, too." With his fingers splayed over the back of her head, her hair spilling over his hands, he brushed his lips over her forehead once more.

Kelsey lifted her palm to his chest. His breath felt warm against her skin. Almost as warm as she felt inside at the restrained need in his touch. She wasn't going to worry about how right he might be about missed opportunities, or even how she should be rejecting the notion. With that need drawing her, all she cared about just then was discovering what mattered to him.

"What is it you want?"

She felt the warmth of his breath on her temple. The brush of his lips followed, causing crazy little shivers to race from her neck to the base of her spine. But just when she thought he might carry that featherlight touch to her mouth, he drew back far enough to see her eyes.

"For you to kiss me first." His finger traced the fullness of her lower lip, then tugged down to touch the moist membrane just inside. "You're not the only one who has fantasies, you know."

She should have known he would bare no more of his soul than he already had. Yet any disappointment she might have felt succumbed to the shameless anticipation skimming along her already sensitized nerves.

She wasn't a bold woman. Not when it came to men. She'd never made the first move. Never taken the lead. But what she did as she reached up and curved her palm over the hard edge of his jaw wasn't about boldness. It was about letting him know he had come to mean something far more to her than just a long-ago memory.

"I can do that," she told him, and raised up on tiptoe to touch her mouth to his.

Surrounded by darkness, she did as he had done the first time. And, as that first time, the brush of their lips led to the touch of his tongue to hers and the liquid heat that flowed through her like warm honey. As before, their breath mingled while his arms slipped around her. As before, she flowed against him, curving her arms around his neck, breathing in the masculine scents of musk and spice. That breath seemed to catch, then escaped on a sigh as her breasts brushed the unyielding wall of his chest.

It shouldn't have seemed so natural. It shouldn't have seemed as if they'd been kissing each other forever. Yet, that was how it felt to her as his hands skimmed down her back, wrapping her in his warmth and coaxing her closer when she was already as close as she could get.

It's just a kiss, she told herself.

Liar, her conscience whispered back. It was so much more than a kiss. It was the first time in her life she felt as if she belonged right where she was. It was the first time she'd felt as if she would die if a man let her go. The sensations he elicited as his hands shaped her body and their breathing grew shallow touched her heart with his tenderness and everything else with a heat that softened her in some places, tightened her in others.

She also knew that in less than thirty-six hours, she would have to leave.

The thought squeezed hard at her heart, made her cling a little more desperately.

A moan caught in her throat.

He seemed to drink that small sound, then coaxed another from her when his hand curved beneath her breast. She longed to have him touch her there. The deeper he drew her into their kiss, the more that longing increased. When his hand eased up, the feel of him shaping her, teasing the tight bud straining against her bra and her blouse nearly buckled her knees.

At the hitch of her breath, Sam felt his blood pool low in his groin. It wasn't enough to feel the shape of her through her clothes. He wanted the barriers gone. He wanted to see her, to know the feel of her skin beneath his palm and the texture of her nipple against his tongue. He wanted July 12, he realized, and edged her back, his mouth still clinging to hers.

Slipping his hand between them, he slowly started slipping buttons from their holes. There had to be twenty of the impossibly tiny things and impatience tugged hard, but he made himself take his time. He wasn't some randy teenager with no experience and less control, though she had him feeling that way as he nuzzled his mouth along her jaw, behind her ear and back to taste the willing sweetness of her mouth.

A raw sort of hunger taunted him as he felt her small hands grip his shoulders and the last button finally gave way. Pushing aside the fabric with the backs of his hands, he curved his fingers around her rib cage and pulled her closer to work the front clasp of her bra.

The feel of his hands on her bare skin turned the longing inside Kelsey to a deep, burning ache. With his breath hot on her neck, he trailed a path of moist heat to where he gently cupped one breast. Lifting its weight, he edged aside thin lace and carried the teasing caress of his lips to its center. She'd never felt anything as exquisite as the rough heat of his tongue. Or so she thought before his free hand dug into her hip and he pressed her hard against the bulge straining behind his zipper.

Her breath caught as he groaned. Through the haze of mind-numbing sensation it occurred to her, vaguely, that she had absolutely no sense of caution where this man was concerned. None of her usual reserve existed around him. None of the sensibilities that would have made her question what she was doing standing in a meadow with her blouse hanging off her shoulders in the moonlight with a man she would never see once she left.

She had no idea where her restraint had gone. But she

knew exactly what Sam was doing. He was acting out the little scenario in her diary. The one where he'd taken off her blouse and they'd been skin to skin in the moonlight. The one where he'd shown her...everything.

"Kelsey." He'd pulled her against him, his lips vibrating against the shell of her ear as he whispered her name. "Do you have any protection?"

She felt herself go still a moment before she shook her head. Her voice thready, she whispered, "No. I... No," she repeated, making it clear she was as unprepared as he apparently was to see that fantasy through.

Her response had his body going as motionless as hers in the moments before he sucked in a lungful of the cooling night air. Blowing it out, he pulled his hands from beneath her blouse and wrapped her in his arms. "In that case," he said, his voice husky, "I think we'd better slow down."

Dragging in a deep breath, too, she let her forehead fall against his chest. With her hands curled against his shirt, she could feel the hammering of his heart, and the deep, deliberate rise and fall of his chest as he sought to calm the hunger she'd felt coursing through him. That hunger had fed her own. Knowing he wanted her as badly as she did him made it almost impossible for her to believe it was better that they stop. Almost. As the night sounds began to register, she realized she had just been handed the best chance she had to protect her heart.

Part of her ached to her core to know the feel of him. But another part, the part she had to live with, knew she was already in trouble where Sam was concerned. And the last thing in the world she wanted was to fall in love with a man who couldn't love her back.

She lifted her head, felt him shift against her as he lifted his own.

"Will I see you in the morning?" she asked.

For a moment, he said nothing. He just took another long breath and reluctantly eased one shoulder of her blouse back into place.

"I don't think so. My uncle is picking me up at five-thirty to help him deliver a load of calves," he finally told her. "It's going to take all day."

She lifted her chin, swallowed her disappointment. "Then I won't see you before I go."

"No." He spoke the word quietly, deliberately, as if he knew they were ending it all right there.

The thought that he didn't seem to mind letting her go jerked hard at her heart. Then, he touched her hair, letting his fingers slide the length of it as if memorizing its feel before he turned his attention to fastening the buttons he'd undone.

"But keep my offer to help you with the mill in mind. And if you do decide to come back," he murmured, "I'll be better prepared for us both."

Kelsey was a logical person. A reasonable person. At least, she considered herself so. But it seemed to her that logic had gone the way of the dodo and reason hadn't come into play lately at all. By the time she'd left Maple Mountain thirty-six hours later, however, she felt certain that her common sense would surface by the time she reached Phoenix, and that thoughts of Sam and the mill would give way to more practical concerns.

Common sense had apparently evaporated, too. Sam and the mill were still resolutely stuck in her mind nine hours, two connections and a bumpy landing later.

She didn't believe for an instant that she and Sam had any sort of future together. No matter how tempting, and despite her earlier penchant to romanticize where he was concerned, she wouldn't let herself even begin to contemplate possibilities in that direction. The life he'd chosen was the antithesis of everything she needed, and he guarded his heart too carefully for the kind of relationship she craved. But he had refused to let her keep her old dreams about the mill buried. He hadn't pointed out all the reasons buying it wouldn't work. He hadn't enumerated all the things that could go wrong. He had encouraged her, helped her find solutions, and had her seriously questioning what she had insisted couldn't be done.

Without those barriers, she was again exploring possibilities. And because the possibility of making the mill work existed, the spark of enthusiasm he'd ignited refused to be extinguished.

That die-hard spark was still glowing under a whole bushel basket of doubt when she let herself into her apartment, dropped her travel bag inside the door and opened the drapes to let in the early evening light.

The drapes were still swaying as she stood by the living-room window, dispassionately studying the orderly space with its deep sage sofa full of fat pillows and vintage art photos on the walls. A scene of wildflowers added soft shades of yellow and lavender to the wall above a small walnut dining table and chairs. With its creams, taupes and greens, its comfortable fabrics and uncluttered feel, the apartment was as serene as she'd been able to make it.

Everything she owned would fit perfectly in the miller's quarters. She could envision it all there now with the windows open to a view of a meadow and the sound of a creek drifting inside.

She had no time to worry about how carried away she was

getting before she noticed the light blinking on her answering machine.

She had seventeen messages. Half of those would be from charities wanting her usable discards. Most of the rest she discovered as she scrolled through the numbers on the caller ID were from her boss at the resort and Doug wanting her to call as soon as she returned. One was from her friend, Amber, the sauce chef who lived in the next unit over wanting her to do the same so she could meet her for a drink.

After calling her mom as promised to let her know she'd arrived safely, she called Amber. Amber was her girl's-night-out buddy. The California native, a transplant like herself, could talk for hours about anything and could fill her in on all she'd missed at work. But Amber wasn't home. Since no one knew Kelsey was back yet, she left the other calls unreturned—which left her with little to do other than unpack while she tried to not think about a man with incredible hands, and wonder where she could learn to grind flour.

Remembering a specialty mill in Oregon she ordered flours from, she idly speculated about whether or not its owner would be willing to talk to her and give her a tour.

Morning brought no respite from her mental tug-of-war.

She awoke wondering if Sam had gone to the diner for breakfast, then rolled over and buried her head under her pillow when she remembered she had to call her boss. And Doug.

She was no closer to a decision now than she'd been when she'd left for Maple Mountain a week ago. All the time she should have spent weighing the pros and cons of each offer had gone to Sam and contemplating what had somehow grown from a wish in her diary into another option for a career.

The fact that she was actually considering it a viable alternative had her throwing off the covers and climbing from bed.

There was only one way she could think of to put the matter of the mill to rest. That was to call a Realtor in St. Johnsbury, since they didn't have one in Maple Mountain, and ask him or her to find out which bank held the property and if they would sell it. If they weren't interested, or the price was too high, she could stop obsessing about it.

The Realtor returned her call as she was getting out of the shower. Since it was barely eight o'clock, she hadn't yet called her boss or Doug. Not that she knew what she would say to either of them. But with the time difference, it was eleven o'clock in Vermont and the Realtor hadn't wasted a minute of his potential commission.

The bank was indeed interested in getting rid of the property it had carried on its books for years. They were also more than willing to negotiate the price.

Still wrapped in a towel, Kelsey sank to the edge of her bed. The whole idea of throwing away certain security was crazy. Insane. It also put a knot in her stomach the size of a lemon.

"I'll call you back," she said, and hung up.

Standing, she nudged back the towel wrapped turban-style around her head, crossed her arms over the one wrapped tightly around her body, stared at the instrument and sat back down.

Vacillating between panic and anticipation, she picked the phone back up, took a deep breath and called directory assistance for Ted and Janelle Collier's number, since she didn't know if the trailer had a phone or how it would be listed if it did. Even as she listened to the line ring, she told herself that if she couldn't reach Sam fairly soon, or if he sounded at all hesitant hearing from her, then the whole idea simply wasn't meant to be.

She had no trouble at all reaching his aunt, who said she'd

be happy to give Sam a message to call. Mrs. Collier also told her that having him call back really wasn't necessary. He was right there having lunch. He'd just helped his uncle weld in a new milk tank, and the two men would be heading for Maple Mountain soon to install the cabinets in Megan's new kitchen. They'd been delivered yesterday.

Kelsey was trying to calculate the odds of having caught him there when she heard his deep voice in her ear.

"Kelsey." A note of concern underscored his tone. "Is everything okay?"

That quick concern was unexpected. So was the tug of longing she felt at the sound of it. "Everything's…a little unsettled," she admitted, missing him already. "I've been thinking about the mill. I just need to know how long you think it would take to make the upstairs livable."

They had never discussed how long refurbishing would take. All they'd talked about was what needed to be done. If he thought it would take longer than a month for her to move in, she told herself, she would take that as a clear sign that the venture wasn't meant to be. He had only that long after he finished his sister's house and before he left Maple Mountain to help her, and she would want to be in her own place before he did.

"That depends on what you mean by livable. If you don't mind the noise of a generator and having cords running to your appliances and ancillary lights while the plumbing and wiring are brought up to code…a couple of weeks."

"That's all?"

"Unless there are problems with getting materials," he qualified. "The windows aren't a standard size, but Sheetrock, insulation and paint shouldn't be a problem." He hesitated. "Why?"

Because I can't stop thinking about this. Because I can't

stop thinking about you, either, she thought, but banished the admission as quickly as it formed.

"Because I might need to take you up on your offer." She gripped the phone a little tighter. "If you're still available."

She didn't know what she'd expected him to say. It was entirely possible that in the three days since she'd seen him, he'd committed himself to something else. Or that he'd lost his enthusiasm for her project.

"I told you I would be. When will you know for sure?"

She didn't allow herself to consider how she felt about the smile in his voice. With the timing obstacle cleared, her thoughts jumped to a few of the other minor details looming in her path. A major lack of knowledge about milling, for one. And lack of a business plan. And a plan for marketing and distribution. Real, solid, flow-chart-and-cost-analysis plans. Not the sort of castle-in-the-sky speculation she'd done talking with him.

She needed to get on the phone and the internet. She needed to call the mill in Oregon. She would talk to her industry friends who'd gone out on their own in their various endeavors. If she ran into a snag anywhere along the way, she would put the idea to rest forever.

"Kelsey?"

"I'm still here." Any snag at all, she emphasized to herself. "Sorry,"

A chuckle came over the line, the sound rich, deep and strangely knowing. "Which are you doing? Trying to talk yourself into it, or out of it?"

"I'm not sure."

"Do you want my advice?"

"Please."

"Ask yourself where you're happiest."

The advice might have surprised anyone else who knew

Sam. It didn't surprise Kelsey at all. She knew he lived by it. And he was happiest avoiding all the things he didn't want to think about.

"Then what do I do?"

"Go with your gut."

"My gut is in knots." Those knots kept getting bigger by the second, too. "I just can't tell if they're knots of excitement or terror."

He chuckled again. "You'll be fine," he assured her. "Just remember how much you've always wanted this. And stop second-guessing yourself."

She took a deep breath, quietly blew it out. "I'll try."

His voice went flat. "You don't try to do something like that," he chided. "You let your instincts take over and just do it."

He made it sound so simple. As if all a person had to do was flip a switch and some sixth-sense would kick in. But, then, she supposed, he'd undoubtedly had a lot of practice letting his instincts take the lead. That, and the man had to be fearless to begin with. He took risks constantly in his line of work. She'd never taken a real risk in all her life.

"Let me know what you decide," he told her. Over the sound of voices in the room with him, he then gave her the number for the phone at the trailer so she could reach him there. "I'm here if you need me."

Thinking she needed him now, she thanked him, told him to take care and with his uncle asking if he was going to be much longer, reluctantly broke the connection.

Go with your gut, he'd said.

Poetic, the advice was not. Practical and wise, however, it definitely was. That pragmatic recommendation also made her acknowledge something her intuition had been nagging her to accept all along.

Of all her options, Doug Westland's offer probably held the most potential for disaster. She would be part owner of a business, which would be a plus for her, but that also meant she would be financially entangled with a man she honestly didn't know how to read. If he truly was interested in her beyond a professional relationship, that relationship could easily suffer when he realized she wasn't interested in anything beyond that with him. If he was just using his charm and dangling himself as bait to get her on board, then he wasn't the sort of person she wanted to be in business with anyway. She hadn't felt totally comfortable with him since he'd come on to her in his bar.

When she reached him later that morning, all she told him was that she didn't feel she would fit well in his organization, and that if she left her current position she would be leaving the state. He hadn't sounded terribly happy with her. She, however, felt enormously relieved with that decision out of the way.

Still going with her gut, she then put off her boss at the resort a few days longer by telling him she had to go out of town again and begging for a few more days' vacation. She had the time coming and the restaurant and resort business was practically dead in Phoenix in the summer anyway. No one wanted to be there when temperatures spiked at over 110, and she had an excellent assistant who had no trouble handling the reduced volume.

Ten hours and as many phone calls later, she had packed for a quick trip to Oregon. The owner of the mill there had been most gracious, considering that what she wanted to do was compete in his market, and agreed to meet with her next morning.

She kept waiting for some obstacle to fall in her path, for some *thing* to happen that would tell her that her gut was all wrong. Yet, nothing got in her way. In a little over two weeks, she had turned down the promotion at the resort and given her notice, sublet her apartment, worked out a purchase agreement with the bank, and sent most of her possessions east in a moving van. She had hesitated at the thought of a three-day car trip alone, but Amber had been up for a road trip so Kelsey bought her a ticket from Albany where she would drop her so she could catch a flight back. Armed with research on everything from grain grinds to market demographics, she loaded her clothes and a road map into her fuel-efficient little silver coupe along with Amber and the trailing ivy that had been her roommate for years, and headed for Maple Mountain hoping she hadn't lost her mind.

She knew her mother thought she had.

"I still can't believe you've done this. I know you said it's somethin' you've always wanted to do," her mother conceded, as baffled as she was displeased as she lifted a blouse from Kelsey's suitcase, "but if it was something that important to you, why didn't you ever mention it? And how much thought could you have given it, anyway? You never said a word about the mill when you were here a few weeks ago."

It was after ten o'clock at night, and Kelsey had been home all of fifteen minutes. Not sure why she'd thought her mom might wait until morning to question what she'd already grilled her about on the phone, anyway, she followed the clearly agitated woman across her old bedroom.

Using the elbow of her casted arm to hold the blouse to her side, her mom reached into the closet for a hanger.

Taking the blouse, Kelsey tried for a temporary reprieve. "You don't have to do this, Mom. You've been on your feet all day." The last thing she needed to do was wait on her. "I can put these things away in the morning."

Ignoring her, her mother took the blouse back and deftly stuffed the hanger into a sleeve. "You know I don't mind helping you," she insisted, clearly intending to get her daughter in and settled before either of them went to bed. "But I do mind that you didn't even talk to me about this."

If there was anything her mother possessed, it was tenacity. Until she got the answer she wanted, she hung on to a matter like a rat terrier with a new bone.

"I did talk to you." It was clearly futile to wish her mother would just accept what she had done. "I told you as soon as I realized it was actually going to happen."

"I know that. You *told* me. You didn't discuss it with me at all." Hurt shaded her tone. "What I don't understand is why."

Heading for the suitcase on her bed, thinking she would have truly appreciated a night's sleep before facing a showdown, Kelsey picked up a stack of underwear and turned to her old white dresser.

"Because," she said quietly, "I knew if I said anything to you, you'd try to talk me out of it."

Wood scraped as she pulled a drawer open and tucked the stack of pastel lace into the space lined with white tissue paper. Beside her, the door opened to a beige living room with maple furniture so old it was nearly antique and a brown plaid sofa with an orange afghan covering a worn spot on its arm. Her mom hadn't bought anything new for her home in longer than Kelsey could remember. As frugal as she'd always been, Kelsey strongly suspected she didn't buy anything new for herself, either, until she had to replace whatever it was she'd worn out. That was one of the reasons Kelsey always sent her pretty clothes for her birthdays and the sort of lotions and powders she'd never splurge on for herself.

At that moment, she was wearing the turquoise caftan

and slippers she'd sent her, along with a look of utter incredulity.

"Well, of course I'd have tried to talk you out of it. This is the last place I want you to be, Kelsey. I love havin' you here. And havin' you around all the time would be wonderful," she insisted, swiping at a strand of hair that had dared to come loose from her braided bun. "But I want more for you than you can have in Maple Mountain. I've always wanted more for you," she stressed. "That's why I made sure you got everything you needed to get the kind of opportunities you'd never have around here." She shook her head, bewilderment firmly back in place. "Now you've thrown away everything you've worked for by buyin' that run-down old mill."

Her mother clearly had her best interests at heart. As much as Kelsey loved her for that, she also hated the guilt she felt for the way her mom made it seem she'd somehow turned her back on all that had been done for her.

"I know what you want for me, Mom. And I appreciate that. I truly do. But I haven't thrown away anything. I'm just using what I've learned in a different way. I can make this work. It's just going to take a while."

"What about what you're losing in the meantime? You're almost thirty, Kelsey. I know girls are getting married later nowadays, but how are you goin' to find yourself a husband at all? There are no eligible men around here. At least not any a girl would want. The Tanner boys are nothin' but trouble and everyone else is either still fightin' acne or wearing a pacemaker. You have no hope at all of meetin' a man like those you'd meet where you just came from.

"And who are you going to get to help you rebuild that place?" she went on, looking as if she wanted to pace, grabbing another blouse instead. "I know Sam's workin' on it for you now, but there's no way on God's green earth he can have it up and runnin' before he leaves."

The thought that eligible men in the city weren't necessarily prizes, either, was cancelled as Kelsey reached back into her suitcase herself. "Sam's already working on it?"

"He has been since last week." Looking as if she couldn't figure out why she didn't know that, Dora hung the second blouse by the first. "Amos found out about it when he was out that way and saw a lumber truck pull onto the old mill road. He thought the driver was lost since there's nothing on that road but the mill, but when he got there, Sam was coming over to meet the guy. Sam told him you two had talked about your plans and that he was getting you started."

Some of the materials Sam had ordered for her had already arrived. Realizing that, Kelsey's expression turned puzzled. She and Sam had talked a few times about what needed to be done and the supplies she'd require. They'd also talked about his sister, the boys and how his sister's place was progressing. But he hadn't said a thing about having started the work on hers.

She was wondering why he hadn't mentioned that when she realized her mom had gone silent.

"Oh, Kelsey," she said with a sigh. "Is *he* why you came back?"

The absurdity of the question kept Kelsey's attention on her unpacking. She could not, however, make herself meet her mother's eyes. "I told you why I came back."

"You hardly know the man. You saw him a few times at the diner and spent a day with him and the Colliers." Having summed up what she and probably everyone else in town knew of their relationship, her voice fell flat with mystified conclusion. "But you talked to him about your plans."

"Yes, I did." They'd seen each other more often than anyone else realized and she knew him far better than anyone thought, but those weren't points she cared to clarify. She especially didn't care to clarify exactly how he'd become privy to those plans in the first place. "I'd always wanted to do something with the mill. And he liked my ideas."

"So he encouraged you."

"It's more that he didn't let me become *dis*couraged." In the process, he'd given her the impetus she needed to turn her life in the direction she knew in her heart she needed to go. "He helped me see that what I wanted was possible."

He'd given her back her enthusiasm, too. Her sense of... passion, she supposed. And for that she would be forever grateful.

"So that's it."

"That's what?" Kelsey asked, absently.

"This is his doing."

Frustration fought patience. Or maybe it was the other way around. Her mom wasn't even trying to understand. She'd simply decided her daughter's less-than-logical decision had to be someone else's fault. Her offspring couldn't possibly have made such a senseless choice.

"It's my doing, Mom. I told you, this is something I've wanted for a long time and I'll never know if I can make it work if I don't try." It was obviously going to take a while for her mother to accept what she'd done. In the meantime, she truly didn't want them arguing. A plea softened her tone. "I made this decision myself. I need to do it. And I've thought it through. I truly have," she insisted, prepared to explain every step in that process if she had to. "Just don't blame Sam. He's only being a friend."

Given her mother's present state of mind, Kelsey halfway expected her to say that a friend wouldn't have allowed her to do such a thing. To her relief, her mother said nothing. She simply stood with her lips pursed long enough to make it clear she wasn't sure what to do with her newly formed opinion, then told her she would go make them some chamomile tea. She was sure Kelsey was tired from her trip and that she wanted to get some rest.

As grateful as she was that the subject had been dropped, Kelsey was willing to bet the new stainless-steel faucet and sink currently en route from Arizona that she hadn't heard the end of it.

She also had the awful suspicion that her mom wasn't anywhere near ready to let Sam off the hook.

Chapter Eight

Kelsey overslept. As anxious as she'd been to get started on her new future, she had intended to be clearing out cobwebs and birds' nests by the time the sun reached the tops of the trees. She'd inadvertently hit Off instead of Snooze on her travel alarm, though. Her mom hadn't knocked on her door before she'd left for work, either. When Kelsey finally woke it had been nearly eight o'clock.

Even running later than she'd planned, she felt good. Better than good, she thought, pulling herself together in record time and practically bouncing down the stairs. For the first time in years, she'd awakened in Maple Mountain knowing she didn't have to leave. What had her nearly grinning, though, was that she was on her way to the mill. Her mill.

Emerging in the storage room, she pushed open its inner door, stuck her head into the kitchen and turned her bright smile to the woman humming to herself at the grill.

"'Morning, Betsy." Curls permed tight and as white as the apron covering Betsy Parker's tall frame were smashed flat beneath her hairnet. "Tell Mom I've gone out to the mill, will you? I'm not sure when I'll be back."

The sixty-year-old choir director and part-time cook smiled back and aimed her spatula toward the door. "'Morning, yourself, Kelsey. And she's right there."

The door had blocked her from her view. Peeking around it, Kelsey saw her rinsing a tray of dishes to be put into the dishwasher. Steam from the long retractable sprayer billowed around her, turning her cheeks a pretty shade of pink. Her expression, however, appeared anything but rosy.

Her greeting was succinct. "You should eat before you go."

Anticipation had Kelsey too excited to even think about food. Another reason existed for that eagerness, too. She was just afraid to let herself fully acknowledge it as her glance shot toward the service window to see who might be on the other side.

"He's been and gone."

Unnerved to know her mom was aware of who she'd been looking for, she didn't acknowledge the comment at all.

"I'll grab something." Thinking to placate at least one of her mom's concerns, she snatched a fist-size poppy-seed muffin from the supply that would refill the pastry case and headed back to the door. On the way, she said goodbye to Betsy and brushed a kiss to her ominously unsmiling mom's cheek. She wondered as she did if the kindly cook had already been privy to her mom's displeasure with Sam.

The thought dimmed the glow on her exhilaration as she hurried out and into her car. She knew her mother, though. Despite the fact that Dora tended to share her every opinion, she didn't think her mom would be inclined to share this particular one. Not as bluntly as she'd shared it with her, anyway. She might mention that she saw the mill as nothing but a money pit that had already swallowed her daughter's nest egg, but she would be careful with what she had to say about how she regarded prospects for her daughter in and around Maple Mountain. She stood to alienate too many of her neighbors, who were also her customers, if she did otherwise.

Many of the locals claimed roots that ran generations deep in Maple Mountain. Those who did were fiercely loyal to their little corner of northern Vermont, and what was good enough for them was good enough for their young people. Many also regarded the cities that her mom had seen as her daughter's salvation as alien civilizations that lured and robbed them of their progeny, so a little discretion on her mother's part would serve her well.

Kelsey headed down the narrow road, past the old-fashioned general store with its display of merchandise in the window, and the single pump gas station by the Maple Mountain Motor Inn. As she waved to Hanna, who was talking to Claire out by the inn's mailbox, she did her best not let her mom's attitude rob her of the anticipation wanting to be felt.

She wasn't sure when she had decided to drive to Sam's sister's house rather than going by the mill first. The practical part of her was anxious to see him because he would be helping her and she needed to know where to start. Another part simply wanted to see him again. Not that she was going to let that matter. Though it had been apparent enough when she'd left that he wouldn't mind a physical relationship, she had no desire for an affair that was doomed before it began. Even if she hadn't known all she did about him, he'd said nothing during their phone conversations to make her believe she'd been on his mind as constantly as he had hers. So while she would be forever grateful for his help, she would remember that all he really wanted from her was the work that would occupy his time while he was there.

She was still reminding herself of that two miles later as she passed the rutted lane to the mill and turned into the driveway leading to the house that now sported the new white aluminum siding Sam told her had been installed last week. All the old Baker place needed was trim paint and it would look brand new.

Music greeted her as she stepped from her car. Heavy metal this time. But he must have seen her pull in. The volume died even as she glanced toward the trash pile that had grown with boxes that had held Megan's new appliances and the empty paint cans that told Kelsey the inside was nearly finished, too.

Sam had even enclosed the back porch. She had just followed the stepping stones leading to it when he emerged through its door wearing his faded NYPD T-shirt, paint-spattered jeans and the deceptively easy smile that never failed to do crazy things to her heart.

Watching him shove his fingers through his dark hair as he walked toward her, she smiled back. His unhurried glance skimmed the short pink T-shirt and worn jeans she'd thrown on to work in, stalling for a moment on the curve of her breasts and her mouth before settling with laconic ease on her eyes.

"I wondered when you'd show up." For one totally irrational instant, she thought he might reach for her. It was that kind of welcome she thought she saw in his too-handsome face. "I heard at breakfast that you were here."

"I had a feeling Mom would mention it," she replied, taking him in, trying not to. The lines bracketing his beautiful mouth looked carved more deeply then she remembered. So did those fanning from the corners of his eyes. He looked tired to her. And far more appealing than she wanted to admit. Thinking of her mom, though, had caution joining the wholly imprudent blend of longing and pleasure she felt seeing him again.

"Actually she didn't say anything until Charlie did. He saw your car on his way into the diner."

Confused by his comment, she buried any equally imprudent stab of disappointment when he killed the possibility of reaching for her by crossing his arms over his chest. "Charlie doesn't know what kind of car I drive."

"He saw your plates."

Of course, she thought. Knowing she was coming, Charlie would have instantly realized the license plate with the purple cactus on it was hers. It didn't matter who had announced her arrival, though. What struck her as odd was that her mother hadn't been the first to mention it. That didn't sound like the parent she knew at all.

The caution she'd felt a moment ago compounded itself as she pulled her glance from the bunched muscles of Sam's biceps. "Did Mom seem okay to you this morning?"

"She seemed fine. Why?"

"I just wondered if she said anything to you about helping me with the mill."

"She hardly said anything to me at all."

That was not good, Kelsey thought. But it had no sooner occurred to her that Sam had completely missed the significance of that silent disapproval when a muscle in his jaw jerked.

"So," he said, as if wanting to shake off whatever thought had elicited that betraying bit of tension. "How was your trip out? Any problems?"

Sam watched her ponytail sway as she shook her head, shades of wheat and platinum shining in the morning sun.

Her scent drifted toward him, clean, fresh, and far too innocent to be so erotic. The whiff he'd caught seconds ago had
jerked hard at his memory. The last time he'd breathed in that
fragrance, he'd been with her in the moonlight and silently
swearing at himself for not being a better Boy Scout.

Though it disturbed him to realize how easily she affected
him, he knew he wouldn't be caught unprepared again.

"It was unbelievably uneventful."

"How about the light fixtures you wanted? Did you bring
them with you?"

"They're on the truck with my furniture. So are the drill
and masonry bits you asked me to get. And I bought a chain
saw. For firewood," she explained, because they hadn't talked
about that particular piece of equipment. "And an automatic
screwdriver, because you said it would be easier for me to
use."

Their conversation wasn't unlike those they'd had on the
telephone. Pragmatic. Matter of fact. And so totally not about
the things that had been on his mind as he'd listened to the
anticipation and worry in the seductive tones of her voice.

As they'd talked about rewiring, he'd remembered kissing
her in the moonlight and how perfectly her breasts fit his
hands.

While they'd discussed insulation and flooring, he'd
thought about how beautifully she'd responded to his touch,
and how badly he wanted her in his bed.

The muscles tightened low in his gut. He would admit that
he wanted her. He would even admit he'd looked forward to
her return. But he was certain that was only because her plans
had given him more to do and the harder he worked, the easier it was for him to avoid the restiveness that had returned
with a vengeance when she'd left. Working to exhaustion
helped him sleep, too. Sleep better, anyway. He doubted he'd

ever go a night without waking every hour wondering where he was.

"What about work gloves?" he asked, determined to focus on something that didn't involve being horizontal.

"I bought two pairs. And I found the decals for the monster trap."

His attention finally shifted. "The decals?" He couldn't believe she'd remembered them. He'd only mentioned his idea in passing. "Which ones?"

"I could only find 'danger' and 'caution.' They didn't carry 'radioactive.'" Almost looking a little cautious herself, her dark eyes softened. "How is your sister doing?"

"I haven't talked to her this week, but my aunt says she's doing okay. How about you?" he asked, searching for some clue that she might regret the enormous step she'd taken. "How are you doing now that you're here?"

An uneasy smile threatened the warmth in her eyes. "I think I'll plead the fifth for now."

"Don't want to incriminate yourself?"

"Something like that."

"Hey," he murmured. Unwrapping his arms, he caught her chin when she glanced away. "You're not still worried about how this all came together, are you?" There had been times on the phone when he'd known she didn't trust how easily everything had come about. It had never occurred to him to question it. "If details fall into place, a goal is meant to be, Kelsey. It's when something has to be forced to happen that it's going to be nothing but problems."

There was no mistaking the uncertainty clouding her expression. It was as obvious to him as her hesitation in the moment before her head moved almost imperceptibly toward his touch. Encouraged by that unconscious need for reassurance, liking that he could offer it, he let his thumb drift to the corner of her mouth. Her lips were unadorned, free of anything that would interfere with the feel of their softness.

He hadn't been able to go five minutes without touching her. But touching her wasn't enough.

"Stop worrying," he insisted, lowering his head to hers. "And welcome home."

Welcome home. He'd been the only one to offer the words that would have made her heart smile had she not been so busy hoping he was right. As smoothly as her transition had gone, she'd had no reason to think anything should go wrong now. Yet, as his mouth covered hers and he drew her into his arms, she knew she already had problems. Her mother, for one. Him for another. She couldn't deny how grateful she was for his encouragement—or how she'd ached to have him do exactly what he did as he drew her up, molding her to him as if he'd missed her as badly as she'd missed him.

Groping blindly for her sense of self-preservation, she'd barely stopped her arms from going around his neck and started to pull back when the honk of a horn penetrated the beat of the pulse in her ears.

The sound had barely registered when Sam lifted his head. A second honk had her glancing toward the sound in time to see Joe Sheldon, the local deputy, driving by in his tan Jeep. He had his khaki-clad arm out the open window and was waving to them as he passed.

She didn't need to see his Joe's face to know he was either grinning or that his eyebrows had arched halfway to his receding hairline.

With a groan, she lowered her forehead to Sam's chest.

"That'll be all over town in about five minutes."

The warmth of his broad palm penetrated her skin as he cupped it over the back of her neck. She knew she should move. She also hated the thought.

"It won't take that long. He has a radio in his car."

Her head came up. "You don't think he'd get on his radio, do you?"

"It's possible," he admitted, looking more interested in whatever it was he saw in her face than with what the deputy had witnessed. "The guy loves to talk. You'd no sooner finalized the deal with the bank than he was out here telling me he'd heard you'd bought the mill. His wife has a cousin at the title company in St. Johnsbury."

She didn't question the swiftness of the grapevine. With the need to protect herself jerking hard, what she was missing was the connection between Sam and Joe. "Why would he come out there to tell you that?"

"He stops by all the time. He likes to talk shop."

"Shop?"

"Trade law enforcement stories," he explained. "I told him the next time he's in New York to look me up. If I'm available, I'll give him a tour of the trenches."

Reminded of the danger Sam would soon return to, she wrapped the need to protect herself a little tighter and finally stepped from his arms. Casting a worried glance toward the road, she was about to ask if there was any chance his new friend would extend a little professional courtesy when Sam stepped back himself.

"Tell you what," he said, Joe apparently forgotten as he moved toward the house. "I have an hour before Charlie gets here to help me hang the molding upstairs. Give me a minute to leave him a note in case he gets here early, and I'll meet you over at the mill. You've got a lot of work to do over there."

The problem with her mother had just compounded itself. It seemed to Kelsey that Sam hadn't been concerned at all with what the friendly local deputy might be sharing with their neighbors at that very moment. But thoughts of the fuel about to be added to her mother's fire filled her with a nagging sort of dread. It had taken her mother less than fifteen minutes last night to conclude that she had returned because of Sam. She *had* come back because of him. His encouragement had been invaluable. She just hadn't come back *for* him. The distinction would be infinitely easier to make her mom understand, however, had Joe not happened by.

Not that there was much Joe could say, Kelsey rationalized as she parked her car in the mill's overgrown driveway and snatched a pair of her new work gloves from the passenger seat. All he'd seen was a kiss. It was entirely possible that as fast as he'd driven past, he hadn't noticed that they'd nearly been wrapped around each other like pretzels.

Possible. But not probable. It was her experience, limited as it was, that those involved in law enforcement noticed details that totally escaped the average citizen.

Remembering from her yoga classes that proper breathing was essential to alleviate stress, she drew a lungful of the clean summer air and slowly blew it out as she climbed from her car. As agitated as she felt, she didn't even look toward the mill that, under other circumstances, would have had her hugging herself at the realization that it was actually hers.

All she could think about was the man she truly had no business being attracted to. There was no denying the pull she felt toward Sam, though. She just needed to believe that the appeal was so strong because of what she'd felt for him before. Nostalgia could be a powerful thing. It had to be. It was at least partly responsible for the gamble she'd taken with her entire future by buying the mill.

The thought of what she'd actually found the nerve to do

with her life finally drew her glance to the stone building rising by the stream. She truly believed that coming back had been the right thing to do. She belonged there. She *needed* to be there. She couldn't necessarily explain why that was but she believed that as much as she believed in her plans for her new business. No matter what her mom or anyone else thought, she wouldn't have done what she had if she hadn't believed she could make a go of it on her own.

She saw Sam cross the footbridge downstream. With his easy, athletic stride betraying the power in his big body, she reminded herself that she also knew she would be a fool to risk the rest of her dreams on a man who was willing to risk his life, but not his heart. She just needed to get through the next month without getting her own heart more involved than she suspected it already was.

"What's the matter?" Sam's eyes narrowed as he approached, his too-keen glance skimming her face. "I thought you'd already be inside."

He watched Kelsey's glance dart away, her expression oddly self-conscious in the instant before she looked back.

"I just thought I'd wait for you."

The woman couldn't tell a convincing lie if the survival of mankind depended on it. Something was bothering her. Joe, he suspected, though, personally, he didn't see what the problem was with what the guy had seen. He and Kelsey were both adults. They were both single. What they did was no one's business but theirs.

He might have told her that, too, had she not just walked away to check out the property she'd recently acquired.

She reached the end of the building. Coming to a halt in the overgrown grass, she spun back with the delight of child.

"You rebuilt the staircase?"

There was more excitement than query in her question.

That unreserved pleasure lit her face, erasing the concern he'd seen there moments ago. She wasn't just a lousy liar, he thought, enjoying the way her smile made him feel. She couldn't hide much of anything she felt. At least, not from him.

"I figured you'd rather use the side entrance to upstairs than to have to come and go through the mill once you're living here," he told her, walking over to where she stood. "It's going to be a mess down there for a while."

Curious to see what he'd done, Kelsey moved to the stairs that hugged the side of the cobblestone building. He had replaced the rotted and broken boards of the steps and railings with new wood. In the warming air, the fresh smell of raw lumber mingled with the sweetness of wildflowers.

Wondering at the hours he must have spent working there, she climbed the now-sturdy stairs to the small, square landing.

Gray paint peeled and curled on the upper entry door's panels. The broken lock, however, had been repaired. New brass screws gleamed against the older brass plate. Reaching for the antique handle, she pushed the door open.

In the pale light, the interior looked much as it had when she'd been there nearly three weeks ago. It still needed to be swept clean of leaves and dirt before she could even begin to scour the century's worth of soot from the outside of the fireplace and strip the hardwood floor. But the rotten wood that had once supported the broken windows was gone. In its place was the thick new furring that would support new windows. The kitchen at the end of the room remained in desperate need of more work than she cared to consider at the moment, too, but it was the little room just off of it that drew her attention.

Skirting the sawhorses that occupied the space where her

dining table would go, she passed the slab of gray-green slate she would keep for her countertop and peeked inside the larger of the two small bedrooms.

She and Sam had talked about how the room needed to be insulated and lined with Sheetrock, but even though her mom had said he'd been working here, she hadn't considered for a moment that he would have done so much without her. All the room needed was paint.

"Sam…" she began, only to turn and notice what she'd missed before.

Across the room was the window that opened to the view of the meadow and the mill pond. The broken glass was gone and the furring around it was new like the rest, but he had repaired the built-in seat that occupied the little bay below it.

She knew he was aware that the bench was where she'd spent so many hours writing of her dreams for this place in her diary. That he had bothered to repair it when he had so much else to do made it nearly impossible for her to remember why she wasn't going be drawn any more to him than she already was.

"I can't believe how much you've already done. And the window seat…" she murmured, walking over to run her hand over its glued-and-sanded surface. She looked up, searching the inscrutable lines of his face. "You didn't have to do this."

The sensation that jolted through Sam was totally unexpected and disturbingly familiar. That quick dread, however, felt totally out of context. He usually only experienced it when he feared he'd blown his cover. Yet, that was how he felt now. As if, somehow, he'd just been exposed.

Frowning at himself, he dismissed the odd sensation and snatched up a scrap of unfinished molding. Tossing it toward the other scraps under the sawhorses, it landed with a clatter and a puff of dust.

"I know you're anxious to get in here," he told her, the cynic in him dismissing any possible significance to what he'd done. He had repaired the bench only because he had known it was the sort of thing she would be sentimental about. That was all. He didn't want her looking for any meaning beyond that. "I just thought it would be easier if we got a head start on some of it. Depending on how adventurous you are," he continued, relieved when she finally turned from what had her looking a little too moved, "you should be able to move in when your things get here. You'll have a bedroom. And the plumbing in the bathroom works. You just need a water heater."

Kelsey watched him nudge aside another scrap of wood with his foot. She'd bumped into the wall he'd built around himself before. "When did you do all this?" she asked, feeling as if she'd just hit it again.

"After I finished up for the day at my sister's. The windows will be in in a few days," he continued, more interested in what remained to be done rather than what he'd already accomplished. "They're a little smaller than those that were in here, but I built a thicker frame so they'll fit. It's the best we can do without a custom order. It could take a few months to get them if we do that, and I want them in before I go."

The reminder that leaving was never far from his mind stayed with her as he moved about the rooms, explaining the order in which he thought things ought to be done, asking if she was okay with his plan. Still aware of that invisible wall, she watched him stop in the middle of the space, dominating it as he stood with his hands on his hips scrutinizing the beams on the ceiling, the condition of the floor. Lines of concentration etched his rugged features as he methodically outlined his plan for making her new home everything she'd ever imagined it could be.

He seemed just as preoccupied when she followed him back out into the sunshine to survey the ivy and brambles that needed to be cleared away.

"I borrowed a wheelbarrow and weed eater from my uncle for you," he told her, hauling open the large main door. "Do you know how to use one?"

"A wheelbarrow?"

"A weed-eater."

"Not without amputating a body part. Show me how?"

"Ain't nothing to it," claimed a rusty voice from the end of the building. Apparently in the process of looking around the place, Charlie emerged from the weeds at the opposite corner brushing at the dandelion wishes that had blown onto his coveralls. "Lot safer than a scythe, too. Wicked, them things are."

"Hey, Charlie." Shrugging off his preoccupation, and the faint tension that had come with it, Sam nodded at his friend. "You're early."

"Yeah, well, the sooner we get that moldin' of yours hung, the sooner you can help me haul out that stump."

"You're helping Charlie?" *Too,* Kelsey might have said. It was no wonder he looked so tired, she thought. Since she'd left, the man had obviously been working day and night and not getting any rest at all.

The lines around his eyes deepened even more with his smile. "Just doing a little friendly bartering. Right, Charlie?"

"Yep," the older man muttered, setting his cap back by its bill to expose a tuft of white hair. "Neither job is one a man can accomplish on his own without a heap of frustration. Easier with two."

Thinking his philosophy applied to a lot of things, and re-minded of how needs were often reciprocated in the coun-try, she glanced from the man who was apparently even more driven to occupy himself than she'd thought to the one now checking out the rusted latch on the main door.

Charlie thinned hundreds of maple trees every summer. She had just acquired a need for something to burn in her fireplace come fall. "What can I barter you for firewood, Charlie?"

The wrinkles in the older man's weathered brow deepened as he withdrew his hand to ponder her query. "Tell you what," he said after several long seconds of thought, "come apple harvest time, you help my Mary pick apples and put up pies and I'll deliver you a couple of cords chopped and stacked."

She held out her hand. "You have yourself a deal," she said, offering her handshake with a smile. "I'm good for applesauce, too"

"Suits me." Clearly satisfied with their deal, he withdrew his calloused hand and nodded toward the open door. "Mind if I have a look around in there?"

She didn't mind at all. She told him that, too, then asked that he be careful before her smile faltered and she turned her glance to Sam.

"What about you?" she asked as soon as Charlie's curiosity had carried him inside. "All the work you've done…all that's left to do…" Her voice grew quieter. "I hadn't considered how much it would cost if I'd had to hire it all out. I don't know what to barter for your work." A man could only eat so many pies and muffins. "Can I help you over at your sister's? Or…pay you?"

The suggestion brought a quick frown. "You have too much to do here before I go to spend time working someplace else. And you don't owe me anything. I'm getting what I want."

Quiet conclusion entered her tone. "Something to occupy your time before they'll let you go back."

He didn't think a lot of her phrasing, true as it was, but it was as clear as the certainty in the depths of her eyes that she understood him. Having never thought a woman would, knowing his family still didn't, she had no idea how he appreciated that acceptance. "Exactly."

"If you're sure…"

"I'm positive." There was something else he wanted, though. He wanted her. As he forced his eyes to remain on hers rather than the fullness of her mouth, he also knew he was not willing to do anything that might make her think he expected her to wind up in his bed. He was more than willing, however, to let nature take its course. "Okay?"

Despite his assurance, the concern shadowing her expression remained. It did, however, seem to shift course as she looked to where Charlie had disappeared.

"What's the matter?"

"Joe must not have gotten on the radio. Charlie would have heard him. He has a police scanner."

"Why does Charlie have one?"

"He has two. One at home and one in his truck. Lots of people around here do. It's how volunteers know there's a fire to fight, or someone needs a rescue."

It was also entirely possible that Charlie had simply missed the transmission, Sam thought, but he didn't point out that little piece of practicality. Charlie emerged just then to tell Kelsey he appreciated the look-see and mentioned to Sam that they should get to their project and leave Kelsey to hers.

He gave no indication that he'd heard anything at all about them. That situation, however, had changed by sunrise.

Sam was greeted by the normal chatter in the diner when he walked in the next morning—only to hear it change quality on his way the counter. As usual, Amos and Charlie had their backs to him as they sat drinking their coffee. Both being a little hard of hearing, neither man seemed to notice the shift in tone as Smiley, the postman, stopped talking to the two other locals seated at his table. The UPS man looked up from his eggs, lifted a hand and went right back to his breakfast, but Sam could have sworn he saw speculation in the eyes of everyone else who nodded to him.

He'd barely sat down on the empty stool between his breakfast companions before Amos leaned closer and poked his bony elbow into his ribs.

"Hear Joe saw you with Kelsey yesterday," he informed him, his conspiratorial whisper carrying the length of the counter.

Charlie poked him from the other side. The white-haired old guy said nothing, though. He just gave him a wink before Dora appeared with a cup of coffee in her hand and a muscle jumping in her jaw.

"Sam," she said by way of greeting, and set the cup down with enough force to send coffee sloshing onto the saucer.

She didn't ask how he was doing as she usually did. She didn't ask what kind of cakes he wanted, either. She didn't do anything other than send Lorna over to finish waiting on him while she disappeared into the kitchen. Lorna seemed different this morning, too. She usually flirted and teased, but this morning she just gave him a smile loaded with what he could have sworn was disappointment.

It was Dora who concerned him, though. The chill she left behind felt as cold as a winter's breeze.

Not at all certain what was going on, he picked up his paper napkin and set it under his cup to absorb what he could have sworn she'd spilled on purpose. It wasn't often that he misread a person. From the way she'd mothered him as she did the rest of her customers, he could have sworn she liked him. Or, at least, that she didn't *dis*like him. This morning, though, he was clearly on her hit list.

Unable to believe she would be so displeased just because he'd kissed her daughter, he tried to imagine what she could have heard. Other than what Joe had seen, there was nothing else for anyone to tell. He hadn't even seen Kelsey since he and Charlie had left her attacking vegetation yesterday. Wanting to finish up at his sister's within the next couple of days, he'd worked far later than usual. By the time he'd walked over to the mill a little before nine o'clock, Kelsey had already been gone.

Considering it best to not be thinking about her now, he asked Charlie if he wanted to come help him again that morning. As soon as he finished hanging the molding upstairs, he could move to the outside trim paint.

He was usually as good at blocking what disturbed him as he was working around distractions. When he worked undercover, he often found himself in situations where he had to appear as if he had nothing to hide. He honestly had nothing to hide now. Yet, as he sat there listening to the older men and aware of Dora's icy glances, he found it strange that the edginess he felt in work situations wasn't anything like the uneasiness he felt just then.

What he felt here was more disturbing, though in an entirely different way. In Maple Mountain, he had no undercover persona protecting him. Here, people knew exactly who he was. He was just a man. And a brother, nephew and friend as Kelsey had so succinctly pointed out to him the day she'd shown up with his favorite pie. He wasn't used to being so exposed.

He made it through breakfast by telling himself to ignore Dora and the more friendly speculation in nearly every pair of eyes he met. But it wasn't until later that afternoon while he was painting the trim on his sister's place that he discovered exactly why Kelsey's mother had treated him like one of the great unwashed.

Chapter Nine

"Mind if I turn that down?" Joe hollered.

From his perch on the roof, Sam saw Joe Sheldon motion to the boom box on the front porch. The guy was big, built like the linebacker he'd been in high school, and wore his khaki uniform with the ease of a man who'd been in it for a while.

Calling back for him to go ahead, Sam finished the last few inches of trim around a dormered window and climbed down the ladder.

The scream of electric guitars gave way to the chirp of birds as he set the bucket and brush he'd carried down with him on the sheet of plastic by the stairs.

Joe's craggy features were screwed into a scowl. "I have no idea how you can listen to that stuff."

"Hey," Sam muttered, feigning umbrage at his musical in- clinations. "Metallica is classic." Glancing at his hands, he absently wiped streaks of Wedgwood blue onto his jeans. "By the way," he added frowning himself, "thanks a lot."

Joe's short sandy hair sported a dent from the ranger-style hat he'd left in his Jeep. Guilt pulled his thick eyebrows low, making his receding hairline look even longer than it was. He didn't have to ask what Sam was talking about.

"Yeah," he began, looking uncomfortable. "That's why I stopped by. I heard Dora's not too happy with you."

"Because I kissed her daughter?" He still couldn't understand why that was such a problem. "She wouldn't even have known about it if you'd kept what you'd seen to yourself."

"Hey. I just thought it was interesting," Joe defended. "Everybody knew you two had been out to your aunt and uncle's on the Fourth. All I said was that it looked like things were heatin' up.

"Look, Sam," he continued, conciliation heavy in his tone. "I think you're a decent guy. And it's not like you're an outsider here," he insisted, sounding as if his loyalties were being torn between the town and a fellow officer. "But I'd lay low around the diner for a while if I were you. Dora's unhappy with you for talking Kelsey into buying the mill. And I heard that the mayor and his wife are upset with Dora for thinking Kelsey wasted her money. Lots of people would like to see that old place up and running again and anything someone can do to boost the economy is welcome. I only saw Kelsey a couple of times when she was home last, but she seems to have a level head on her shoulders, and I'm hoping like some of the other folk around here that she can make it profitable.

"I can't blame you for being interested in her, either," he admitted, bluntly. "She's one attractive lady. But you might keep in mind that you're not her mother's favorite person right now."

He'd come to spare him another dose of the Big Chill. That much was clear. Joe's advice, however, barely registered in Sam's confusion.

"What do you mean I talked Kelsey into buying the mill?" he demanded, his tone flat with denial. "I didn't talk her into anything. All I did was tell her to follow her instincts and go with what she felt was right." That hardly qualified as coercion. "Buying that mill is something she's wanted since she was a kid."

"You're helping her fix it up."

Sam felt as if he were getting more lost by the minute. "Yeah..." he confirmed, slowly drawing out the word while he waited for enlightenment as to the particular problem there.

The best Joe could do was deepen his scowl. "Well, she's not happy about that, either." He held up his hands, palm out. "I'm just telling you what I've heard, Sam. She thinks you're responsible for Kelsey buying the place, and she doesn't like that you're helping her with it. Just thought you ought to know."

Looking sympathetic, he nodded toward the endless yards of bare trim still needing paint and hitched his thumb toward his patrol Jeep. "I'm on my way out to the lake. Someone's stealing campers' fishing gear. Best let you get back to work, too."

For a full minute after Joe left, Sam stood frowning after him. If he was responsible for something, he took the credit or the blame he deserved, but it grated against his basic sense of integrity to be unjustly accused. No way was he responsible for the decision Kelsey had made. No way had he talked her into anything she hadn't truly wanted to do to begin with.

Dora's attitude that morning made more sense to him

now. But even as annoyed as he was at the woman for giving him the deep freeze when she was the one whose facts were screwed up, he fully intended to let the matter go. This thing had "family problem" written all over it and that was the last thing he wanted to get involved with. He had enough trouble with his own family and he knew from experience the dead-end sort of conflict that came when both sides tried to change the other's mind. Emotions ran high, no one walked away happy and someone inevitably left feeling lousy because he wasn't living the way someone else thought he should, or feeling cheated and resentful if forced into a change.

Avoiding conflict was the easiest way to prevent it from escalating. That had been his experience, anyway, and he fully intended to rely on it now. Since he would only be around for a few more weeks, he didn't need to concern himself with any of it. Or so he told himself in the split second before he thought about Kelsey.

If Dora was that unhappy with him, she was equally unhappy with her daughter.

Sam swore. Shoving his fingers through his hair, belatedly remembering they were splattered with paint, he swore again. He wasn't at all prepared for the protectiveness he felt toward Kelsey just then. But it was there, pulling as hard as the more familiar instincts jerking him in the opposite direction. Those instincts had always kept him from getting any more involved in a personal situation than he was comfortable with. They were the ones that insisted now that he needed to stay out of it, that there was nothing he could do, and that Kelsey would have told him if the situation was really as bad as Joe had made it sound.

It was because he felt certain she would have confided in him, since she'd confided so much else, that he picked up the paint to finish the trim around another window—only to remember that one of the first things she'd mentioned yesterday was her mom. She'd wanted to know if Dora had said anything to him about helping her.

Swearing silently again, he set the paint back down. He'd already intended to go over earlier than he had yesterday, just to make sure she would still be there. Since checking up on her was something he'd planned to do, anyway, he might as well do it now.

He found her not far from where he'd left her the day before with the weed-eater. The large swath of vegetation she'd cleared from the doors, stairs and directly in front of the building sat piled in heaps off to one side waiting to be mulched or burned. In the late afternoon light, he saw her adding to the nearest pile as she tipped a wheelbarrow beside it, dumping twigs and leaves and broken boxes from inside the mill.

"How's it going?"

She turned at the sound of his voice, her preoccupation fading to a smile. A dusty purple ball cap covered her pale hair and a streak of dirt slanted across her cheek. What he noticed most was that she didn't seem sorry to see him.

Taking that as a sign that the situation with her mom couldn't be all that bad, he watched her leave the wheelbarrow to walk toward him, pulling off her gloves as she did. She had dust on her jeans, too, and on the shoulders and front of a big white T-shirt that practically swallowed her whole.

The thought that the loose garment might have belonged to an old boyfriend caused a twinge of something unwanted, unfamiliar and faintly unnerving—until he read the logo. It was for a women's medical research run-walk she could well have participated in herself.

Not trusting the unexpected twinge of jealousy any more than he did the protectiveness that had brought him there, he watched her motion to the mill's large open door.

"I think there's as much dirt in there as there is out here." Using her gloves, she swatted at her jeans. Dust puffed and drifted off. "I could plant seeds and grow things."

"You could start with wheat."

She tipped her head, her smiling eyes shadowed by the brim of her hat. "Grown and ground on site?"

The streak of dirt on her cheek ended at her jaw. Thinking to wipe away the small smudge, he reached toward her— only to notice the paint spatters on his hands. He'd wiped them, but he hadn't taken time to wash.

"Paint," he murmured, dropping his hand, feeling oddly cheated. "I don't want to get it on you."

The temptation to tell him she wouldn't mind tugged hard. Instead Kelsey told herself for the umpteenth time since yesterday that she truly needed to exercise a little more restraint where Sam was concerned. Even some would be good, since she'd been pathetically lax in that department.

"I'm a mess, too," she murmured, just glad he was there.

"So," he said.

"So," she echoed.

Not sensing anything at all unusual about her, he put his hands on his hips to keep from reaching for her again. Even with every curve hidden and dirty from the long day's work, she looked as tempting to him as sin itself.

"You'd already gone when I came over last night. I just wanted to make sure everything is going okay."

She turned to the open door, blocking her expression, leaving him with only the view of her delicate profile. "Everything is fine," she replied easily. "I want to start cleaning upstairs, but I can't do that until I'm finished clearing storage space down here. I need a ladder to pull down the nests on the rafters, but I can get the rest cleaned out so I have someplace to put my things when they get here."

"How about with everything else?" he asked, not overly anxious to ask about her mother outright. He'd rather take on a felon than personal matters any day. "Have you run into problems anywhere?"

"Everything else is fine, too," she assured him. "Or will be when my things get here." *So I don't have to listen to my mother tell me what a mistake I've made,* she thought, promptly attempting to dismiss the admission. She truly did not want to think about her mom just then. She most definitely didn't want to think about all she'd had to say about Sam last night.

Purpose in her step, she headed toward the mill's wide-open door. Reaching it, she motioned Sam inside with her.

"Do you think there's enough room back there to store a living room set, an entertainment center and about twenty packing boxes? I'm going into St. Johnsbury tomorrow for paint so I can finish my bedroom," she told him, moving into the dim light and the dust swirling in the sunbeams. "Then, I'll move in my bedroom set and the kitchen table and chairs and live up there while we finish the rest.

"I've decided I am adventurous," she confided, thinking of what he'd said yesterday, thinking of all she'd done in the past couple of weeks. "So I'm moving in as soon as my things get here."

Adventurous and maybe even a little daring, she decided. Having only been daring in her dreams before, she loved that she'd actually moved beyond them—thanks to the man her mother insisted hadn't a scrap of conscience in his body.

She truly wished her mother would stay out of her head.

She took a deep breath, banished the thoughts.

Passing the huge grinding stone and its broken casing, Sam followed her to an area that had been swept as clean as the oil spots on the floor would allow. The windows down here were still in their original cracked or broken and rain-splattered condition, but she'd opened them all to let in as much light as she could.

"You don't want to wait until we get the kitchen in?" The uncomfortable and insistent protectiveness began to ease. She sounded fine to him, and not concerned about anything other than her mill. She hadn't mentioned her mother at all.

"How long will that take?"

"From now?" Overlooking the fact that he could have pushed harder, or asked outright, he latched onto what he felt far more comfortable dealing with. "Cabinets, appliances, the tile backsplash you want. Ten days, give or take."

"I'll buy a hot plate."

"You're welcome to use mine."

"Your hot plate?"

"My kitchen."

"Would that mean I'd have to cook for you, too?"

He mirrored her teasing smile. "Absolutely."

A car door slammed.

Precariously close to getting paint on her and dust all over himself, he made himself step back. "I think you have company."

She did. It was her friend from high school, who also happened to be his cousin, Cathy, coming to welcome her home with cookies and a request for a tour of the mill everyone was talking about. She didn't seem at all surprised to see him there, which told him she must have heard either from her mom or through the grapevine that he was helping Kelsey. Since he wasn't doing anything productive for her at the moment, and he had accomplished his original mission, he told them both he'd see them later, and headed back to tackle trim.

Kelsey didn't bring up anything about her mom when he checked on her the next day, either. Or the day after that. There had been people around each time he'd stopped by. Her friend Carrie who was helping her clear the driveway of weeds while her three small children picked wildflowers one day. His cousin and Carrie, the next. He wouldn't have expected her to mention a problem with her girlfriends around, but even alone with her when they went inside the mill to store the ladder he brought and he asked how she was doing, she didn't say a word about her mom.

The fact that she didn't mention having any particular trouble with her relieved him. At least until he realized she wasn't talking about Dora at all.

Had there not been a problem, she would have mentioned her mother somehow. The fact that she didn't, gave him the certain and strangely uncomfortable feeling that she was protecting *him* by staying silent.

In the five days since Kelsey had returned, she had spent nearly every waking hour at the mill. Because the only locals she saw were those who dropped by, she hadn't realized until Charlie came to check on her progress that Sam hadn't been eating breakfast at the diner. The older man mentioned it only in passing and then only because Sam's absence was the reason he was there. Without Sam at breakfast, Charlie wasn't getting his usual morning reports about how things were going at the mill and over at the old Baker place, as the house would probably forever be known, so he was checking on both himself.

Had Kelsey thought about it, logic would have told her Sam would avoid the diner. She knew from Carrie and Cathy that word was out about her mom's displeasure with him. What they didn't know was that her mom was now blaming Sam for Claire and her husband, the mayor, being upset with her about not being supportive of the community. Her mom had insisted just last night that she most certainly did support the local economy and that she had no problem with the mill being put to work again. She even thought it was a fine idea. She'd apparently even told Claire that. She just thought it was a fine idea for someone other than her daughter.

It seemed to Kelsey that the woman had gone totally deaf to her insistence that the mill was her dream. And she wasn't being rational at all where Sam was concerned.

Defending him had been a mistake, too.

More concerned at the moment with what she'd just learned from Charlie, she watched him head to his truck to drive over to visit with Sam—who was putting the finishing touches on the house since his sister was moving in tomorrow.

She didn't believe for a moment that Sam was going hungry. Still, guilt hit like a brick.

Between working to finish his sister's place in the mornings and installing the new windows and water heater in the mill in the afternoons before going back to his sister's, he was working even harder than she was. She knew he bought his lunch from the Burger Haven by the high school, which she'd been frequenting, too, and that Cathy occasionally dropped off dinners from his aunt. She'd just been so busy keeping a judicious mental distance from him that she hadn't considered his care and feeding in the mornings.

She knew that his uncle would be helping him that evening, so his aunt would have again sent food. Since he wasn't going to starve in the next several hours, and she was desperately in need of a shower before she could go anywhere near a stove, anyway, she would make sure he got a decent breakfast first thing tomorrow.

Her intention should have been simple enough to implement. Anywhere other than in Maple Mountain, it would have been. But there were no supermarkets open twenty-four hours a day for her to anonymously pop in to buy ingredients for what should have been an uncomplicated meal. The nearest supermarket was nearly an hour and a half away and the only place to buy food locally was the Waters's general store. Even if the store hadn't been closed by then that evening and wouldn't be open before she returned in the morning, Kelsey would have hesitated to stop there. Agnes Waters, nosey as she was, would want to know if her purchases were for the diner and, if not, what she planned to do with them since everyone knew she didn't have a kitchen yet. Agnes had already mentioned to Charlie how much cold cereal Sam had bought lately.

Being closed, the store wasn't an option, anyway. That left her mother's pantry and refrigerator—those in the diner's kitchen, since the tiny one upstairs was rarely used other than to make tea or heat leftover day's special for a late supper.

All she needed was bacon and eggs and ingredients for pancakes.

She didn't know which offended her mother more when she asked if she minded her borrowing them. That she was obviously cooking for Sam—though she never said so, nor did her mother ask—or that she told her she would replace or pay for them. Since Betsy had just arrived, her mother's only response was that she didn't need to be spending whatever money she had left on "that man."

"Does that mean I can take them, or not?" Kelsey quietly asked.

"Suit yourself," her mother replied, sounding as if her suddenly headstrong daughter was going to do as she pleased anyway. "You know how I feel about all of this."

Kelsey stifled a sigh. Though she doubted Betsy could hear over the splash of water running while the cook washed up at the sink, she lowered her voice even more. "I wouldn't have to do this if he still felt welcome here." Her mother wasn't being fair at all. "He's working with me. The least I can do is make sure he gets a decent breakfast."

Ignoring what she didn't want to hear, her mom's voice dropped as well. "Are you paying him?"

"He doesn't want money."

"Well, then." Her lips momentarily thinned. "I think we both know what it is that he does want."

Kelsey opened her mouth, shook her head, closed it again. She had no intention of arguing with her mother over whether or not some man was after her body. Nor would she attempt to explain what motivated that particular man to stay as busy as he did. It wouldn't get her anywhere, anyway.

She shouldn't have felt so incredibly guilty, Kelsey told herself. But as she quickly gathered what she needed and left with her mom muttering something to Betsy, she did. She would have felt just as bad leaving Sam to eat cold cereal when he was used to fueling his body in the morning with protein.

Still feeling totally torn, she pulled up in front of Sam's trailer a little after six o'clock fearing there was no respite in sight. Her mother's attitude would only get worse as long as Sam was there. She knew that as well as she knew what a gamble she'd taken coming back.

The sounds of the stream tumbling over the rocks in its bend behind the trailer filtered through her car's open window. Telling herself to focus on the stillness and to just breathe in the fresh air, she tried to move past the agitation clinging to her like moss to stones. In no way had she romanticized how her life would be when she came back. She'd been brutally honest with the amount of work and risk involved and not for a moment had she expected things to progress with the almost eerie, straightforward ease of her move there. But she hadn't thought the glow she'd awakened with that first morning would have dimmed so rapidly, either.

"How long are you going sit out there?"

Dropping her hands from the steering wheel, she glanced over to see Sam in the doorway of the single-wide trailer. With his arms crossed over a white T-shirt, his jeans missing their belt and in his bare feet, it appeared that he hadn't been up for long.

She reached for the bag on the seat beside her, scrambling as she did to focus only on why she was there.

"I was just trying to decide if you'd be up or not," she told him, climbing from the car with the bag in her arms. "I figured you would be, though." He'd been hauling away the construction debris off and on all week. He'd told her yesterday that he'd wanted to be at the dump when it opened that morning to get rid of the last of it before his sister arrived. She was to be there at noon.

"You said you wanted to leave by seven." She nodded toward what was left of the pile at the end of the drive. "I can get started while you load that up."

Meeting her at the bottom step, he pulled back on one edge of the bag. "What's this?"

"Breakfast."

One dark eyebrow slowly arched. "You're cooking?"

"If your stove works."

Giving her a sleepy version of his killer smile, he took the bag from her. "It works just fine. Coffee's already on."

A sleep crease slashed one cheek. A tuft of damp hair that had escaped his efforts when he'd splashed water on his unshaven face and dragged his fingers through it stuck up on one side. Ignoring the tug she felt at that small vulnerability, she followed him to the long space divided into a living room at one end, a bedroom at the other and a little kitchen in between.

She knew the modest trailer with its navy-blue furnishings and beige everything else was a rental. But she had the feeling the flat-screen television and the music system that practically overtook the sofa and single easy chair were his. The electronics and wires and yard high tower of CDs didn't surprise her. What did as he set the bag down on the short, beige breakfast bar dividing the rooms and opened the curtains over the sink, was how tidy he kept everything.

She didn't know what she'd expected. A little careless bachelor clutter perhaps. Dishes in the sink, at least. A wadded up burger bag on the coffee table, perhaps. But other than two plates and some flatware that had been left to drip dry in a drainer and a haphazard stack of *Rolling Stone, Newsweek* and *Motor Trend* magazines on the floor by the sofa, the place was neat and ordered and everything was right where it should be.

Which is just how he likes his life, she thought, a moment before she caught a glimpse of his bed through the open doorway.

What appeared to be a wall-to-wall mattress was a tangle of sheets and blankets and a pillow that looked as if it had been beaten into submission.

The restiveness she sensed in him sometimes during the day obviously followed him into his sleep.

"Pretend I'm not here," she told him. She didn't like the thought that he didn't rest well. As hard as he worked, he needed his sleep. "Just point me to your pans and go do whatever you were going to do."

"I was waiting for the coffee."

Reaching into the sack, Sam pulled out a smaller brown bag containing a half a dozen eggs. With a thoughtful frown, he also removed a clear plastic Baggie of what looked like flour, another holding strips of raw bacon, and syrup in a pitcher that looked very much like those on the counter and tables at the diner.

Wondering what Dora thought of her daughter raiding her diner to feed him, he watched Kelsey pull out a Baggie containing a small amount of a white substance he didn't recognize at all, a handful of foil-wrapped butter cubes, and a take-out soup container holding some sort of liquid. He heard it slosh when she set it down.

"What's this?" he asked, lifting up the Baggie.

"Baking soda."

No wonder he didn't know what it was. "Does your mother know you have all this?"

Her glance dropped from his. "She knows," she said, turning to the cupboards. "I figured you'd have salt and pepper, but I didn't know about real butter," she went on, indicating the foil cubes. "I hope plain buttermilk pancakes are okay. Do you have a bowl?"

"Mind if I ask why you're doing this?"

Because I hate that you have to give up something I know you enjoy just because my mother thinks you're ruining my life, she thought. "Because I know you're not eating at the diner and you need more than cereal for breakfast," was all she told him.

"How do you know I eat cereal?"

"Agnes told Mary."

"Mary?"

"Charlie's wife," she reminded him, snatching open another cupboard when the first proved fruitless. "She said you've gone through two boxes of grain flakes in the last week."

"Agnes? At the general store?"

"There are no secrets in this town."

The man's kitchen equipment was abysmal. He was apparently a strictly heat-and-eat sort of cook. "Don't you have a mixing bowl?"

Hearing what sounded suspiciously like a hint of frustration in her voice, Sam moved behind her. Reaching past her shoulder, he took a salad bowl from the top shelf. He'd only brought the minimum of what he'd thought he'd need from his apartment. He'd become used to living spare.

Handing the bowl to her, he watched her take it without so much as the questioning lift of an eyebrow and turn away to start cracking eggs. Beneath the clean faded pink T-shirt that now sported a rip on one sleeve, her slender shoulders rose and fell with the deep, deliberate breath she drew.

She seemed different to him this morning. Working with her the past couple of days, he'd been aware of a deliberate sense of purpose about her as she'd painted and scrubbed, and hammered the trim around the windows he'd installed. He'd been drawn by her willingness to tackle every task she could handle, her quick grasp of things he'd had to explain and the hints of enthusiasm that had leaked through her grit. Now, all he sensed was a grim determination. Or, maybe, what he sensed was simply agitation.

He didn't know if the faint strain in her features was new or if he simply hadn't wanted to acknowledge it was there, but he couldn't avoid noticing it now. It was as apparent as the impatience in her movements as she pulled a pan from beneath the stove and went back to beating the daylights out of the eggs.

"Since there are no secrets, do you want to tell me what's bothering you?"

"Nothing's bothering me."

The coffeemaker sputtered behind him, signaling that the coffee was finally ready. Instead of reaching for cups, he reached for her.

Taking her by the shoulders, he turned her around, set the bowl she held on the counter and settled his hand back on her shoulder.

"Try again."

She said nothing. While his glance moved over the baby fine strands of hair at the crown of her head, he thought about staying silent himself. He might have, too, had it not been for the protectiveness that had yet to disappear. If anything, it had grown—without his permission and in spite of his attempts to ignore it, but there was no denying that the feeling was there. So was the realization that, at that moment, he was far more interested in protecting her than he was himself.

Too concerned about her to acknowledge that dangerous shift, he nudged up her chin with his finger. In his gut he knew what the problem was. It was the only thing they hadn't talked about since her return.

"What's going on with you and your mom?"

He could practically feel the tension shift through her muscles as she stepped away to open the bags of flour and baking soda. "I really don't want to talk about my mother. Okay?"

"Why not?"

Kelsey picked up the baking soda, quickly opened the bag. She didn't want him doing this. All she wanted was to fix his breakfast so she wouldn't have to feel bad about what her mother was doing. She didn't want him looking at her as if he already knew her secrets. She didn't want him touching

202   *CONFESSIONS OF A SMALL-TOWN GIRL*

her as he had so casually over the past few days, either. Now as then, she'd had to pull away and make herself be busy because when he touched her the temptation to lean on him was too strong. Every time he would nudge up her chin and asked if she was okay, he reminded her of how badly she wanted to be in his arms, and of how she wanted his reassurance that everything would be all right. But she couldn't let herself want him. And she couldn't rely on him any more than she already did because soon he wouldn't be there to rely on at all.

"Kelsey?"

"Because the only time I don't feel that I've made a terminal mistake coming back here is when I'm at the mill working on it or with you. Okay?" She hadn't meant to verbalize the "with you" part. Feeling pushed, it had simply slipped out. "I'd just appreciate it if we could talk about something else." She peeled the lid from the soup container of buttermilk. "Please."

For a moment, Sam said nothing, he just stood there, watching her in that steady, unnerving way he had while she let out an exasperated breath. She hadn't mixed her dry ingredients. She needed to do that first.

"Just answer one question for me, will you?"

She grabbed a dry plate from the drainer. "What's that?"

"What does she want you to do?"

"As of last night, she wanted me to put the mill on the market. She's sure I won't have any trouble getting my old job back."

"And what do you want?"

She'd started spooning flour onto the plate. *What I've always wanted,* she thought to say, only to go still when she realized that, just then, she felt more uncertainty than conviction.

You've never run your own business before, Kelsey. This isn't what you've trained to do.

With her mother's voice echoing in her head, she resumed her task. "To know that I haven't made a huge error in judgment."

Sam knew he could be sorely lacking in sensitivity at times. Part of that was genetics, he was sure. His mom had accused his dad of the same thing on more than one occasion. Part of it, he suspected, was just being male. Then, there was the fact that he'd had little practice being sensitive since his typical modus operandi was to avoid situations where employing it might be necessary. All of which combined to make him feel rather awkward when he found himself wanting to remove the disquiet that had robbed the light from her eyes.

Not knowing what else to do, he could only offer what he'd learned from his own experience.

"The only mistake you're making is doubting yourself, Kelsey. You asked yourself all the right questions going into this. You did your homework and your heart is in it. Once a decision is made, you need to stick with it and not let anything…or anyone," he quietly emphasized, "stand in your way."

She turned the disquiet in her eyes to him.

"No second-guessing?"

"None," he replied, wondering at how her mother must be wearing on her. "You're the one responsible for the direction your life takes. Uncertainty is totally self-defeating."

"You never have doubts?"

"Sure I do." He doubted situations and people all the time. People especially. He'd just never doubted her. "I just don't second-guess myself once I've decided what I need to do. If I don't have faith in my decisions, I have no power to act on them. No one does."

He had the feeling he wasn't helping at all. The disturbing disquiet remained as she looked away.

"Hey," he murmured, settling his hand on her shoulder once more. "You never would have taken this on if you hadn't had faith in yourself." He was still blown away by the guts it had taken for her to make such a move. "You need to shut down that doubt and put that faith of yours back to work. Okay?"

The coffeepot gave another sputter. Above her head, the roof creaked as the morning sun heated its surface. Kelsey barely noticed the sounds. Searching the strong lines of his face, she desperately wished she possessed his confidence. More than anything else, she wished he would hold her.

"How?"

At her typical insistence, the light of a smile entered his eyes. "Repeat after me," he instructed, looking very big, very male as he turned her to face him. "I have no doubts. What I'm doing is absolutely right."

She'd never known anyone who had his faith in her. Amazed by his power to calm her fears, she touched her fingers to the soft cotton covering his chest.

"Is that the mantra they taught you at the police academy?"

The smile in his eyes deepened. "I could tell you, but then I'd have to put you in solitary for the rest of your life. Come on," he coaxed, "Say it."

She took a deep breath. "I have no doubts…"

"Not like that," he muttered, cutting her off. His smile turned serious. "Try it again. It will only work if you really mean it."

She needed to believe it. In her heart, she knew she did. So, she closed her eyes, concentrating on that conviction while the warmth of his hands seeped into her shoulders, and started over.

"I have no doubts," she repeated, thinking of each of word as she spoke it. "What I'm doing is absolutely right."

"Better. Now," he said, squeezing her shoulder. "Promise me you won't ever forget that."

Considering all he'd done for her, giving him her word was the least she could do. Eyes still closed, she gave a little nod. "I promise."

"Good," he murmured, seconds before his lips brushed hers.

His kiss was featherlight, the merest whisper of skin to skin. Yet, the quick heat was immediately there. Kelsey felt it shimmer through her as she breathed in the scents of toothpaste and warm male and told herself she should move. And she would, she insisted, in the moments before his mouth settled more fully over hers and he drew her into his arms. Soon. Right now, she wanted to absorb his strength and let herself lean on him. Just a little. And just for a while.

Sam thought she might do what she'd done nearly every time he'd reached for lately and find some excuse to pull away. If she had, he would have let her go. Reluctantly. But he would have done it. Yet, instead of that subtle retreat, she lifted her arms, winding them around his neck, and kissed him back as greedily as he was suddenly kissing her.

With her firm breasts flattened against his chest, he slipped his hand down her spine and cupped her hips to draw her closer. He nearly groaned at the feel of her body seeking his. The woman was like a drug in his blood. One taste of her was all he needed to crave her more. One taste, and his judgment was altered. He'd intended to offer her reassurance and, if he was capable of it—a little comfort. It was just hard to remember his purpose with her kissing him as if she felt the same slow-burning heat that threatened to turn his control to ash.

"Hey." He whispered the word against the shell of her ear, kissing the soft skin behind it. "Are you okay?"

He felt her hesitate a moment before she lowered her head to his chest. The bones in her back felt incredibly fragile as he skimmed his hand over them.

"I am now," she whispered back. As if savoring his touch, or drawing something from it, she gave a little sigh. "Thank you," she finally said.

"My pleasure." He pressed his lips to the crown of her head. Breathing in her scent, he realized his whole body felt as taut as a bowstring. "You should probably fix my breakfast."

"Probably," she agreed, though she didn't seem terribly anxious to move.

With her arms still around him, he nuzzled the side of her neck. "Breakfast would be good," he murmured, "but you know what I'd rather have?"

"Help loading the truck?"

He chuckled against her hair. "That would be good, too," he conceded. "But in all honesty…I'd rather have you."

The phenomenon was interesting. He felt every muscle in her slender body go motionless in the long seconds before she lifted her head. Still, to his relief, she didn't retreat.

"What I'd really like," he clarified, slipping his thumb over the moisture he'd left on her bottom lip, "is to pick up where we left off on July twelfth. Only this time," he told her, his eyes dark on hers, "I want to get to the bottom of the page."

She had wanted him to show her…everything.

He was giving her fair warning. If he kissed her again, he wouldn't want to stop. Kelsey sensed that as certainly as she did the heat flowing between their bodies. It moved through them, surrounded them, drew them closer still.

She wouldn't want him to stop, either.

The admission should have had her easing away. At the very least, it should have given her pause. But she was right where she'd wanted to be since the moment she'd last stepped from his arms and moving was the farthest thought on her mind.

"You'd have to show me where we were." Her heart beat wildly at her stunning lack of caution. "I don't remember…exactly."

Something feral slipped into his expression. "I'll refresh your memory."

He would have no problem doing that at all. That night at the mill had fused itself in his brain, haunting his sleep, adding an entirely different sort of frustration to his restlessness. His eyes steady on the control-wrecking need she didn't even try to deny, thoughts of it now sent heat, poker hot, racing through him as he slowly tugged up the hem of her shirt.

This time there were no buttons to contend with. All he had to do to feel her in his hands was coax the fabric over her head. The shirt had barely hit the floor before he leaned down to kiss her, softly, making himself take his time while he unfastened the clip of her pink lace bra.

The bra had landed soundlessly beside the shirt when Kelsey felt his lips trail down the front of her throat. His hand eased over one bare breast. Cupping it, he did exactly as he'd done before and flicked his tongue over its tight little bud.

Her nerves already sensitized, she dug her fingers into his shoulders as he closed his mouth over her. Apparently realizing he'd just made her knees go weak, he slid one arm around her back. Just before they threatened to buckle completely, he lifted his head.

"Remember now?"

She swallowed past the pulse hammering at the base of her neck. She'd lied. She remembered exactly what he'd done.

"Perfectly," she assured him and raised on tiptoe, kissing him as she had before while she pulled the hem of his shirt from his pants.

As if impatient to be skin-to-skin himself, Sam grasped a fist full of white cotton between his shoulder blades and dragged it over his head. But even as the garment joined hers and he reached to pull her back to him, she noticed the scars bisecting the hard, honed muscles of his beautiful chest.

Her glance flicked to his. There was no mistaking the hesitation in his carved features before she touched her fingers to the inch-long scar under the right side of his jaw. Below it ran the raised ridge that angled from above his right collarbone to six inches below the flat, brown nipple on the other side.

Thoughts of the pain he would have once been in had her lightening her touch as she slowly traced that gash its long, disturbing length. The texture felt hard compared to the smoothness of his skin, and slick. Yet, it didn't feel as satiny as the pink, quarter-size disk of flesh high on his left bicep.

She kissed that puckered disk first, leaving her palm curved over it before touching her lips to the slash. Even as she did, she heard his slow intake of breath.

She wasn't allowed to ask what had happened. She'd barely lifted her head before his hands were in her hair, his mouth was on hers and she wasn't thinking of anything at all but the raw hunger she felt in him as he invaded her senses as thoroughly as he had her heart.

I have no doubts. What I am doing is right.

The words drifted through her mind as she stretched against him, rough skin to soft, heart hammering. She knew he had intended the affirmation as encouragement for her decision about the mill. And heaven knew how grateful she was for his unrelenting confidence. Yet, as he backed her across the kitchen and through the door to his bedroom, what was happening now felt absolutely right, too. She had started falling in love with him thirteen years ago. As they fumbled with the snaps and zippers of each other's jeans and tumbled, clinging, onto the tangle of sheets, she knew she had now fallen for him completely; body, mind and soul.

The admission held no surprise. Not even the faintest hint of shock or dismay. All she felt was a sense of inevitability, as if she'd been destined to fall in love with him all along. Beyond that odd certainty, she was mostly aware of the daring he encouraged when she followed his lead and pushed away his clothes, kissing her way down his body after he'd stripped away hers and kissed his way back up.

With him, she could somehow be the woman she wanted to be. Someone more courageous, more fearless, and infinitely less restrained than she'd ever been around anyone else. With him, she could be bold.

She loved him for that. She loved him for so many reasons. She just couldn't think of them just then. With his hands and mouth escalating the need deep inside her, she could barely think at all.

She had once wanted him to show her everything. And he would, he promised himself, dragging his mouth from her breasts to her belly. He wanted that, too. He wanted to take the time to explore and linger. He wanted to know every seductive inch of her. He couldn't get enough of her taste, her scents, her softness. As long as it had been for him, as badly as he wanted to be buried in her, he just couldn't do it now. Especially not with her small hands roaming his shoulders as he moved back up to drink the sound of his name on her lips.

The need for release pounded like a pulse.

Sheets rustled. The clock on his nightstand bumped the lamp with a metallic clink when he groped for the handle on the nightstand's drawer. They needed protection. The thought of having to use it with her battled some primitive instinct that didn't feel familiar at all, but the functioning part of his brain overrode that dangerous impulse. Finding one of the small foil packets he was looking for, he ripped it open with his teeth.

He was beyond the fantasy. All he cared about was the moment as he rolled the condom over himself and she rained urgent little kisses along his neck. All that mattered was seeking her when she slipped her fingers through his hair to meet his mouth, urging him closer as their tongues mated and he settled his weight over hers.

She arched to him, threatening the control that already felt razor-thin.

He asked her to slow down.

She wanted to know why.

He couldn't respond. He didn't trust the raw, demanding need he felt for her. He didn't trust the threat she had over his control.

It's just sex, he told himself, but the claim felt more like protest than conviction as he eased inside her. Hanging on to that control, he clenched his teeth against the exquisite feel of her, only to find that control no longer mattered. All that did was the way she clung to him as they moved, and the heat they created that seared its way clear to his soul.

He hadn't trusted the need. Lying with her in his arms while his heart rate slowed and his breathing quieted long minutes later, he didn't trust the peace he felt with her, either.

He hadn't recognized the feeling at first. But the odd and quiet stillness that settled over him couldn't have been anything else. It had just been so long since he'd felt it that he hadn't known it for what it was.

He didn't know which one of them had pulled up the sheet that covered them both. He lay on his back with her curled at his side, their legs tangled and her head on his chest. Her tousled hair tickled his chin, its gentle scent filling his lungs with each breath. It had been a full minute since she moved. When she stirred now, it was only to lift her hand and touch the puckered pink flesh high on his muscled arm.

"What happened?"

He didn't think much about his scars, except to keep them covered. He didn't mind the questions. He'd just never been comfortable with the way some people stared. "Got in the way of a bullet."

"How long ago?"

"Three years." It had been longer than that. "Maybe four."

"And here," she said, tracing the long scar on his chest.

"A guy had a knife. I didn't move fast enough."

Kelsey pulled back her hand, laid it over the quieted beat of his heart. He made both incidents sound as if they were his fault—as if he should have been in a different position, that he should have moved faster. He was a man who took responsibility for his actions. He would blame no one but himself when things went wrong.

There had been a time when she might have thought he shouldn't be so hard on himself. Knowing him now, she realized it was how he survived. Every incident was a lesson.

She touched the scar under his jaw. "And this?"

"I fell off my bike doing wheelies."

Raising up on one elbow, she looked doubtfully into his eyes. "Seriously?"

He lifted his hand, pushed her hair from her cheek. What he'd just told her was his usual, blow-off explanation for his most visible scar. Remembering the tender way she'd kissed his old wounds, he gave her the truth, instead.

"It's where the guy with the knife started. He had me in a neck-hold from behind."

The vision of a knife to his throat before he'd turned and been slashed formed in an instant. That vivid scenario also had her glance falling back to his chest. It shook her to her core to think his skills would have failed him in such a way.

As if he knew what she was thinking, he tipped her chin back up. "There were three of them. I was the diversion so my partner could go for backup. It all turned out okay."

Disbelief colored her quiet tone. "That's how you judge the success of something? By whether or not you walk away alive?"

He hadn't exactly walked. "What else matters?"

Kelsey had no answer for that.

"All we have are moments, Kelsey. And all we really have is the one we're in."

The past was over. The future wasn't there yet. She supposed his pragmatic approach served him well, considering how he lived his life. But she didn't want to think of how hard it had been not recalling fond memories or having dreams beyond tomorrow. She especially didn't want to think of his life away from her. As she kissed the scar on his chest, praying he would stay safe, all she wanted was to hold reality at bay for a little while longer.

Sam wasn't sure what it was, but something seemed to squeeze at his heart at the feel of her lips on his skin. Some of the women he'd known over the years had been fascinated by his scars. One had even seemed a little afraid of them. But none had kissed them the way Kelsey did. And not one had made him want to simply lay with her while his body, so recently sated, began to stir again.

He glanced at the clock on his nightstand, tucked her a little closer. It was barely eight o'clock. They had nearly four hours to slake the hunger that was building already.

Or so he thought a moment before he heard the slam of car doors and his sister's voice yelling for the boys to slow down.

Chapter Ten

"Trevor! Don't you dare jump off that porch rail! Tyler, don't run with that stick!"

Kelsey could hear Megan hollering at her offspring as she scrambled to dress at the edge of Sam's bed. He had already handed her her jeans and underwear and was pulling on his own on his way into the kitchen to retrieve their shirts.

Standing with the sheet in front of her as she snapped her own pants, she saw him swipe up pink cotton and white, then bend to look through the slats of the blinds over the tiny kitchen table.

"She's chasing the kids right now," was all he said before heading back to hand her the rest of her clothes. "I think we have a minute."

Her bra dangled by one strap from his finger. Snatching it, she turned away to put it on, only to have him turn her right back around.

"I've kissed every inch of you," he reminded her, lifting his hands to cradle her face. "You don't have to turn away to dress."

He wanted her to be comfortable with him, and to know she had no reason to ever feel self-conscious where he was concerned. Desperately relieved to know that, she whispered a shaky, "Okay." The tension in his body had been almost palpable when he'd bolted from bed. It was clear now that it wasn't there because of any regrets he had about her.

He looked very much as if he were about to kiss her when the muscle in his jaw jerked and his hands fell.

"She was supposed to be here at noon," he groused, stuffing his shirt tail into his jeans. "Not at half past the crack of dawn."

"I'm sure she's anxious to get into her house." Quickly fastening her bra, she reached for her shirt and stuck her head through its neck. "I would be if I were her," she confided as her head popped through.

This time he did kiss her. With his hands in the mess of her hair, he pulled her to him, kissed her hard, then turned to grab clean socks from the built-in dresser drawer. "I'm sure she is. But her timing sucks."

"Sam? You in there?"

"Yeah, Sis. Hang on."

Kelsey reached for her own socks, pulled one on. "I need a comb."

"In the bathroom. Through there," he said, pointing to the door just outside the bedroom. And Kelsey," he said, catching her by the arm before she disappeared. His glance moved from her mouth to her eyes, promise heavy in his rugged face. "We'll take longer next time."

The thrill that shot through her coincided roughly with the sharp knock on the door.

"Sam? I've got to get back to the kids. Do you have any coffee in there?"

"I'll bring you a cup."

"And some aspirin if you have any."

"Got it."

With his hand still on Kelsey's arm, he gave a little squeeze. "Can I have a rain check on breakfast?"

Kelsey told him of course he could and slipped into the bathroom, leaving him to pull on his boots. By the time she had made herself presentable, he was already outside and she was left to make as graceful an exit as possible with his sister standing twenty feet from the door.

The boys were running around like wind-up toys beside the orange trailer his sister had pulled behind her SUV when Sam heard the door of his temporary residence open. Megan stood beside him, cradling her coffee mug as if it contained the elements of life itself. She had just started to take another sip when she noticed the door open, too.

"'Morning," Kelsey said, appearing as if she were trying not to be self-conscious as she descended the stairs. She looked as neat to him as she had when she'd first shown up. Except that her hair was down now instead of in a ponytail. Apparently she hadn't been able to find the little fabric thing he'd pulled out and tossed somewhere.

"Well," his sister murmured. A smile joined the fatigue in her eyes. She'd said she and the boys had been too excited to sleep. That was why they'd left so early. "I see now why you weren't so happy to see me."

"She came by to fix breakfast."

"Looks like you didn't get very far. With breakfast, I mean." Her voice dropped at his puzzled frown. "The ingredients are still on your counter."

"How do you know that?"

"The curtain wasn't pulled all the way on the door window. There's also a car parked right there," she pointed out, motioning to the little sedan beside his truck. "It's obvious someone's here. I was looking to see who it was.

"'Morning, Kelsey," she called. Her knowing smile turning friendly as she glanced to the woman walking toward them. "Sorry about the interruption. Oh, jeez," she muttered, shoving her mug at her brother before she turned. "That kid is going to kill himself.

"Trevor! I told you not to walk on the railings! Get down before I buckle you back into the car and make you stay there forever!"

"Lookit what I got, Uncle Sam!" Oblivious to his older brother's impending fate, little Tyler walked toward him with his hands cupped together. "It's fuzzy!"

Kelsey touched his arm, quickly eased back her hand. She didn't know if she should offer to help or just get out of the way. "I'm going to go," she decided, as the little boy drew closer, his expression rapt. "Unless it would help if I stayed to help your sister."

Sam's attention, clearly divided, cut to her.

"Thanks," he murmured, "but we'll call my aunt and cousin. They're coming, anyway. And my uncle's going to help unload the heavy stuff, so I should be finished by midafternoon. I'll be over to help you then."

"Uncle Sam?"

At his nephew's plea for attention, Kelsey smiled at the child, then looked back to the big man beside him. "Don't worry about me."

She offered the assurance as she backed toward her car. She was in trouble here. Deep trouble, she realized. She didn't regret for a moment what her appalling lack of restraint where he was concerned had led. She knew she should. She could practically feel the void he would leave once he was gone waiting to open. But she wasn't going to think about that now. She had always planned ahead, always considered consequences, but for now, she was going to adopt the philosophy he apparently lived by and stay focused only on the moment.

At that particular moment, he was smiling at her in that deceptively easy way he had as his nephew held up his treasure for his perusal.

"Just take care of Megan," she said, taking another step away. At the moment, too, she had soot to scrub from a fireplace and he had a sister who definitely needed his assistance. "She has her hands full."

Sam would have agreed with her had Tyler not been elbowing his knee to get him to look at what he held so gently.

"That's a great caterpillar," he told him, only to look back to see that Kelsey had already turned and was headed for her car.

He'd just watched her head down the drive for the road when he heard his sister behind him. She had Trevor, in full pout, by the hand. He knew the kid was just wound up. But he really didn't want him breaking an extremity, either.

"I like her."

"Yeah," he muttered, making himself focus on the people surrounding him. "She's…"

"Special? That's okay," she told him when his only response was protective silence, "you don't have to answer that. I can see it. And it's nice to see you with her."

Bending at the waist, she glanced down to see what her youngest son was holding up for her inspection. "That's a big one," she told Tyler, praise in her voice. "Are you going to quit the force and stay in Maple Mountain?" she asked her brother.

Sam blinked at the top of her dark head. "You know me better than that."

He couldn't believe she'd asked such a question. Apparently, she couldn't quite believe his response. Puzzlement crossed her face as she looked up.

"Then why would you talk her into moving back here if you aren't staying yourself?"

Disbelief shot into his voice. "Where did you hear that?"

"That you talked her into staying? I heard it from Aunt Jan, and from Cathy," she explained speaking of their cousin. "They said everyone around here is talking about it."

For a moment, Sam said nothing. He knew from experience that the first words to come to a person's mind weren't necessarily the best to verbalize. Since those that immediately came to his involved several with four letters, he had the foresight to shield them from tender ears.

The annoyance Sam had first felt toward Dora did not diminish, however, as he chose what he said with a little more care.

"What you heard is her mother's interpretation," he explained, when explaining anything about his personal affairs wasn't something he tended to do with his family. "I didn't talk Kelsey into anything. Buying the mill is something she's wanted since she was kid," he maintained, telling her exactly what he'd told Joe—who apparently hadn't done a very good job of spreading that part of the story.

"But you're helping her with it, aren't you?"

He all but gritted his teeth. "Because I need something to do while I'm stuck here now that your house is done." His exasperation was with Dora. Not with his sister. For that reason, along with the fact that his already beleaguered sibling didn't need to bear the brunt of his frustration, he did his best to keep that exasperation from his voice. "All I'm doing is working on the place while I'm here."

He didn't know if Megan believed him or not. In the moments before Tyler asked if he could keep his find as a pet and Trevor said he had to go to the bathroom and wanted to know if Uncle Sam could show him where it was, he was more concerned with putting an end to the rumor that, by now, people were apparently accepting as truth.

Like stemming the flow of a broken dam, the best place to stop a rumor was at its origin. Dora had started it. With Dora was where it would end.

By five o'clock that afternoon, all of his sister's boxes and furniture had been unloaded and moved into their respective rooms and his aunt was helping her unpack her kitchen. Since Sam knew Kelsey would be at the mill until the sun set and she could no longer see to work, he figured the time was as good as any to talk to her mother about her glaringly erroneous assumption.

He didn't bother to wonder why he was deliberately walking into the sort of family clash that normally would have had him diving for cover. All he did as he parked in front of the diner and walked down the graveled side driveway to its back entrance was consider his approach. An operation was only as good as its planning. Dora possessed a basically warmhearted nature, which she had passed on to her daughter. She also had an obsessively practical side which Kelsey had likewise inherited in spades, but had softened with a huge dose of imagination. Considering those qualities, he'd decided that Dora would best respond to the direct approach.

He was wrong.

"I'm not sure you want to talk to her right now," said the white-haired woman in the hairnet who answered his knock on the back screen door. The inner door had already been open. She'd simply appeared on the other side of the screen. "Claire just left."

Claire would be the mayor's wife—the woman who thought Dora wasn't being civic-minded because she disapproved of her daughter's plans to rejuvenate the mill. That meant Dora's mood would not be good.

"When do you suggest I come back?"

"The turn of the next century comes to mind," came Dora's response.

Appearing at her cook's elbow, Kelsey's mom crossed her arms over the bib of her white apron by resting her still-casted arm atop the other. Her actually rather pretty features looked as tight as the braided, figure-eight bun at the back of her head. "It's all right, Betsy. I'll take care of this."

Sam had met Betsy through the serving window. The woman had cooked his breakfast all the time Kelsey had been gone, and while they'd never had a conversation, he'd thought her rather pleasant. That was obviously before her employer had gotten to her. The look she gave him before she turned away was nearly as thin-lipped as Dora's.

"Unless you're here to tell me you're stayin' to see Kelsey through the start up of that mill, I have nothin' to say to you."

She hadn't bothered to open the screen door. With the clank of pans drifting from the kitchen into the storage room behind her, she just stood there, staring at him through the metal mesh, waiting for him to vindicate himself.

"I never planned to stay," he told her, his tone as reasonable as he could make it. "Kelsey knows that."

"Then why did you talk her into moving back here?"

A muscle in his jaw bunched. "That's what I want talk to you about," he advised her, masking his surge of annoyance with practiced calm. "I never talked your daughter into anything. All I did was encourage her to follow a dream she's had since—"

"That's not what you did at all," she cut in, cutting him off. "What you've done is set her up for a whole lot of discouragement. You had no business encouraging her to do anything, much less buying that mill.

"No one knows better than I do how hard it is to run a business alone," she informed him, apparently finding plenty to say after all. "It takes all your time and every bit of your energy. I don't think Kelsey realizes what she's sacrificed buying that place. Doing what I do here, I have a social life. But she's going to be stuck out there alone. Day in, and day out. She won't see anyone who doesn't make a point of stopping by. Heaven knows she won't have time to get out and do the things a single girl ought to do.

"Not that there's anything for her to do here," she continued, clearly upset by that circumstance, too. "We don't have the opportunities here that she had in the city. On top of that," she persisted, squeezing her arms as if to hold herself back from going through the screen at him, "she'll be out there working off her backside trying not to lose her money. This would all be different if she had a partner. Life's just plain easier that way all the way around. But she doesn't, and she isn't likely to have one given the pickin's in this county. I hate to think of all she's thrown away. She had a wonderful future ahead of her. Now all she has is that…that…mill."

Kelsey was right, he decided. Talking to her mother was like talking to a brick wall. Only there was no conversation involved. She'd barely let him say a word.

The last thing Sam wanted to do was cause more problems between Kelsey and her mom. That was the only reason he didn't tell the woman she should back off and let her daughter live her own life. Or, at the very least, that she should give her a little credit for having a brain of her own and not bending to her mother's expectations just to keep the peace. Had she been anyone else, he would have said just that. But he wouldn't have talked that way to his own mother, and having Dora more upset with him would only make her more unhappy with her daughter.

"You're underestimating her," he said instead. "Her plans for the mill are solid. I don't think you realize how committed she is."

Offense joined indignation. "I know my daughter, Sam MacInnes. You're the one who doesn't. I don't doubt that she'll work herself to the bone making a go of that place. That girl's never shied from hard work. But there's more going on here than whether or not I think what she's done is right."

As if to make sure her cook or waitresses weren't lurking behind her, she tossed a quick glance over her shoulder. When she turned back, she lowered her voice a terse notch.

"I can tell from the way Kelsey defends you that she cares about you far more than you care about her. I know you're after her," she snapped. "After Joe saw the two of you, there's not much of anybody in this town who doesn't, and I don't think much of you for messin' with her heart the way you're doin' when you know you're just going to walk away. That girl is fallin' in love with you. If you don't care about anything else, you might at least consider her feelings and her reputation and behave yourself while you are here."

Standing at the back of the old, converted house, Sam couldn't see the street. But he could hear the sounds of a car driving by and another pulling up to the diner in Dora's sudden, condemning silence.

Of all she had said, what she'd unloaded last clearly angered her the most. He held the potential to hurt her daughter. Watching her glare at him, there was no doubt in his mind that she resented his lack of respect for that above and beyond everything else.

Sam often didn't say what he thought. That didn't mean he didn't have an opinion or a defense. It just meant he didn't choose to waste his breath offering it. At that moment, though, he had no defense. He was also at a total loss for words.

Dora seemed to know that, too. Looking as if she dared him to deny her conclusions, she held his eyes long enough to do what no man had done in longer than he could remember. She made his glance fall. That accomplished, she turned away to take care of her customers.

He'd gone down in flames as far as accomplishing his initial goal was concerned. He did, however, now understand the root of her protective fury.

Sucking in a breath that smelled faintly of meatloaf, he stepped back himself and plowed his fingers through his hair. At that moment, he wasn't honestly certain which disturbed him more: the question both Dora and his sister had asked about why he'd encouraged Kelsey, Dora's announcement of how Kelsey felt about him, or her insinuation that he could be ruining Kelsey's reputation.

Then there was the realization that he had the power to cause Kelsey pain.

The defensive sensation suddenly knotting his gut felt all too familiar. His jaw working, he headed past the row of metal garbage cans and out to the street.

The only reasons he'd encouraged Kelsey about the mill were because her ideas clearly excited her, and what she was doing was something she'd always wanted—in one form or another. As he climbed into his truck and pulled onto the narrow main road, he insisted that to himself as forcefully as he had to everyone else.

He just didn't bother to wonder why what she wanted mattered to him. He was too busy refusing to accept responsibility for the decisions Kelsey had made. She was a big girl. She was bright, stronger than she thought she was and quite capable of making her own choices.

He was, however, also beginning to feel an acute sense of accountability where she was concerned.

Despite Dora's claim, he did know Kelsey. And because he knew her, he had the uneasy feeling that what had happened between them that morning wasn't just about fulfilling a sexual fantasy. Not for her. She'd gone too far out of her way in the beginning to make sure he knew she was more conservative than he might have suspected reading what he had of her diary. In the time he'd known her, he'd also come to realize there was a lot about her life and her dreams that she had shared only with him.

Her mom's claim that she had fallen in love with him tightened the knot in his gut. Whether things had gone that far, he didn't honestly know. Kelsey certainly had never said anything to him about it herself. But he didn't need to hear the words that would have sent him running, anyway. He knew she never would have slept with him had her feelings somehow not been involved. And that was a complication he'd never counted on.

Complications were never a good thing. It had been his experience that one always led to another, and the last thing he wanted was for her to start believing there was anything more between them than what they already had. He didn't want anyone else speculating about them, either. And people would if their relationship continued as it now was. He had never considered the effect an affair would have on her, or how it could affect her reputation in the small, conservative community.

Considering it now, guilt hit him square in the chest. Though he didn't want to admit that Dora was right about much of anything just then, he would concede that she did have reason to be slightly furious with him where her daughter's reputation was concerned. In her mind, his intentions were definitely less than honorable and Kelsey would only suffer more talk after he'd gone. Especially since he wouldn't be there to defend her.

The responsibility he felt toward Kelsey jerked a little harder.

He didn't drive to the mill as he had planned to do. He didn't go to his sister's house, either. Partly because he didn't want her and his aunt asking why he was there instead of helping Kelsey. Partly because it was always possible Kelsey could come looking for him there if she worried about him not showing up.

He made a U-turn a mile from the mill road and drove out to his aunt and uncle's farm instead. He had some arrangements he needed to make with his uncle Ted. He could use the phone there, too. He was due back on the force in a couple of weeks. Knowing it was always safest to put a quick end to an operation that had gone out of control, he would call his supervisor and ask if he could come back now.

The disappointment Kelsey had felt when Sam's sister had come over last night to tell her he'd needed to help his uncle had been replaced the next morning by anticipation as she listened for the sound of his truck. She'd also begun to feel a certain uneasiness. It was already noon and he still wasn't there.

Reminding herself that his sister might have needed his help moving something heavy, or that whatever project had taken him out to his uncle's last night required more time than he'd thought, she continued rolling sealer over the new wallboard in her bathroom and tried to ignore that taunting sense of disquiet.

Live in the moment, she reminded herself, only to find her thoughts promptly sliding straight back to the past. The man had probably always been her ideal, she'd come to realize, her hero and, subconsciously, the man by whom all others had been measured. It seemed monumentally unfair to her that she would only be allowed a couple of weeks with him when a lifetime was what she wanted, but she knew she couldn't think that way. She'd promised herself that as long as he was there, she would live only in the moment. At least, as far as their relationship was concerned.

Since her efforts didn't seem to be working, she would also pray for a miracle.

The breeze carried the warm August air through her open and sparkling new window. Yesterday, she'd scrubbed the soot from the hearth and the stones above the fireplace and shown up at her mother's last night looking as if she'd spent the day working in a coal mine. Her mother had even commented on the soot, though, mercifully—and surprisingly—she'd said little else before Kelsey had showered and fallen into bed. She didn't know if she could have taken her mother's criticism of Sam now without somehow betraying how she truly felt about him. Knowing how her mother felt about Sam herself, Kelsey could only imagine what her mom would have to say if she realized she was in love with him. She also wouldn't stand a snowball's chance in Hades of convincing her that he wasn't the reason she'd come back.

With one of the dirtier jobs out of the way, the next task on her list was to seal the new wallboard in her small bathroom so she could paint now that her bedroom was finished. Sometime in the next couple of days, she and Sam needed to go into St. Johnsbury to pick up the fixtures that had been on back order when she'd picked up her paint.

The list of tasks seemed endless. The moving van bringing her kitchen sink, new appliances and the rest of her possessions was to arrive tomorrow. Sometime between now and then, they needed to install the remnant of deep sage carpet she'd found for her bedroom on sale at the home improvement store where she'd ordered new unfinished fronts for her kitchen cabinets.

Leaving the sealer to dry when she'd finished, she headed into the kitchen, still listening for some sound that would tell her Sam was there. Hearing nothing but Mrs. Farber's geese, she picked up a screwdriver and sat down on the floor to remove the half-dozen old cabinet doors. With half of her attention on how messy it was going to be to strip off the old layers of paint and refinish the cabinets themselves, and half on the lengthening silence outside, she tried again to shake the unease that told her something wasn't quite right.

When Megan had come over last night, she'd said only that Sam had called and asked that she tell her he wouldn't be able to make it out until morning, but that he would see her then. His sister, who was now her new neighbor, had then invited her back to her house with her and her boys, both of whom had devolved to the cranky stage, to share the tuna casserole her aunt had left for them. Since Sam wasn't coming, and as much as Kelsey enjoyed the young widow's company, Kelsey would have loved to join them. She told Megan that, too, but as dirty as she was and with more of the grimy task left to tackle before night fell, she'd needed to pass.

Megan had understood completely. She'd also said nothing to indicate that Sam planned to be so late. Since it was Sunday and everyone else was either at the community church or with their families, no one had stopped by to mention whether or not they had seen him that morning, either.

Noon came and went. Then, twelve-thirty. Then, one.

By two, Kelsey was beginning to worry that something had happened to him and was about to head for Megan's when the muffled growl of his truck's engine had her bolting to the new window that overlooked her driveway.

Looking down on the roughly cleared strip of overgrown meadow, she watched his truck stop directly below.

It was no wonder he was late, she thought, anxiety fading to a grin as she headed for the door. The long bed of his pickup truck was loaded with boxes of bathroom fixtures. He'd driven to St. Johnsbury. Round trip alone took up three hours.

By the time she made it to the bottom of the stairs, she had forced her grin to a smile. Sam was already out of the truck, muscles bunching and shifting beneath his chambray work shirt as he pulled off the ropes that held the load in place. Seeing him toss one end of the rope to the other side, she headed to that side herself to start untying the rope where it had been anchored there.

"You didn't have to pick these up," she told him, wondering why he'd made the trip without her.

Hidden behind boxes, she heard his easy, "Yeah, I did. Ernie is going to help me install them this afternoon."

Ernie Beauchamp was his uncle's right-hand man at the farm. The grizzled, fortysomething-year-old Vermonter barely had two words to say to much of anybody, but the man did the work of ten. He was also one of the few men she'd ever encountered who tipped his hat to a woman. She'd met him and his wife at the Colliers' barbecue.

"I thought we were going to install the bedroom carpet today."

"We are," he said over the chug of another vehicle pulling into her meadow. "Ernie's bringing the tack strips with him now."

The faded red truck that parked not far from Sam's looked as old as the hills surrounding them. Its engine still sounded healthy enough, though, and judging from the load of lumber in its bed, it could still carry its weight. But Kelsey's attention was on Sam as he emerged by the rear fender and gave her a faint smile.

Using her forearm to swipe back the hair that had come loose from her ponytail, she smiled, too. Only a little more hesitantly this time. He'd barely met her eyes before his glance cut away.

She thought for certain that the telltale muscle in his jaw jumped.

"I've only got Ernie for a few hours," he said, lifting the latch to lower the tailgate, "but that'll make a big dent in what we have to do." Metal clanked as the gate locked into place. "Did you get the wallboard sealed?"

"It might even be dry by now," she told him, searching his guarded profile. "I just need to get the roller and paint tray out of there."

"That would be good," was all he said as the chug behind them died.

As distracted as he sounded, she wondered if he wasn't just preoccupied with what he was doing. Now that his sister's house was finished, it was entirely possible that he'd simply thrown himself headfirst into her project and wasn't thinking of much else at the moment. She'd seen that intensity in him before when he'd worked, the concentration that made him seem almost…distant.

That concentration seemed firmly etched in his face as his uncle's slightly bow-legged handyman climbed from his truck. Ernie's ruddy features were shadowed by the same Vermont Dairymen's Association cap he'd worn when she'd met him. The white T-shirt and overalls he wore might have been the same, as well.

Seeing her, he gripped his cap by its bill, lifted it off his flattened brown hair and muttered, "Ma'am."

"Hi, Ernie," she replied, and told him it was nice to see him again, but he was finished socializing. His cap was already back on his head and he'd joined Sam at the tailgate to pull on a box the size of a refrigerator marked This Side Up.

"We'll need all the room we can get to maneuver," she heard Sam say as Ernie gave a tug and a grunt. "We'll put in the shower stall first. What do you think?"

Ernie apparently thought the plan was fine. All Kelsey knew for certain was that he didn't say otherwise before she hurried up the steps to clear away the can of sealer and the paint tray and roller she'd left to soak in a bucket.

While the men cut away the cardboard container to wrestle the molded fiberglass up the stairs, Kelsey decided the best way she could help was to stay out of the way. Sam and Ernie clearly knew what they needed to do and how to do it. Since her experience with caulk and silicone was limited strictly to repairs, she returned to scraping layers of paint from the cabinets in the kitchen and soon found herself listening to male voices and various bumps from the other side of the wall.

"You have a shower," Sam announced over an hour later, only to disappear out the door with Ernie before she could do anything more than look up.

Five minutes after that, she heard him thud back up the stairs. This time he carried a sink. Ernie came behind him, bearing variously shaped pieces of pipe and a large wrench that apparently hadn't been in the green metal toolbox Sam had carried in before.

She thought Sam might come back after he'd set down the heavy white porcelain, maybe crouch beside her and do what he'd always done when he was there and ask how things were going. She wouldn't have expected him to touch her or kiss her with Ernie working so near, but after what they'd shared yesterday morning and the unsettling distance she'd begun to sense in him, she was beginning to feel a definite need for some reassurance on his part that yesterday morning hadn't been a mistake.

He didn't come back, though. Thinking of how preoccupied he still looked, she wanted to believe he was just intent on taking advantage of Ernie's help while the man was there. Knowing he only had use of the older man's experience and brawn for a short while had to be why he didn't seem to slow down at all, much less take a break. After the sink was in, they carted up the toilet tank and bowl, installed them, then went back down to get the roll of carpet from where she and Sam had stored it on a tarp near the grinding stone.

By the time her carpet was in, she had two cabinets ready to sand and a new blister from scraping. It was while she was digging an adhesive bandage out of the box she'd learned to keep on hand, along with antibiotic ointment and tweezers for pulling out slivers, that she heard Ernie in the other room mention that he'd best get home to supper.

She had one of the bandage strips in hand when, seconds later, he walked past where she stood by the slate counter.

"Ernie," she called, heading after him. "Thank you so much for your help."

"Glad to do it," was his only reply before, tipping his hat, he walked out the open door.

His footsteps on the stairs had barely started to fade when heavier ones had her turn back around.

Sam had stopped behind her.

Seeing what she held, he reached for the adhesive strip.

"What's this for?" he asked, his focus on peeling off its paper jacket.

She held up her right hand. Even though she'd worn gloves, the pad below her fingers had been rubbed red. A spot in the middle sported the blister that had already broken.

Seeing it, he frowned. "Where's the ointment?"

She'd left the tube on the countertop. Retrieving it, she removed the cap and deposited a small blob on the rectangle of gauze he had exposed.

The same concentration that had carved his features before seemed fixed just as firmly as he positioned the bandage over the sore and pressed the ends into place with his thumbs. Held in his big, masculine hands, her own looked very small, and despite the nicks and scrapes she'd earned over the past week, almost as fragile as she suddenly felt.

The movements of this thumbs were gentle. But it was the way those motions slowed and how his brow furrowed in the moments before he looked up that stalled the relief she'd started to feel at his touch.

"I checked at the home improvement store," he told her, letting her go to check out the work she'd done that afternoon. "Your cabinet doors won't be in for another month, but they can install the carpet you ordered for the living room and the other bedroom the first of next week if you're ready. I put you down for a week from Tuesday just to get you on their schedule, but you can change that if you don't have the painting finished by then."

It seemed to her that he was getting way ahead of himself. "Do you think we'll have the insulation and wallboard up by then?"

"I asked Ernie if he can do that next weekend. He has a brother who can help him."

She hesitated. She'd never intended to impose on anyone else for the work they'd talked about doing themselves. She knew she would have to hire help later, but Sam was talking as if enlisting more help had suddenly become essential right now. "I thought you said we could do that ourselves over the next couple of weeks."

It took a moment, but as his glance met hers and she caught the telltale tightening of his jaw once more, the reason for the unease she'd felt slowly began to register.

He wasn't going to be here that long.

The breath Kelsey drew felt almost painful. When she let it out, she felt as if she wasn't breathing at all. "You're leaving."

Apparently he didn't feel confirmation was necessary.

"I think I have everything covered here," he told her, glancing around as if he wanted to be sure he hadn't overlooked some detail. "When your things arrive tomorrow, have the movers bring whatever you need up here. If you decide later that you want something brought from downstairs, call my uncle and he and Ernie or Ernie and his brother will move it for you. Uncle Ted will be in and out helping Megan, so you can coordinate with her."

He turned away, tension radiating in waves from his big body. Planting his hands on his hips, he nodded to the far corner of the kitchen.

"I asked Charlie if he could recommend a carpenter. You'll need one to build your pantry over there."

"Sam..."

"If you like his work, you can use him to rebuild the casing around the grindstone and the chute. If you can't find packing tables, he can probably build those…"

"Sam…"

"…for you, too."

"Sam, stop! Please," she added, more quietly.

She didn't care about who would build what. She didn't care about carpet or cabinets or the mill itself for that matter. Not just then. For the first time since she'd attempted to adopt his cynical philosophy, she honestly didn't care beyond that particular moment. At that moment, all she wanted was to know why he couldn't seem to get away from her fast enough.

It also seemed imperative that he not realize how big a hole that knowledge ripped in her heart.

"You didn't have to do all this. Make all these arrangements, I mean." She kept her voice low, forcing calm over the swift and sudden ache. "And you didn't have to take Ernie away from his family to get all this done today."

His guilty glance skimmed her face.

"Yes, I did. I know how important it is that you get moved in here. You have the basics now. Except for your hot plate," he said, wincing when he remembered. "I forgot that."

She had thought she would borrow his stove. To cook for them both.

The thought deepened the ache, made her more desperate to know what had gone wrong. She held that desperation in check, masked it beneath the calm she clung to just as urgently. "Did you get a call to go back to New York?"

Sam could have told her he had. He could have said that something had come up and that they needed him back at the precinct as soon as he could get there. Such an explanation would have taken the onus of the decision off of him and left her with someone else to blame for his walking out on her before they'd planned. But even if he hadn't always accepted responsibility for his actions, there was no way he could lie to her. If he owed her anything, it was the truth.

"No one called me." He spoke the admission quietly, hating the hurt she couldn't hide in her eyes, hating that he'd put it there. "I asked my boss if I could come back early. He told me to come in and we'd talk about it."

Anyone else would have asked why he had done that. The lovely woman turning from him didn't seem to think an explanation was necessary.

"Please tell Ernie I'll pay him for today."

"Kelsey. Don't," he said, catching her by the arm when she turned away.

Beneath his hand, he felt her muscles stiffen. She might not want to hear it, but he needed to explain, anyway.

Since she refused to turn back, he stepped in front of her. "You know I never intended to stay here."

"I never said I thought you would."

She didn't want the defense she heard in her voice. She didn't want the hurt she felt, either, but there didn't seem to be a whole lot she could do about that at the moment. It was her own fault it was there. All the time he'd encouraged her, worked with her, helped her, her old dreams had slowly crept back. She'd known all along that those dreams were impossible. She'd known he would want no part of them. But that hadn't stopped her from longing for them, anyway. And she'd wanted them all. Everything she'd dreamed of all those years ago. Him. His children.

She would never be able to live in the moment. There was too much about what a person did with each second that affected the future.

"I never said I expected anything from you," she reminded him, easing from his grip. "So please don't make it sound as if I said or did something that pushed you into leaving."

"It wasn't you." Her withdrawal had him withdrawing himself. "I went to see your mother yesterday. I wanted her to understand that you know what you're doing here," he told her before she could ask why he would do such a thing. "And I wanted her to stop telling everyone that I talked you into buying this place."

Disbelief robbed the strength from her voice. "You talked to my mother?"

"I'm surprised she didn't tell you."

"What did she say?"

"Basically, that I'd be doing you a favor to get out of here."

The tension taunting his muscles demanded that he move. Kneading the cords knotted in his neck, he headed for the bathroom to load up the tools he and Ernie had used. They were his uncle's, but he'd leave them for Ernie to use later when he installed her kitchen sink.

Kelsey was right behind him.

"You're leaving because of my mother?"

"I'm leaving because I was going to anyway. And because she's right," he admitted, crouching to swipe up a couple of wrenches. They landed in the toolbox with a rattle and a clank. "If I stay, I won't want to keep my hands off of you," he told her bluntly. "I don't care how careful we think we are, someone around here is going to figure out what's going on and the talk will escalate." He snapped the box, carried it in to where he'd left the sawhorses in her unfinished living room and headed for the bedroom to pick up carpet scraps.

He suddenly stopped, turning in the doorway. As he did, something protective moved into his eyes, entered his tone. "You're reestablishing yourself here, Kelsey. You're starting a new business. You don't want everyone around here talking about how you had an affair with some guy who talked you into moving back here then abandoned you. It won't matter that you and I know that's not what happened. That's what they'll say. You know that as well as I do."

His tension snaked toward her, wrapping around her, fed her own.

She couldn't deny his conclusions. She couldn't believe how blinded she'd been by her feelings for him, either. She hadn't considered consequences at all.

She wasn't ready for this, Kelsey thought, hugging her arms more tightly. She wasn't prepared. She felt robbed, cheated of the time they would have had together. But as much as she wanted to blame her mother for what he was doing now, in her heart she knew he wasn't doing what he wouldn't do a few weeks from now, anyway.

He might have made it sound as if he were leaving to protect her, but he was leaving to protect himself, too. She knew how he felt about commitment. She knew how he'd shut down the parts of himself she wanted most. As he quietly studied her face, she had the feeling he also knew how she'd come to feel about him. Heaven knew she'd done a lousy job of hiding it. And that, more than anything, had hastened his need to leave.

"I'll clean that up," she said, nodding to the scraps in her newly completed bedroom. If he thought he should leave, then by all means, he should. "It might be best if you go now."

The dark slashes of his eyebrows pinched. "Hey," he murmured. Looking torn, clearly struggling, he lifted his hand toward her face. "Don't do that. Okay?"

It was not okay. Her sense of self-protection finally, belatedly, asserting itself, she stepped back. He couldn't have it both ways. He couldn't push her away with one hand and reach for her with another.

"Be careful out there. Okay, Sam? I know you don't like to hear it, but there are people who care about you."

"Kelsey…"

"Call your sister once in a while, too. One of these days, you might even realize that you need her and her boys even more than they need you.

"I'm going to work downstairs for a while," she concluded softly. "I appreciate all your work here, Sam. I really do. And all your support, and your encouragement and I just…need to go."

Still hugging her arms around herself, she turned and headed out the open door with the warm breeze blowing after her. She didn't slow. She didn't look back.

For a moment, Sam heard nothing but the light and hurried sounds of her sneakers on the steps and the distant honk of Mrs. Farber's geese. All he felt was the guilt that had brought him there, and a strange and unfamiliar ache behind his breastbone.

He hated that she'd run from him. He hated that they'd had to end so abruptly. He knew he had no finesse, and he hated that, too, but he'd known no pretty way to tell her things would only get more complicated if he stayed. He knew only that clean breaks healed the fastest, and that there wasn't a doubt in his mind that leaving was the best thing he could offer her.

He waited until she'd had time to get inside downstairs before he jogged down the steps himself and climbed into his truck. He didn't look back, either. He never did. He would do nothing but load up his things, arrange to have the trailer picked up, and head for the city in the morning. He needed to get back to work. Once he did, he felt certain the demands of his job would make him forget all about the unfamiliar void that had just opened in his chest.

Chapter Eleven

Imagination. It had gotten her where she was, Kelsey thought. It would get her where she needed to go.

Standing beside the furniture and boxes she'd stored at the end of the large and open mill room, she closed her eyes and tried to use that intrepid imagination to envision the work space as it would be. New walls, painted white. New floor, industrial gray rubber. Tables for packaging, stainless steel so they could be sanitized. A boxing and storage area separate from the grinding and packaging area to avoid contamination. She had government safety rules to follow that hadn't been in effect a century and a half ago.

When she opened her eyes, she groaned. It would take her another century and a half to make it all happen.

In the month since she'd returned to Maple Mountain, she had discovered two hard and fast rules about remodeling, renovating and starting a business. Everything cost twice as much as planned and took twice as long to accomplish.

The good news was that she had all winter to get the mill up and running. The better news, as far as she was concerned at the moment, was that she'd figured out how to raise and lower the one ton top millstone from the equally heavy bottom one to change the grind of grain from course to flour fine. She had no hopper to pour the grain into the hole in the middle of the top stone, though, and she still had to replace the belts to the waterwheel outside that would slowly turn the stones with the grooves that would carry the ground meal to the discharge spout. She needed to have that fabricated, too, but Sam had said that would be the simplest part of the whole project.

Sam.

There wasn't a day gone by that he didn't creep into her thoughts, or an hour that she didn't miss him, wish she'd never laid eyes on him and felt enormously grateful to him for her mill.

He'd been gone three weeks, two days and about an hour. Not that she was counting.

"I'm leavin' now," Ernie called from the other side of the large and open door. "Want me to carry some of that wood upstairs before I go?"

"Oh, that's not necessary," she called back, turning from the cartons she'd come to search for the box of sweaters she'd packed. It was nearing the middle of September and she needed her warmer clothes.

Reaching the open door, she saw him stop by his faded red truck. "But thank you," she continued. "Does the stove work now?"

He pushed back the brim of his cap. "Yup."

"And the sink?"

"That, too," he added, downright talkative today.

"Thank you so much, Ernie." She'd had the appliances and the kitchen sink for weeks. Ernie just hadn't had time to install them until now. "Can I pay you tomorrow? I need to go into St. Johnsbury to the bank," she told him, and to the warehouse store, she thought. Her kitchen cabinet doors had come in just as Sam had said they would.

It wasn't that she couldn't go a day without thinking about him. She couldn't even go five minutes.

With a mental sigh, wondering how she would ever get over him if she couldn't get him off her mind, she smiled at the man lifting his hand toward her. Telling her tomorrow was fine, he said goodbye by tipping his hat and climbed into his truck.

She could hear him pulling out of the drive even as she returned to her search. As soon as she found the box, she would carry it upstairs, then take up some of the firewood Charlie had brought that morning. The skies were a clear, sharp blue, but the air had turned crisp and cold almost overnight. The maples had even started to turn.

She could use more blankets, too.

She'd just found the first box she was looking for when she noticed the rumble of a truck growing louder rather than retreating. Wondering what Ernie had forgotten, she dragged the large cardboard carton up and over the top of a half dozen others and turned with her arms wrapped around it.

She'd made it to the doorway when she realized it wasn't Ernie at all.

Bending slowly, her heart bumping her ribs, she set the awkward carton at her feet.

From behind the wheel of his truck, Sam watched Kelsey straighten in the last of the day's sunshine. Her pale hair was clipped low at her nape, but strands had worked themselves free. She nudged them back, only to immediately snake her arms around the loose top of her gray sweats.

The guardedness in her stance was equally evident in her expression when he killed the engine and climbed out.

He had walked into stings that didn't have his nerves feeling as tight as they did just then. He couldn't quite believe what he was doing. But, then, he couldn't quite believe what he'd already done.

He moved toward her, his hands in his pockets, his gait easy despite the trip-wire tension flowing through his veins. "Hi," he said, stopping in front of her to slowly scan the caution in her pretty face.

"Hi," Kelsey replied. She swallowed. Hard. The slate-gray sweater he wore made his shoulders look huge and turned the silver in his unreadable eyes to pewter. He looked as big and compelling as he always had to her. But he also looked a little uncertain as he tried to gauge her reaction to his presence. And that didn't seem like him at all.

"Did you come to see Megan and the boys?"

"I'll go over later. I wanted to see you first," he admitted, still working on finesse, still not sure he had a handle on it. "And your mom."

"My mom?"

"Actually, I've already talked to her." As meetings went, the second had gone considerably better than the first. He didn't think he'd redeemed himself completely in Dora's eyes, but he had the feeling there was hope—depending on how receptive her daughter was to what he had to say.

"Why would you want to talk to my mother?"

At a loss, Kelsey studied the strange hesitation in the handsome lines of his face. She and her mom had finally come to an understanding of sorts. Her mother still thought she'd traded her best opportunities to become a slave to a mill, but she had come to realize that Kelsey always had been happiest when she was home, and that Sam had simply given her the courage to return to where she needed to be.

That she be happy was all her mom really wanted for her.

"Because I want her to know my intentions are honorable."

Aware of her sudden confusion, more aware of his sudden need to move, he nodded toward the box at her feet. "Where are you going with that?"

"Upstairs." Her confusion remained firmly in place as she shook her head. "What intentions?"

He stepped toward the carton. "Do you have anything else you want taken up?"

Still hugging herself, Kelsey blocked his path. She had spent every single one of the past twenty-three nights wondering when the emptiness she felt without him would begin to ease. She'd spent those same nights wondering how long she could bear to put off asking his sister if she'd heard from him, if he was safe, if he was even still alive. Thoughts of where he could be and what sort of danger he might have put himself into had left her tossing and turning as much as missing him had. He wasn't going to show up out of nowhere, totally undo what little emotional progress she'd made, and just start moving boxes.

"I don't need you to carry anything, Sam." An unwanted bubble of hope bumped into the potential for fresh hurt. Having recently mastered the ability to protect herself, she needed to keep that hope in check. His return could mean anything. He could have been told to take more time. He could have returned to help his uncle or his sister and because he would be around, he'd wanted her mother to know he had no designs on her. He could have come to tell her that himself. "I just need to know what you want."

Sam pushed his hands back into his pockets. The temptation to reach for her was strong. But he had no desire to have her pull away from him. He wasn't going to push. He wouldn't rush her. He would give her whatever time and space she needed, and pray that he wasn't too late.

He stepped back, his jaw working.

"Do you still believe in your dream for this place?"

Her brow furrowed at the unexpected question. "More than ever," she replied. "Why?"

"Because I do, too." It seemed safest to start with the practical side. More comfortable, anyway. "Could you use an investor?"

"You want to invest in the mill?"

"I haven't had much to spend my money on the last few years." The last ten, to be exact, he thought, starting to pace. "So I have a hundred thousand or so I could contribute. And you still need muscle around here," he noted, glancing through the open doorway to the broken casing around the millstone. "I'm good for the labor."

"You want to work here?"

His glance lifted to the new windows he'd installed before he'd left. With the setting sun now half hidden by the treetops and reflecting like fire off the sparkling panes, he couldn't tell whether or not she'd hung curtains.

"That, too," he replied, but let the rest of his thought go. Telling her he also wanted to live here would definitely be getting ahead of himself.

Restive, he glanced back at her, kept pacing.

"They put you on leave again," she concluded.

"Actually, I quit."

For the first time since he'd arrived, her caution slipped. "But you love what you do."

"I used to," he agreed, relieved by the sudden concern in her eyes. "There was a time I honestly couldn't imagine doing anything else. But I have no business going undercover anymore. I'm not safe. And I have no desire to jeopardize someone else because my head's not in what I'm doing."

"What happened?"

At her unmasked concern, he stopped six feet in front of her.

The last time he'd seen her, he'd been dead certain his work would make the void that had opened up inside him go away. Instead the void had affected his work in ways he would never have thought possible.

He'd been two days into his new assignment when he'd found himself distracted by thoughts of her clearing birds' nests from the high rafters of the mill room. Worrying about her falling, he'd missed the suspect he'd been waiting to spot and two days of surveillance had gone down the tubes.

He'd been two weeks into that same operation when his lack of concentration had nearly gotten him shot.

He'd lost his edge. More important, he didn't care.

Everything he cared about was in Maple Mountain.

He could have told her that. He could have told her what he was supposed to have been doing on the stakeout and what he'd been doing instead. It seemed easiest to cut to the heart of it all.

"You." He paused at the simple truth of it. "You happened."

It was because of her that he'd realized how the work that had become his way of life had simply become a way to avoid the parts of his life that hadn't worked out. He suspected she'd already known that, though, as he moved closer, wanting to erase the quick disbelief in her expression. He needed her to understand that he understood more about himself now than he ever had. What he understood most was that he'd been slowly dying inside—until she'd come along.

She had spoken of breathing life back into the old building rising above them. He'd never realized that, all along, she'd been breathing life back into him.

"When you came back, you knew exactly what you wanted and how you would make it happen. We'd talked about it all. It just hadn't occurred to me that while you were sharing your dreams for this place, you were making me realize what all I was missing."

He offered the confession quietly, slowly withdrawing his hands from his pockets. He'd missed her, missed working with her, missed the feeling of working toward something positive. "I want to be around my family." He missed them, too. "Especially the boys. You were right when you said I might need them as much as they need me," he conceded, bracing himself. "But I need you more."

Feeling totally exposed, he watched her dark eyes search his, her slender shoulders rising with the deep breath she drew.

"You had the insight and the courage to change what was wrong about your life." He remembered how she'd struggled against that change at first, how she'd questioned and fought it. He'd struggled these past weeks, too, fought and denied. In the end, his need to survive had won. "That's what I'm trying to do with mine now."

The restlessness that had plagued him since he'd left began to fade even as the tips of his fingers skimmed her cheek. The need to touch her was too strong to avoid. But she didn't pull from him as he'd feared she might. The relief in her eyes told him she needed that contact as much as he needed it himself.

Drawn by the need she sensed in him, hope shoved hard. She wouldn't have had that courage without him.

"You're staying?"

"I am if you're willing to take a chance with me," he told her, feeling the tension ease from his body as he slipped his arms around her.

"What if you want to go back to the force?"

"I don't want to go back," he insisted, conviction heavy in his tone. "I'll help out Joe if he needs me, but I want what I found here. If you want time, I'll go to work out at my uncle's." He'd already figured that as his contingency plan. "I always liked working for him. But I'm talking about a real chance, Kelsey. We don't have to rush into anything. And I know I'm coming out of the blue at you with this. But what I really want is to build this place up with you, and maybe work on a few dreams of our own.

"I want to marry you." He thought he should warn her of that. "And I'd like to have kids." She deserved to know that, too. "That's the kind of chance I'm talking about."

Kelsey's heart felt as if it were about to pound out of her chest at the certainty she saw in his eyes. Sam wasn't a man to speak of family or dreams. He wasn't a man to make promises he wouldn't keep. Yet, he'd just told her he wanted her old dream. All of it.

"You said no rush?"

"None."

Feeling as if she could float right up to her toes, she slipped her arms around his neck. "How long do I get to make up my mind?"

"How long do you think you'd need?"

"Considering that I've waited thirteen years for you?" she asked, lifting herself higher. "About a minute."

There was no mistaking the possessive light that entered his eyes at her admission. That same possession was in his touch as he pulled her against him, and in his kiss as he lowered his head and covered her mouth with his.

It was like coming home. Wrapped in his arms, feeling protected and desired and more cherished than she could have imagined, Kelsey knew she was finally, completely where she needed to be. Yet, as he robbed the strength from her knees and the breath from her lungs, she also knew that it wasn't the place that filled her with that wonderful sense of belonging. It was the man. She'd just needed to come home to find him.

Just as he'd needed to return to find her.

His hands had somehow worked their way into her hair. With it spilling over his hands, her clip now on the ground, he lifted his head and smiled into her eyes. "Your mom was right."

"She was?"

"Yeah. She said you were crazy about me."

She rolled her eyes, tried not to smile. "She did not."

"Honest. She did. Not a while ago," he conceded. "But the last time. She said she thought you were falling in love with me."

Her mother was far more astute than she'd thought. "My mother can't keep anything to herself."

"I know," he muttered, leaning to nuzzle her neck. "I imagine by morning everyone around here will know I love you, too."

Kelsey went still. Maybe it was because he'd protected his heart so fiercely. Maybe it was because of the cynicism that had always run beneath his deceptive easy manner. It could have even been because the admission would make him vulnerable and being vulnerable wasn't something a man like him would ever care to be. But she'd never thought she would hear those words from him.

Hearing them now, she lifted her head, her heart shining in her eyes. "You do?"

He smiled his easy smile, the one that had always charmed her. Only now the latent tension behind it was gone. "Yeah. I do. I think it started when I was reading your diary," he admitted, tightening his hold. "I'd never been the subject of fantasies before."

Kelsey truly doubted that. He might not have been aware of it, but there were women right here in Maple Mountain who would blush the shade of a beet if he knew what they thought about him. She didn't doubt women had thought about him in such ways for years.

"Which reminds me," he murmured, tracing her jaw with his fingers. "What ever happened to it?"

"My diary?" she asked, distracted as his touch drifted down her throat.

"Yeah," he murmured, seeming distracted, too.

"I still have it."

"I think I'd like another look at it." Letting his hand fall, he drew her closer. A devilish light glinted in his eyes. "I still feel pretty partial to July twelfth," he admitted, shifting her body to better align it with his, "but there may be another fantasy in there I'd like to fulfill."

She now knew for certain that he'd never read parts of August.

"You know what?" Thirteen years ago, standing in the very spot she stood in now, she never would have thought that her wild imaginings could ever come true. But impossible as it seemed, Sam loved her, he wanted to marry her, to live with her in the mill, to have their children. Tightening her arms around his neck, she smiled against his lips. "You just did."

* * * * *

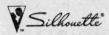

If you enjoyed what you just read,
then we've got an offer you can't resist!

Take 2 bestselling
love stories FREE!
Plus get a FREE surprise gift!

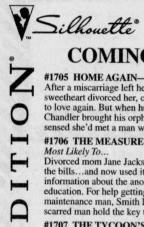

COMING NEXT MONTH

SPECIAL EDITION

#1705 HOME AGAIN—Joan Elliott Pickart
After a miscarriage left her unable to bear children and her high school sweetheart divorced her, child psychologist Cedar Kennedy vowed never to love again. But when humble construction company owner Mark Chandler brought his orphaned nephew, Joey, in for treatment, Cedar sensed she'd met a man who could rebuild her capacity for love....

#1706 THE MEASURE OF A MAN—Marie Ferrarella
Most Likely To...
Divorced mom Jane Jackson took a job at her alma mater to pay the bills...and now used it to access confidential records seeking information about the anonymous benefactor who'd paid for her education. For help getting to the files, she turned to the school's maintenance man, Smith Parker. Did this sensitive but emotionally scarred man hold the key to her past—and her future?

#1707 THE TYCOON'S MARRIAGE BID—
Allison Leigh
When six-months-pregnant Nikki Day collapsed on her vacation, she awoke with former boss Alexander Reed by her bedside. Alex devoted himself to Nikki's care, even in the face of his estranged father's attempts to take over his business. Their feelings for each other grew—but she was carrying his cousin's baby. And Alex had a secret, too....

#1708 THE OTHER SIDE OF PARADISE—Laurie Paige
Seven Devils
The minute Mary McHale arrived for her wrangler job at a ranch in the Seven Devils Mountains, her boss, Jonah Lanigan, had eyes for her. Then Mary, orphaned at an early age, noticed her own striking resemblance to the Daltons on the neighboring ranch. After discovering her true identity—and true love with Jonah—would she have to choose between the two?

#1709 TAMING A DARK HORSE—Stella Bagwell
Men of the West
After suffering serious burns rescuing his horses from a fire, loner Linc Ketchum needed Nevada Ortiz's help. The sassy home nurse brought Linc back to health and kindled a flame in his heart. But ever since his mother had abandoned him as a child, Linc just couldn't trust a woman. Now Nevada needed to find a cure...for Linc's wounded spirit.

#1710 UNDERCOVER NANNY—Wendy Warren
As nanny to restaurateur Maxwell Lotorto's four foster kids, sultry Daisy June "D.J." Holden had ulterior motives—she was really a private eye, hired to find out if her boss was the missing heir to a supermarket dynasty. D.J. fell hard for Max's charms—not to mention the unruly kids. But would her secret bring their newfound happiness to an abrupt end?

SSECNM0805